Richard Waters grew up in Birmingham, England, where he worked in various roles in property and financial services before migrating to Australia in 1996. He then turned to travel and features writing, and now works in marketing communications.

In 2012 he completed a research masters degree in creative writing at the University of Technology Sydney, during which he wrote *Where There Is Darkness*, his first novel. He lives in Sydney with his wife and two daughters.

richardwaters.com

WHERE THERE IS DARKNESS

A NOVEL

RICHARD WATERS

ANSOVA PRESS · Sydney

First published in 2016
© Richard Waters 2016

ISBN 978-0-9946021-0-7

Cover, internal design and typesetting: Jessica Le

For Vanessa

Life is the sum of all your choices

Albert Camus

BIRMINGHAM, WEST MIDLANDS

5 NOVEMBER 1981

$$- 1 -$$

The match flared alight with a sulphurous puff, casting a vivid pool of light on the wet grass and plunging everything beyond to a blackness that ran even deeper than before. The foggy air was so still that the match flame was unwavering, steady, needing no cupped hand to shield it as it hovered beneath the neat twist of blue touchpaper.

The firework hissed into life, its fuse glowing red with a wisp of smoke that was abruptly snatched away as an arctic breeze moaned down the hillside. There was an explosive whooshing noise and a spray of flame split the darkness. Pete's head jerked towards me, and his hands flew up in horror.

Instead of shooting upwards as it was meant to, the rocket shot out horizontally from the hillside. It flew in a perfect smooth flattened curve, like a fiery arrow. For what can have only been a few seconds but seemed more like a minute, it kept on flying, surprisingly slowly. For a surreal moment I almost believed that our rocket might keep cruising forever, maintaining its perfect low orbit above the earth. But gradually the angle of its golden comet tail tilted upwards as its nose dropped and it dipped towards the ground.

The saliva dried from my mouth instantly as I realised what was about to happen. I bobbed up and down, urging it to explode.

But it hurtled on, much farther away from us now, heading towards the centre of the park. With only seconds of its life remaining, it flew faster but steeper, spearing down through the smoky air as its nose dropped towards the vertical and it fell from its orbit, pulled back to earth like a dying star.

I tried to close my eyes, but I couldn't. Someone was saying 'oh fuck oh fuck oh fuck oh *fuck*.' It might have been me.

Perhaps the rocket wouldn't explode when it hit the ground? Yes! Surely it would just stick in the wet mud and fizzle out. I exhaled, realising I'd been holding my breath.

It was only a glowing pinpoint, like the angry eye of some mythical creature, when it plunged into the sea of bobbing heads between the fairground and the food stalls, just where everyone was surging to go home. Among the family groups and the pushchairs. For a millisecond, nothing happened except some agitation of the crowd around the point of impact: a breaking of the surface tension, an outward ripple of energy as if a pebble had been tossed into a black lake.

There was an upward mushrooming silver flash, silhouettes and shadows and what might have been stark white faces, frozen in time. A thought struck me: why hadn't it made any noise? Had it not exploded properly?

The crack and rumble of the explosion echoed up the hillside and rolled over us like a breaking wave on a dark, frozen beach.

Someone shook my arm, nearly jerking me off my feet.

'Dave! Dave! Come on! *Move!*'

'Oh god, what happened? What do we do?'

'Let's go. Now. Come on.'

Pete dragged me away, heading along the crest of the slope in a wide arc, away from the crowds and the fairground. The slope ran down until the ground flattened out by the reservoir, in the far corner of the park.

My mouth was so dry I could hardly swallow, my throat squeezed so it felt like my Adam's apple would jam it closed. The residue of the Southern Comfort we'd drunk earlier was a sugary slime in my mouth.

'What are we doing? Let's go home!' I said.

'Not yet. We can't get out of the park here. There's no gates in the bloody fence. Anyway, we have to get back into the crowd, else we're stuffed.'

'Let's just climb the fence. I want to go home!'

To our right, the high spiked fence ran down the slope to meet the brick wall bordering the reservoir.

'No. Even if we climbed over and legged it someone might remember two kids running away. It's too risky. We need to get down there,' he pointed back towards the chaos, 'and get lost in the crowd again. That's our only hope. *Fuck.* Let's go. *Now.*' He yanked on my arm.

The flat ground by the reservoir was a morass of frosty grass and frozen puddles. We squelched along, trying to hop between the spiky clumps of grass. It was so dark we mostly misjudged and went up to our ankles in water. Up ahead, the fairground rides cranked to a standstill, their cheery music became grotesquely distorted as it slowed and finally died. Now there was screaming: shrill and piercing and laced with the howling of a dog in agony. This hideous din was joined then mercifully consumed by the swelling wail of sirens before the flashing lights of several emergency vehicles emerged, bumping towards us through the murky drift of smoke and freezing fog.

I was suddenly desperate for a piss.

'Pete, I've got to go to the bog.' The words were clumsy in my dry mouth.

'Not now! Fuck's sake!'

'I've got to go, right now! Pete, can I stop?'

My bladder was already relaxing. But my frozen hands were too clumsy on my zip. As I was pulling myself free I burst and sprayed hot piss on my left hand and down my thigh. I leaned forward with one hand on the fence's flaky ironwork, eyes drooping, pissing into the long grass along the fence line, not caring about the steamy smell or the cooling wetness on my leg. I looked to my left, at the reservoir. The string of lights along the dam, far away on the opposite shore, cast a wavy yellow glow on the black water. It looked beautiful through the liquid blur of my half-closed eyelids. It was like something I'd done in art last term that Mr Scott had put up on the school's art room wall, to the derision of my classmates. I smiled. Maybe I'd do another similar one. Perhaps I'd try oil paints this time though…

The creaking leather of Pete's coat startled me. He grabbed my collar.

'Come *on* Dave! Wake up! Jesus Christ!'

My trouser leg clung to my thigh, wet and cold. I could no longer feel my feet. But the discomfort was easing as increasingly I felt drugged, poisoned, my senses going into shutdown. Even with Pete dragging me along, I couldn't stop my eyes closing. A sharp image of the explosion was imprinted on my retina. I kept blinking, but the silvery flash wouldn't go away.

I tried to think, to grasp the implications of what had happened. I glared at Pete's back, cursing my best friend, hating him for his wild ideas and schemes, and for the catastrophe we were now running from.

But we weren't running from the catastrophe. We were running towards it. Because I knew, even though we hadn't yet seen exactly what had happened, that we had done something terrible.

SYDNEY, NEW SOUTH WALES

31 DECEMBER 2012

– 2 –

'This is *awesome!*' my brother says, repeatedly scanning the neon city skyline behind us and the curving grey-green hulk of the harbour bridge to our right. Insects swarm around the streetlights in drunken spirals, while the lights on the hundreds of boats cast parallel lines across the black rippling water. Shouts and music and laughter drift to shore through the humid air in a continuous buzz.

The crowds are dense on Pyrmont Bridge as we merge with other groups trekking from the city train stations to the waterfront parks. Children squeal and giggle, clutching parents' hands, thrilled to be out so late. A faint tang of gunpowder lingers in the air from the early fireworks display, trapped under the low cloud, slowly dispersing in the easterly breeze off the ocean. The smoky tickle in my throat makes me shudder. I fight down the feeling of unease that has been building in me all day and that now occasionally surges up into mild panic at the thought of what the evening holds. We round the bend past the Maritime Museum and Lydia points out our destination. Tony's mouth drops.

'Bloody hell.'

Beyond the rows of renovated wharves rises a curved, six-storey apartment building of dark concrete and glass, designed rather too obviously to resemble the stern of a ship nudging out into the water.

Farther along the waterfront promenade the crowds are thinner. A few early arrivals are claiming pitches for the midnight fireworks show, spreading blankets on the trampled grass and unpacking eskies and hampers. I give Lydia's hand a squeeze. Despite everything even I'm not immune to the excitement in the air, the sense of anticipation.

Tony and Gail are thrilled at being in Sydney for New Year's Eve. Since they arrived two days ago he has pestered me constantly about whether tonight's show will be the biggest New Year fireworks display anywhere in the world. I've promised him that Sydney's is always the biggest, which probably isn't true, but it has kept him happy. He and Gail are also delighted that we've been invited to a party at the penthouse apartment of one of Lydia's colleagues at the magazine. 'A proper *penthouse?*' Tony had asked, cackling, when Lydia told them.

Gail slips her arm through Tony's. 'It's still only lunchtime at home,' she says. 'Isn't that funny?'

Maybe it's one of those drab, mild English December days, with none of the clear snap of real winter. I briefly wonder what Mum's doing for New Year but jerk back to reality and the ordeal to come.

A row of palm trees fronts the building, squeezed into the

strip between the roadway and the timber boardwalk that lines the waterfront. They have perilously skinny trunks on which their jagged fronds sway fully four storeys high. Tony stops and stares at them for a while, as if struggling to summon his thoughts, while Gail tugs at his arm.

'Class,' he says in the end. 'Like something out of *Miami Vice*.' He nudges me. 'What's this penthouse worth, Dave?'

'No idea. Two or three million dollars, easily.'

'Never!'

I can see him furiously doing sums in his head, calculating exchange rates, before muttering in Gail's ear. She shakes her head in disbelief.

Inside the penthouse there is a lot of glass and marble and deep cream carpets and the winking lights of electronic gadgets. Symon, our host, (he changed the spelling from Simon) is as annoying as I'd remembered. I'm glad Tony and Gail are here and that they don't know anyone, since it gives me an excuse to look after them and not talk to anyone else.

My survival plan is going to be tricky to implement. But then Tony unknowingly does me a big favour. He whispers in Lydia's ear with the urgent air of a small boy desperate to know where the toilet is. She laughs.

'I'm sure he will,' she says. 'Symon, Tony and Gail want to know if they can have a stickybeak around the flat.'

'Sure,' says Symon, throwing his arms wide, a bottle of Moet in each. 'Sorry I can't give you the guided tour,' and he inclines his head at the guests out on the balcony. 'Are you right to find your own way around?'

'You go with them Dave,' Lydia says to me. 'I'd better go outside and say a few hellos.'

'Outside' consists of a balcony three times the size of our backyard, with a long curved edge where it overhangs the street. The apartment is gigantic: four bedrooms, study, home entertainment room, huge lounge and kitchen area, multiple bathrooms. The walk-in wardrobe in the master bedroom is a room in its own right, like a mini warehouse full of clothes in racks and dozens of pairs of shoes in wire drawers. Gail's mouth hangs open and I can see Tony mentally preparing an inventory of everything: the styles, the décor, the gadgets.

By the end of our inspection, I've learnt what I need to know to get me through tonight, and Tony and Gail are like a couple emerging after a tour of the Queen's private rooms in Buckingham Palace.

'Dave, can I talk to you about something?' Gail whispers, leaning in close. Her breath is sweet with champagne. Lydia is inside and Tony is telling one of his travel stories to a group of people who if not enthralled are at least listening.

'Sure.'

Gail and I move away and lean on the balcony railing looking down at the street. There's a champagne bottle wedged in the crown of one of the palm trees. I point it out and we laugh. Then I wait.

'I lost my daddy recently.'

Bloody hell. I'm not up for this. I don't know Gail nearly well enough to hear a confession about how she wished she had known him better.

'Gail, I'm sorry about your father, but isn't this something you're better off talking through with Tony…'

'Don't worry, I don't want to talk about my father. I want to ask about yours.'

'Dad? Ask away, but why me? Why not ask Tony?'

'Because Tony acts like you never had a father. Even when your mother mentions him, Tony cuts her dead or ignores her. I must say, your mum does talk about your dad an awful lot. But still.'

I try to make sense of this. My head is spinning. Gail goes on, perhaps taking my silence for disapproval.

'I'm sorry for being a nosy parker. For ages after Tony and I met, I just left it alone. But now we're a proper married couple I think I've got a right to know about his family. *Your* family.'

'Well, has Tony told you anything?'

'Hardly. Just that your father died when you were children. When I ask Tony how or when, he gets angry, or he pretends to get sad — and I know he's only pretending, I can tell — and says he doesn't want to talk about it. But your mum talks about your dad a lot, as I said. So I know a bit about what he was like, and I know he used to work down the road at the British Leyland car factory, and that he left there suddenly and went to Scotland to work on the oil rigs.'

'That's right.'

'I think, too, from talking to your mother that… well, that him going off to Scotland was difficult for her. Maybe for all of you?'

Confusion and sadness and vague scraps of fleeting images from early childhood memories swirl briefly in my head and then subside.

'Probably. But I was very young when that happened. Only four or five.'

Gail takes her time with her next question.

'What happened to him, Dave? Something always stops me asking your mum, although I'm sure she'd probably tell me.' She grabs me by the arm. 'Dave! Sorry. You mightn't want to talk about it either. How rude of me!'

'It's okay. I don't mind talking about it. He was killed in a helicopter crash, on his way out to one of the sea platforms. It was night time, in a storm.'

'My god! How terrible.' Gail's hand flies to her mouth. I have known her just long enough to see that this is a genuine gesture. 'How old were you?'

'Ten. Tony was about thirteen.'

'Why do you think Tony doesn't talk about your dad? It's like he just doesn't care. Did they not get on or something?'

'Gail, I was very young. I can't remember much. But Tony wasn't exactly an angel when he was a kid. I don't think I'm giving anything away in saying that.'

Gail smiles, although some effort is involved.

'He was often in trouble with Dad,' I continue. 'So Dad and I did lots of things on our own, without Tony. I can remember that.' I shrug. 'Hell, I don't know. Yes, probably Tony and Dad didn't get on.'

'But why not? Did something happen?'

Something in my brain, some tiny beacon of recollection, tells me that there's something to this. Something specific, an actual event. I grasp for it, but the flickering pulse of memory fades and dies.

'I don't know, Gail. Or rather, I can't remember.'

'Yep, it's a big dealership we run. Audi. Fleet and private sales. And parts and servicing, of course.'

Tony is now in business mode, standing erect, legs apart, pushing his bony shoulders back. Someone says it must be tough in the UK for new car sales, what with the GFC and now a deep recession.

'Not so bad. Europe is stuffed, of course. The Krauts are running the show. I always said Thatcher was right, keeping us out of that euro time bomb. Our market, the top end, is holding up well. What do you drive, by the way?'

Soon he is virtually handing out business cards. I'm tempted to make a joke about Tony being a second hand car salesman (well, they do sell the demonstrators), but remember doing so years ago and Tony being livid, later calling me a stuck up idle student wanker and punching me in the chest in the pub car park.

I get heavily into the beers, chasing them down with a couple of margaritas. It's too easy when the drinks come to you on a tray. I'll regret it tomorrow. But it's part of my survival plan for tonight. The humidity has worsened and the sky is a strange luminous grey, low cloud swelling over the city, reflecting the light back, hardly any wind.

Despite everything I relax in an alcohol-assisted way and even begin to enjoy myself. Some of Lydia's female colleagues are absolutely stunning, so there's plenty to look at after I quickly tire of Tony crapping on about traffic cameras in the UK or the price of petrol. My head is whirling by the time a tray of champagne comes past but I grab a glass, swigging it back and enjoying the frothy rush over my teeth and up my nose.

All this makes me forget to watch the clock, until Lydia comes over and puts her arm round my waist.

'Are you okay, babe? Only half an hour to go!'

My guts start fluttering, the terror returning in a rush. Lydia rears back, arm still round me, and makes a half joking – but only half – face of disapproval.

'Christ, Dave, how much have you had?'

I wave my arm vaguely and luckily she is dragged away by her hag of a boss, Judith, a self-styled fashion 'maven', a word I loathe. She looks at me like I'm the janitor.

More guests have arrived and the balcony is packed with bodies. The noise is intense, a high drone of shouts and chatter and laughter, champagne corks popping. There's a swell of excitement as midnight nears. People glance at their watches, scanning the crowd to check where partners and friends are. Everyone drifts towards the eastern side to get the best view, facing the great looming curve of the bridge's arch. A couple of champagne buckets full of party poppers are passed round and everyone grabs a handful.

I down another champagne and clumsily dump the glass, snapping it at the stem, and twist the top off a beer. The adrenaline is kicking in, my temples pounding, shirt sticky on the small of my back. I look at my watch – three minutes – and launch my plan into action. Lydia is still giggling with Judith and a bunch of cronies. Perfect. I gesture to Tony and Gail, beckoning them across. They've hardly moved all night but have befriended a couple Lydia and I know vaguely. Gail drags Tony towards me, her face shiny and beaming, their new friends following.

Someone turns up the radio and the presenter begins shouting the midnight countdown, a ragged, swelling roaring crescendo, echoed by the crowds in the park below us, across the water and the coloured lights, round the harbour's jagged rim, around the nation, as a year ticks to a close. I put my arm round Lydia and I'm pumped now and breathless. *Three, two, one* and there's a massive roar of 'Happy New Year!' and 'Wooohh!' and an explosive *crummphh* cracks the air, and a firework flash of green light floods the balcony, reflecting off glass and metal and tile, a freeze frame of dazzling brightness and black shadow.

Moving fast, I do what I have to do. First, Lydia. A crushing hug and a kiss.

'Happy New Year. Love you.' We look into each other's eyes for a second before she's swept away by her friends who close in with hugs and kisses and handshakes and slapping of backs. Party poppers crackle like gunfire, draping everyone's heads with strands of coloured paper. Next I deal with Tony and Gail. My arms tremble as I pump Tony's hand and give Gail a hug and kiss.

'It's so wonderful to be here,' she says. 'I can't believe I'm in Australia!' This sounds like the start of a gushing speech so I wheel away as if keen to get back to Lydia. And now everyone's eyes are drawn upwards to the fireworks, to the explosions of crimson and gold and white. Thunder rolls across the water and reverberates off the city buildings, trapped in by the pressing cloud cover, echoing off the concrete. There's a fresh surge of people towards the balcony's edge. I have to get out of here, *now*. I weave back through the crowd, bearing an empty glass as if on an urgent mission to find more champagne. I'm shaking badly as I slip inside into the sudden air-conditioned chill. Nausea rises in my throat and I break into a fast stride.

Thanks to our earlier tour, I can ignore the main toilet and cloakroom off the corridor, and dart into the guest bedroom farthest from the balcony. I slam the door. I scuttle to the windows, which rattle as another crackling bang sounds outside and a ruby red burst of light fills the room. I drop the blinds with a crash — I may have broken them, who cares — and yank shut the drapes. Then I'm in the en-suite bathroom, door shut, sitting on the toilet with my hands over my ears. A windowless room in one of the few high-quality apartment blocks in Pyrmont guarantees good sound insulation. In my panic I can't work out which of the eight switches turn on the lights. An extractor fan comes on with a solid whine and that'll do. I'm set. I sit in the dark on the toilet with my hands over my ears. I can't see or hear anything now, conscious only of the swirling rush of blood in my head. After a while I think I smell the tang of gunpowder, and see a few soft silver flashes on the inside of my eyelid. I can't believe the smell has got in here, at the same time knowing that it hasn't. I press two fingers hard onto my left eye, sliding the eyelid back and forth, smooth curved lubrication, feeling the give at the back of the eyeball as I push. So delicate, so easily damaged. I imagine the smooth pink hollowed-out scoop of the eye socket, the holes in the flesh where the optic nerves and blood vessels run back inside, towards my brain. Towards the black silt of memories and a thirty-year-old secret.

I jerk off the toilet, crash the lid up and shove my head inside the bowl. The room is pitch black, but even through the waves of vomit and bile and bitter regret I register that I mustn't throw up on the marble floor. I retch and heave and sob. Finally I slump back onto the floor, shivering. I can't see the hands of my watch. I shuffle backwards across the floor until I hit the side of the bath. I draw my knees up to my chest, lean my head in my hands and cry some more. I'm still there when the door cracks open and a widening sliver of light spills across the floor.

'Dave! For fuck's sake! Are you in there?' Tony's voice is sharp even through the slur of alcohol. 'You couldn't have timed that worse, could you? You've missed the fireworks.'

Lydia pushes past him and clicks on the lights.

'Don't worry Tony,' she says grimly. 'Dave isn't a big fan of fireworks.'

$$- \; 3 \; -$$

I hate the way hangovers are depicted in movies: character wakes up, looks at clock radio, groans, sits up in bed, holds hand to temple, shakes head ruefully, stumbles to bathroom, looks in mirror, groans again, takes handful of Panadol, and slinks out of the house. Then within the hour they're chasing someone across a roof or seducing Angelina Jolie. But two hours after Lydia forced me out of bed I'm still green and sick, head spinning, body drained of not only energy but also basic human strength: my neck can barely support the weight of my head. I want someone to shoot me. Lydia would be happy to. Even through my pain and self-pity I know this.

I stopped the taxi twice on the way home last night to throw up in the gutter. Lydia was in the front seat and the rest of us crammed in the back, all New Year excitement gone, just tired and sick and nothing to say. Gail briefly tried to say something polite and neutral – 'lovely apartment, wasn't it?' – before passing out on Tony's shoulder, drooling.

These thoughts, and other blacker ones too, swirled in my head after Lydia and I crashed into bed. Around dawn I was dragged awake when she grabbed her pillow and stomped out of the bedroom.

'Jesus, Dave, you're a mess.'

'Huh?'

'You're grinding your bloody teeth again. It's horrible.'

'I'm sorry. Hey, don't go…'

The door crashed shut. I rolled back onto the bed, groaning at the light filtering into the room.

From when Lydia and I first shared a bed I lied and told her I started grinding my teeth as a child for no apparent reason and never grew out of the habit. At her insistence I've tried every known medical treatment and quack remedy. Even now just to keep her happy I eat an apple or couple of carrot sticks last thing at night. It's supposed to relax the jaw. I do it to please her and show I'm trying, even though it's futile.

I rarely drink heavily these days but when I do I never suffer from memory loss. On the odd occasions like last night, when I get totally pissed and do or say things I regret, I never need to rely on Lydia or someone to tell me. Even through a killer hangover I can always remember everything in excruciating detail.

I get up around mid morning and we slouch around watching the New Year celebrations from around the world – Paris, London, and New York a couple of hours later. I can just about tolerate fireworks on television. There's no smell, for one thing.

Tony isn't feeling much better than me. He lies on the sofa, yawning and scratching his balls, wearing only a pair of flapping boxer shorts and an England football shirt, the shiny white fabric stretched taught across his belly. He's irritable and snappy with Gail. She isn't looking great either. She's made an effort but her hair is lank and lifeless, her face puffed and shiny and her sunburned shoulders have gone blotchy.

'Looks good, doesn't it?' Tony says, indicating the hulking chocolate-brown wooden elephant that sits on our glass coffee table. He and Gail bought it in Thailand on their way to Sydney and presented it to Lydia and me as a present when they arrived, the day before New Year's Eve. I suspect it is teak or some forbidden hardwood. Its tusks look alarmingly like real ivory, too. It looks terrible amid our mostly modern furniture.

Our house and its decor are very much to Tony's taste.

'Nice,' he'd said, after having a good poke round on his arrival. 'Bit on the small side though.'

'There's only two of us. Anyway, Sydney's very expensive for property.'

'Oh yeah? What's this place worth?'

'I don't know. Well over a million.'

'No way!'

I'm discovering a lot else about my older brother aside from his taste in home furnishings. Seventeen years apart is a long time. I'd seen photos of him, but waiting at the airport for them the other day I wasn't even sure if I would recognise Tony. But suddenly there he was, emerging from customs, and I immediately recognised the pointed shape of his face, the slight roundness of his shoulders as he pushed the laden trolley, the impatient way his head was inclined as he barked at the woman trotting next to him. My new sister-in-law.

I've got everything to discover too about Gail. I expected Tony to have married someone younger, but she's about the same age as him. This realisation is comforting, for some reason. She's different from Clare, the first Mrs Anthony Truman, who was a female equivalent of him – loud, confident, flirtatious, occasionally hilariously funny, often not. Very much one of the boys. She was blonde and attractive in an obvious kind of way, the type that men always liked (I was probably the exception) but whom other women detested on sight. Their relationship began after a drunken one-night stand in the Christmas holidays after my first university term. I was never comfortable with Clare for many reasons but mainly because at a pub lunch the day after they met Tony informed his mates and me that he had just enjoyed the dirtiest night of sex he had ever had. Presumably at the time he thought it would only be a one-night stand. How he must have come to regret those words, especially the first time he actually introduced her to the same lunchtime pub crowd. I could never look her in the eye. Tony and Clare divorced after three years. She later married an anaesthetist and had three children.

Lydia and I have already seen plenty of pictures of Gail, mostly from their wedding. Mum sent us hundreds. They got married in St Lucia, which Tony claimed was to make it easier for me to come because the Caribbean is roughly halfway to Australia. I told him we couldn't afford it. I don't think we missed out on much. One photo is from the ceremony: everyone self-consciously barefoot on the beach, lots of unfashionably crumpled linen suits, the white ribbons round the cabana, people brick-red with sunburn, scraps of ribbon from previous ceremonies littering the sand, the next wedding party already beginning to congregate back in the hotel foyer, the sky looking stormy. They went in the wet season, when it was cheaper.

Then the surprise news in one of Mum's letters following her usual chat about the weather and the noisy students next door and how her dog training classes are going and how she hopes I'm coming home for a visit soon. Just a few words in her neat, girlish writing in blue biro. *Isn't it exciting, Tony and Gail coming to see you? She's ever so nice. And aren't they lucky, coming for New Year's Eve and everything!!!*

I phoned her that evening. She seemed surprised that Tony hadn't yet told me he was coming, then apprehensive. She probably detected the ominous edge in my voice.

'Dave love, he's been busy, I think they only just decided…'

'What's Tony's email address?'

She got his business card from her fridge and laboriously spelled it out.

And so contact – the occasional Christmas card or holiday postcard excepted – between the brothers Truman was restored, and Lydia and I prepared for the arrival of Tony and my new sister-in-law. While I was nervous about having Tony to stay, mainly because I was worried about him and Lydia, I was looking forward to seeing him. But I just wish we could have one drunken weekend together and go our separate ways afterwards. I'm not so keen on three weeks of him. I don't want Tony inside my head, inside my life. I've come too far, gone to too much trouble to get away.

The front door slams and Lydia appears, red faced and panting. She clutches the doorframe for balance and does some leg flexes, pulling one foot hard up behind her, then the other.

'God, it's hot out there already.'

'Have you been *running*?' Gail asks, incredulous.

Lydia nods and swigs from her water bottle. She's one of those people who never get hangovers. She eyes me pitilessly.

'You'll be alright for lunch at Mum and Dad's, won't you Dave,' she says. It isn't a question.

'What time are we due there?' I stifle a groan.

'One o'clock, latest.'

There's no way.

'Should be fine. I'm sure I'll feel better in an hour or so.'

We watch television in silence while Lydia drums her nails on the doorframe. Soon I can take no more and slink off to bed again, her eyes boring into my back.

– 4 –

Lydia fiddles with the lock and finally throws open the sliding doors onto the deck. Tony and Gail rush outside.

'Wow,' Gail says. '*Wow!*'

'Cor,' Tony says. 'This is a bit of alright.'

The house perches on an escarpment high above the bay. From the back deck the ground drops away to a tree-lined coastal pathway and the rocky shore beneath, with a strip of beach to the left. Port Stephens stretches out in front of us, a broad blue expanse dotted with boats. Tiny waves crunch on the beach.

'So your old man just bought this place as a holiday home?'

Lydia nods. 'We used to have a house at Byron, but it was too far away for a weekender. So they got this place. Port Stephens is nicer.'

'What did it cost, if you don't mind me asking?'

'Tony, give it a rest, man,' I say.

'I don't know, Tony,' Lydia says. 'A lot.'

He turns to Gail, who is mesmerised by the view.

'Hey, maybe we could get a second home. Spain. Or maybe Majorca?'

'Sure, love. Good idea.'

A flock of lorikeets explodes from a gum tree like little green meteors, screeching madly.

'Christ, those birds are noisy, aren't they?' says Tony. He sees our faces. 'They're nice though. Don't get parrots in the wild at home.'

'How's that for a barbie, Tony?' I ask, pointing.

'Holy shit, look at this thing!' He runs to it like a child on Christmas morning. It's a ridiculous size, an immense stainless steel outdoor kitchen on wheels.

'About five thousand dollars, Tony,' Lydia says, giving me a sly look.

****

Tony is hunched over, one foot up on his chair and his chin resting on a hairy knee, clipping his toenails, ignoring Gail's half-hearted murmur.

'Tone, you don't have to do that here, do you?'

After a pause he makes a show of clumping his chair round so his back is to the table, but this somehow makes the ritual even more repellent. After each loud clip, he turns and grabs a swig of coffee or a noisy mouthful of toast.

'I'll pick them up,' he says, seeing Lydia's face.

'You'd bloody better,' I say, making a show of disapproval for her sake. 'What are you going to do next, trim your nasal hair?'

For a second Tony looks as if this is a great idea, then flips me a v-sign and returns to his toenails. We've seen a lot of Tony's bare feet over the last few days. They are disgusting: deathly white and knobbly with hideous long toes with cracked yellow nails. His second toe extends a good half inch past the tip of his big toe, as if his middle fingers had been transplanted onto his feet. I've been hinting that he should buy a pair of thongs, but he won't – 'I hate flip flops' – and goes around in a pair of bulky reef sandals, which look ridiculous on the ends of his spindly legs.

The timber deck is already hot underfoot and the sun's glare is strong even through the umbrella.

'How was Christmas in Thailand?' I ask Gail.

'The hotels and bars didn't make much bloody effort,' Tony grunts, still with his back to us. 'No decorations. Not even a tree. You wouldn't have known it was Christmas.'

'It was lovely.' Gail's face shines. 'I'd always wanted to go to the beach on Christmas day. Like you can. You're so lucky.'

They've spent plenty of time at the beach since they've been in Australia. The back of Tony's neck is the colour of cheap strawberry ice cream. Gail is wearing a strapless sundress which reveals that she has also gone at it too much, too soon. Her shoulders and arms are a strange, deep orangey-red, a lurid contrast to her silvery-blond hair. They've stubbornly ignored my advice that the Australian sun is even more ferocious than in Thailand, and certainly than in Europe. Maybe I laboured the point, but they didn't want to know. 'We're here to get a tan, no point coming all this way otherwise is there?' they say before heading off to lie on the beach for hours. I should warn them that even sitting out here under the umbrella is dangerous, but I think *fuck it*, and keep quiet.

When not at the beach Gail has spent much of the past two days sitting on the deck with a pair of binoculars, looking for dolphins. They're so common, especially at dusk when they come closer to shore to feed, that for Lydia and me, they're just part of the scenery here. They'd have to do tricks for either of us to get excited any more. Yet every time she spots the glint of sunlight on a dorsal fin, Gail shrieks.

'Oh, Tone. Tone! Aren't they beautiful?'

Tony couldn't care less about dolphins. At first he'd been interested too, letting Gail scan the bay while he lounged next to her drinking his beer. He snatched the binoculars from her whenever she spotted one, but only because he hoped it was a shark. In the car on the way up I told him that this area was famous for Great Whites and that there'd been lots of gory deaths, all hushed up by the tourism authorities. I couldn't resist. When we went down to the beach yesterday he refused to do anything more than potter at the water's edge, saying we were mad to go beyond knee deep. He's partly right, since there's a good chance here of treading on a sting ray. But I don't tell them that.

Tony turns out to be a very good cook. He loves the whole Aussie barbie thing. So he's become our chef, revelling in his role, wielding the big tongs, flipping the steaks or sausages, even making elaborate salads involving chick peas or pine nuts.

I have to keep well away when the barbie's going, and that's tricky. I usually go for a run or a swim just when he's firing it up and come back when the smells have died down.

But today I return five minutes too soon to find that he's only just finished cooking my tuna steak. It's a calm night, barely a breeze off the water, and the smell on the deck is bad enough anyway, the oily meaty smoke still hanging in the air, mosquitoes buzzing happily.

'There you go Dave,' he says, sliding the fish onto my plate with a flourish. 'Cooked to perfection and I kept it well away from the meaty part of the barbie, you big girl.'

I'm the only one having tuna. And it looks perfect, the dark parallel lines from the griddle showing as neat diagonal indents, the flesh still intact, not flaking away at the corners. The hot smell drifts up at me, and it starts: the rising wave of nausea and the churn of bile. I look at Lydia but she just shrugs. Holding my breath, I cut the tuna open. The top and bottom layers are cooked, but the middle is still pink and moist. I see Gail's sunburned shoulders, red and vivid, and heave violently and jump to my feet so quickly that I jar the table. Then I'm inside, in the toilet and it's New Year's Eve all over again.

I want to go and lie down but I have to face them. Tony shakes his head at me in a 'what the hell?' expression.

'Sorry about that,' I say.

Gail smiles at me, worried.

'Lydia was saying you're often like this, Dave,' says Tony.

'Oh, not often. Just sometimes, the sight and smell of meat... even seeing it on TV sometimes – makes me sick. Physically sick.' I can't explain it.

'We've had some fun and games at parties and barbeques, haven't we Dave?' says Lydia.

I nod and force a smile. The smells are fainter now and I can stand to sit at the table, as long as I don't look too closely at their steaks. Gail pats my arm.

'When did you stop eating meat, Dave?'

'Years ago. I was still at school.'

'I remember one Christmas time,' says Tony, waving his fork at me, his mouth full of chop. 'We went to Auntie Sandra's and you made a fuss about one strip of bacon on the turkey. You wouldn't touch it.'

We fall silent. Tony's right. I need to change the subject but am too slow because Gail steps in.

'So why did you stop eating meat, Dave?'

I've had to answer this question a thousand times but never sound convincing.

'We did a thing at school about how they're clearing the Amazon rainforests to make way for cattle grazing. That made me decide.'

'Funny how it makes you sick,' says Lydia. 'Having an environmental conscience is one thing, but feeling sick about it, I don't understand.'

'Good point,' said Tony. 'You used to love meat, Dave. We all did. I remember fighting with you over who got to have the last burger.'

'I know. I can't explain it.' I try to rouse myself, sound convincing. 'Look, it doesn't matter. Let's not worry about it, please. I'll cook my own stuff, inside on the stove.'

Lydia waves her hand in a 'whatever' kind of gesture and goes back inside to get more wine. But Tony isn't done.

'It created lots of problems for Mum, you becoming a poofter vegetarian, Dave.'

'No it didn't.'

'It bloody did! You probably didn't realise. Having to cook special things for you, always in a separate pan, always having to have the kitchen door open to let the meat smells out, winter or summer. It was fucking freezing in there for poor Mum.'

Lydia returns and I hold out my wine glass.

'It was a bad time for you to suddenly develop a bloody environmental conscience,' Tony continues. 'She had a lot on her mind at that time. She wasn't herself.'

'How long was this after your dad passed away?' Gail asks.

Tony glares at her.

'It was five years and ten months after Dad died,' I say. 'The disaster was 1976. March the 8th. A Friday. And he didn't pass away. He was *killed*. Either in the crash, or drowned. We never found out which.'

'That's so terrible,' Gail murmurs, without looking at Tony.

There's an awkward pause which we fill by watching Lydia open another bottle of wine. The hiss of cicadas seems to have got louder, an infuriating buzzing in my head. It's almost completely dark now, just some pale moonlight flickering out on the bay and a couple of winking red and green lights out in the channel. The treetops, level with the deck, swish in the breeze.

'Mum was funny around that time you gave up meat, Dave. You have to admit.' Tony puts his knife and fork down. 'Nobody was themselves around then, were they? I probably wasn't.'

Is that guilt, or anger, or remorse in his voice? Or just too much wine on top of too much beer?

'Why not?' Lydia's voice is softer now, because Dad's name has come up. She knows what happened to him, and what it has meant to me. Tony and I look at each other. He raises an eyebrow and gives a half shrug.

'Oh, just the culmination of a few things that happened at once,' I say. 'It was just a bad time all round.'

I wait, but Tony says nothing. He stares out into the darkness.

'Let's go inside,' Lydia says. 'I'm getting eaten alive out here,' and she slaps her arm, for effect. 'Let's go and watch the news. It's nearly on.'

It is like a light has been snapped on. Everyone is animated again, standing, clearing the table, balancing plates and glasses and bowls and carrying them inside. I try unsuccessfully to catch Tony's eye. I don't know what I want or expect, anyway – maybe a reassuring smile, a sympathetic face, something to mirror what I want to signal to him.

****

Lydia elbows me awake. For a few seconds I'm groping upwards from deep underwater.

'Dave! Please, no more!'

Face-achingly bleary as I am, I know that with no spare room to retreat to, she will have been tossing and cursing me for ages before waking me. My head throbs and my jaw is stiff and aching. Even my actual teeth seem to hurt, like hot little coals have been hammered into my gums.

'Sorry sweetheart.'

She shrugs and sighs and rolls over, pulling the sheet tight. In the morning she'll be nice about this. But right now there's no way she'll offer any words of sympathy.

I creak out of bed, pull on a tee-shirt and tiptoe out to the lounge room. I find some Panadol in the kitchen cupboard and drink a glass of water. I splash some on my face and the back of my neck, soaking my tee-shirt. It's icy cold down my back but it feels good. The room is flooded in silvery light from the floor to ceiling glass that forms the beach-side wall of the house. The sliding patio door is open a couple of feet, making the blinds tug and sway. I stand in the doorway in the cool clear air and do some deep breathing, eyes closed.

There's a cough from out on the deck. I nearly drop my glass.

'Alright, Dave.'

My thudding heart slows.

'Shit, you made me jump.' I step outside and sit on the sofa. It's chilled with dew.

'What time is it?' Tony doesn't sound like he cares.

'Dunno. Three, four.'

'Can't sleep?'

'Nah.'

'Me neither. Still can't, half the time. Must run in the family, eh?' Tony laughs mirthlessly.

After this exchange we settle back into an uncomfortable silence.

The moon spills glowing silver corrugations across the inky water of the bay. Waves hiss along the beach.

'It's good that you've come to Australia, Tony,' I say, feeling that I'm the one who will have to start a conversation, although my jaw aches and my head throbs and I don't feel like a brotherly chat. But it's just too surreal otherwise: the two of us, who haven't been together for nearly twenty years, sitting silently together staring at the night sky.

He waves an arm.

'No problem,' he says, as if his visit has done me a great favour. 'Sydney's the place to be, isn't it. New Year and all that. Gail took some persuading, a flight this long. Furthest she'd ever been before was the honeymoon.'

I'm about to say 'same for you' when I remember that Tony once went to Florida with Clare in their early days. We never heard the end of it.

'How's things at home, Tone? How's work?'

'Sales aren't great, but things could be worse. But zero Christmas bonus this year. And I had to let some of the youngsters go the other week. Gen-fucking-Y. Big wake-up call for them. Welcome to recession reality.'

'Gail's nice,' I say, not feeling up to a discussion about youth unemployment at 3am.

Tony grunts. I try another conversation starter.

'Tony, I've been meaning to say thanks for looking after Mum all this time. I know you're busy. Gail told me how good you are with her.'

'I can't deny it's not easy. I'm forever having to go round and unblock her drains, repaint the back room, fix the clutch.'

'I know you spend a lot of time with her, Tone. She always tells me how lucky she is to have you.' I laugh. 'The doting elder son, while the black sheep ran off to the colonies.' I instantly regret this throwaway remark.

'Yes, ran off indeed. Why did you come and live out here, Dave?'

How many times have I had to fend off this bloody question.

'Oh you know, Tone. The weather. The lifestyle.'

'Alright, so the weather's good. And it does seem a nice place, I'll grant you. But I'm still as mystified now as I was then,' he says. 'To leave your mates, the place where you grew up... to leave your *family*.'

'Family? You mean Mum! You mean how could I leave when she was on her own, don't you?'

He shrugs.

'Look, it wasn't an easy decision, Tony.' I shudder at the memory of the stages my mother and Tony went through at hearing my news: shock, disbelief, anger, and finally a bitter acceptance. 'You have to do what's best for you, don't you? It's my life. Anyway, it was better me than you. If you'd left the country Mum would have followed you.'

'Huh?'

'Oh, forget it.'

The favourite son wouldn't have been allowed to disappear, like I was. It's not that our mother doesn't love me. It's just that Tony will always be the cherished first born, the eldest son. As a child

I used to wonder which of the two of us Mum would have saved in a house fire, if she'd had to choose. I always ended these stupid macabre visions with the conclusion that if the house caught fire it would be better for me if it was a time when Dad was home – although statistically that was less likely. Certainly now, Mum couldn't manage without Tony, and I accept that in my absence, his position as head of the family and Mum's favourite son is unassailable.

'No, come on Dave. No one suddenly decides to move to the other side of the world just because they don't like the cold and rain. And Christ, it's not like you were the outdoors type anyway. You're a crap swimmer. You always just had your head in a book – and all you need for that is central heating.'

These words don't go anywhere, but dissolve slowly into the darkness and now deafening cicada chorus.

'Funny,' he continues, 'the only people who used to end up here at the arse end of the world were criminals.'

'Ha ha. The old "you lot live in a convict colony" joke. I've been to the cricket. I've heard the Barmy Army giving it some.'

The ragged outline of a fruit bat arcs across the sky.

'All right Dave, I suppose it is your life.' He sounds more conciliatory. 'It's just that as time goes by, the old girl gets more depressed than ever. It's all doom and gloom. She mopes around, surrounded by thousands of pictures of Dad. She puts a new one in a frame every week.'

'That's strange,' I say. 'Lots of her friends must be widows now too, but she seems sadder about Dad than ever.'

The next question comes out of my mouth from nowhere. Perhaps the commonsense part of my brain is still asleep.

'Why did you and Dad never get along, Tony?'

'Huh?'

'I know I was only ten when he was killed… but even I can remember that you and Dad didn't get along that well. Why was that?'

'What the fuck are you on about?'

Suddenly a name comes into my head, spiralling to the surface from the deepest recesses of my most distant past. It startles me.

'Did something happen? Something to do with you and Dad and that little girl, Janice?'

Tony's voice is steely.

'You're talking crap, Dave. Nothing happened. Anyway, you couldn't possibly remember a thing. You were just a little kid. And Dad and I got along fine.'

My heart is hammering.

'How many photos of him have you got up in your house, Tony?'

'How the fuck would you know?' he snarls. 'You've never once in twenty years come home to visit!'

He raises his knees and in one movement rolls upright from his prone position and strides to the edge of the balcony. There's a faint splat as he gobs onto the pavers below. He spits again, properly this time, jerking his head back and snapping his neck forward for extra distance.

'Sod this, I'm off to bed.' He strides past, crashing his shin against the edge of the glass table.

'Fuck!'

I've got no spit. My mouth is like leather.

A cloud bank rolls across the moon and the darkness in front of me stretches out endlessly, with just a couple of faint yellow dots far out in the bay.

****

Tony is still irritable in the morning. He sits apart from the rest of us at the cafe table, complaining that his coffee's too strong, scowling at the waitress, fiddling with his phone, sending suddenly urgent work messages. The prospect of going on a dolphin spotting cruise, which has Gail fizzing with excitement and checking the settings on her camera already, has done nothing to rouse him. Not even when I untruthfully tell him there's a good chance we'll see sharks as well.

They arrive in a melee of pushchairs, kids, bags and toys. We jump to our feet – or three of us do, at least. Tony drags himself upright and forces himself to shake hands with my best friend Jeremy and his wife Penny. Their kids – two girls, five and three – cluster round me, jumping up and down, Chloe wanting to be picked up.

'Dave! Dave!' She holds her arms up, imploring. 'We're going to see dolphins!'

Tara, the three-year-old, takes one look at Tony, bursts into tears and buries her face in Penny's skirt.

'She mustn't be a Blues fan, Tony,' I laugh, indicating the royal blue Birmingham City football shirt he's wearing. He looks more morose than ever and I remember that Tony was never comfortable around little children.

After another coffee we gather our gear and wander round the rim of the bay alongside the strip of beach to the wharf where our dolphin boat awaits. The sun is fierce already and the sky is that improbable Australian blue that you just don't get anywhere else in the world and makes your photos look like they've been digitally altered. Gail, Lydia and Penny are ahead, the kids skipping and weaving between them, Gail bending to talk to them and taking Chloe by the hand with Penny on the other, swinging Chloe along in big looping jumps. All of them are laughing. We boys are further back. Jeremy and I try to include Tony in conversation but we quickly give up on his monosyllabic grunts and ignore him. So he trails behind us, head down. As we pass beneath a street light he lets out an angry bellow. The girls are too far ahead to hear, but Jeremy and I whirl round. A seagull has shat on him from its perch on the light, depositing a gleaming white streak across his shoulder, stark against his blue shirt. Jeremy guffaws but I know better than to laugh at my brother in such situations.

'Hey, that's good luck, remember,' I say, but Tony isn't listening. Head flicking to and fro, searching, he grabs a pebble from the side of the pathway. He looks up, eyes narrowed, at the bird on the streetlight, sizing it up, but then spins round and hurls the stone at a flock of seagulls mooching at the water's edge, only twenty yards away. He throws the stone low and hard in a whipping sideways action. The birds rouse themselves and flap squawking into the air but they aren't fast enough and the stone hits one of them just as it spreads its wings to fly off. The force of the blow spins the bird around and for a few seconds it writhes on its back, wings outstretched and legs flailing. Its comrades land about thirty yards up the beach, cackling indignantly. The injured seagull scuttles to join them, its wing trailing out to the side, repeatedly catching on the peaks of sand, toppling it onto its chest. Eventually it joins its friends and collapses in their midst. As if from instinct, it half-heartedly preens the feathers of its outstretched broken wing, but gives up, forlorn. The other birds look at it without interest.

'Tony!' I shout.

And suddenly he's all whining contrition.

'Shit, I'm sorry, alright? I only meant to give them a fright.'

'For fuck's sake, Tone!' I can't bear to look at the doomed bird. 'You bloody psycho! What's the matter with you?'

'Christ, I'm sorry! It'll be alright anyway. I only clipped it.'

'You've bust its wing! The poor thing will die, won't it!'

'Oh come on, it's only a seagull. They're a pest, aren't they? Like pigeons.'

Jeremy snorts and shakes his head. Instantly my brother gives him the old Tony Truman stare, the narrowed eyes and clenched jaw. Jeremy turns away.

We start walking, the girls well ahead of us now. Tony quickly falls behind again.

'How long since you last saw Tony?' Jeremy asks. 'Or even spoke to him?'

'I talked to him only last year, when he tried to make me feel bad about not going to his wedding. But I haven't seen him since I moved here.'

'I can't believe you haven't once wanted to go home in seventeen years.'

I say nothing.

'Has Tony changed much?'

'He's become far more domestic,' I say, struggling with truth and loyalty. 'Gail seems to have been really good for him. She's nice. And he's great with Mum. But otherwise, he seems the same old Tony. I mean, no-one really changes, do they?'

– 5 –

We come off the freeway and hit late Sunday afternoon traffic grinding down the Pacific Highway into Sydney. Tony cheered up the day after the dolphin cruise, even pulling me aside to mutter 'sorry about yesterday', and the rest of our stay was fun and relaxing. So we're all sorry to leave Port Stephens: the roomy house, the peace and quiet, the blue water. Everyone's gloomy, and a stifling flatness pervades the inside of the car. I'm back at work tomorrow, which depresses me further. By the time we cross the harbour bridge conversation has petered out and I'm desperate to be home and out of the claustrophobic car. I'm also desperate for water. Tony drank the last of what we had while we were back on the freeway.

I screech into our car port and brake hard so everyone jerks forward and Lydia looks at me, surprised. I'm dying for that drink and am first to the front door, keys at the ready. But something is wrong.

Down the side of the house, past the garbage bins, the side gate swings open. I walk through to the back yard, and stop abruptly. The sliding doors from the lounge room to the patio are wide open. I've forgotten about being thirsty. The others approach up the path.

'Come on Dave, never mind checking your tomatoes, just let us in,' says Lydia.

She sees my face.

'Dave, what is it?'

We stand in a huddle.

'We didn't leave the doors open, did we?' I say.

I already know the answer. We eyeball each other. Gail's hand is at her mouth.

'Come on Dave,' says Tony, jerking his head at the house. 'Let's have a look. Just you and me.'

Shit. He means that the burglars — I've now grasped it must be burglars — could still be inside.

We step through the sliding doors into the lounge, listening like deer for the slightest sound. There's a savage dent in the timber doorframe, and the lock itself has been prised away from its housing. The television is gone, leaving a couple of trailing electrical leads and a neat dust-free oblong on top of the cabinet. The Bang & Olufsen is gone too. There's a smashed vase on the floor and a pile of books cascaded on top of the pieces. Tony strides through to the kitchen, then into the hall with me trotting behind. He stops abruptly, cocking his head, and I bump into him.

In that instant, we know that the intruders are long gone. The air is too still, too quiet. And it's late afternoon on a Sunday, with half the neighbourhood outside watering their lawns or slurping beer on hot patios. We giggle at our collision. The inappropriateness of our sniggering only fuels it as we move through the downstairs rooms. We end up pretending to be cops checking a house like on those silly television crime shows: our hands clasped, forefingers extended like guns, going into rooms, and shouting 'clear!'

Our losses and damage aren't too bad. A couple of drawers have clearly been rummaged through, a few bits and pieces missing, things knocked over. But there is none of the mindless vandalism you hear about – spray paint on walls, shit on the carpet, piss in the cupboards.

'Wonder why they didn't take the elephant,' says Tony, patting its back. 'Too heavy, I suppose.'

'Probably.'

'I'll just check upstairs,' he says. 'You go and tell the girls to come in.'

Tony's footfalls sound on the stairs as I go back out to the patio. I smile reassuringly and am about to say 'it's not so bad', when there's a shriek from upstairs.

'Dave!'

I take the stairs two at a time. Tony stands in the doorway of the first bedroom, hands on hips, shoulders slumped. Oh, *shit*. It's like the burglars did upstairs first but ran out of time – or perhaps they got spooked – and fled, just doing a quick look round downstairs and grabbing the television and stereo on their way out. But upstairs they were thorough. Every drawer and cupboard in each of the three bedrooms and study has been ransacked and their contents tipped onto the floor. Bookcases have been pushed over and rest precariously on top of the debris, face down, a few paperbacks sliding casually down the piles of clothes and shoes.

'Bastards,' I say.

'I'm sorry mate,' says Tony, patting me on the shoulder. 'I didn't think this sort of thing happened here.'

In our bedroom, the familiar comforting clutter that sat on Lydia's dressing table – her powders and lotions and lipsticks and a wedding photo of us – has been swept off onto the mounds of clothes and shoes and books that already covered the floor. Our feet slide on the hundreds of coins where my champagne magnum bottle, in which I save loose change, has been emptied. Even the bathroom has had the full treatment, probably in a search for hidden jewellery. The drawers are empty and all the components of a domestic bathroom, the toilet rolls and cotton wool balls and toothpaste and tampons, are scattered across the tiles. Everything reeks eye-wateringly of mouthwash. I glance into the study – which is basically mine, since Lydia rarely uses the PC on the desk, preferring her laptop – and turn away with a moan. My iMac is gone and there's not a square foot of carpet visible under a teetering mountain range of books and stationery and papers. It's utterly depressing.

Lydia and Gail join us and Gail sobs and clasps Tony's arm.

'Oh, Lydia, you poor things,' she sniffs.

'Thank Christ we had our passports and stuff with us,' Tony says, patting Gail's hand.

Lydia's face is pale and she looks tired. Together we go back into our bedroom. There's a strong smell of perfume, spillage from the dressing table carnage. I put my arm around her.

'At least we're insured. And I always wanted an excuse to buy a bigger TV,' I add, trying to sound light hearted. 'Erm, how about your jewellery?'

Lydia picks her way to the dressing table. On its polished surface lie a couple of rings and a scattering of beads from a broken necklace. Nothing else, and no jewellery among the mess on the floor. She slumps on the bed with her head in her hands.

The rest of our Sunday is spent in trying to clear up and showing two unsympathetic police constables round the house. They talk in that annoying way that cops now adopt when interviewed on television.

'So, have you located where the persons have gained entry to the premises?' one asks, as if the burglary is still in progress.

I point at the shattered patio doors. Tony makes a 'wanker' gesture behind their backs.

'The offenders are most likely juveniles. Males. They probably absconded in a vehicle,' adds the other.

I become irritated so Lydia takes them round while I phone the insurance company. Later the four of us tidy up most of the downstairs mess and order pizza, pretending we're hungry. In our bedroom I get on my hands and knees and shove the coins and books and everything else to one side to make a narrow strip of carpet for us to navigate from doorway to bed. We're exhausted, and Lydia has a big work day tomorrow, and the television's been nicked, so we go to bed early.

'Don't you two worry about clearing up tomorrow, right?' I tell Tony and Gail as we say goodnight. 'You've only got a few days left. Go out and enjoy yourselves. I'll sort it out when I get in.'

****

I sleep amazingly well. Partly it's from tiredness. But it is also that the effect on my nocturnal mind of a recent trauma or big event is to leave no room for the past to intrude. So there's no teeth-grinding, or periods of blank, tossing wakefulness, and when Lydia's alarm goes off at 5.15, its jangly tune hauls me awake from a deep pit of sleep. From the extremity of her yawn and the heaviness of her sigh, it's obvious that she's hardly slept at all. I've just got time to roll over groggily and give her warm body a squeeze from behind before she switches the alarm off and swings herself out of bed. I reach out to pat her on the back but am too slow and my hand swipes at empty air and flops onto the mattress.

'What time's your flight?' I ask.

'Six forty-five.'

'Do you have to go?'

'Yep. The meetings are locked in, and I'm presenting. God, you snored last night.'

'I know. I've not slept that well in ages. Sorry. It's weird, considering. What time will you get home tonight?'

'Around nine, hopefully.'

She pads to the bathroom. I can tell from the rhythm and volume of her bare feet on the floorboards that she's terribly depressed.

As if being burgled wasn't enough, I've got the usual Monday morning depression and that returned-from-holiday flatness to overcome. I've got hundreds of emails to sort through at work, having had Thursday and Friday off. I'm at my desk later in the morning sighing and cursing and tapping away when Gail phones.

'Ever so sorry to bother you at work,' she says. 'We just wanted to know what flowers Lydia likes.'

'Why?' I ask.

'We're tidying up and thought we'd nip round the corner and buy her some nice flowers to come home to.'

Damn, wish I'd thought of that. Can I tell Gail not to bother, and steal her idea?

'She was ever so upset last night,' Gail says. 'And having to go to Melbourne and back today.' She can't believe that anyone would fly somewhere and back in one day.

'Tulips are her favourite,' I say. 'Gail, that's a lovely thought, but no need to bother. Anyway, you two are supposed to be out and about, enjoying your last few days.' From our eighth floor windows, an oblong of blue sky shows between the other office towers. 'It looks lovely out. Go down to the beach, or out for lunch. Don't hang around doing our clearing up for us. I'm coming home around four to meet the insurance bloke.' I try to sound stern. 'Don't let me find you guys at home!'

'Alright, if you mean it, we'll just do some more tidying, and then we'll go. I'm doing downstairs, and Tony's doing upstairs.'

Maybe Tony's trying to atone for his part on our nocturnal row at Port Stephens. My Outlook calendar flashes a fifteen minute reminder about a meeting I arranged last week and am completely unprepared for.

'Gail, shit, I've got to run. Look, please don't worry about tidying up.'

'It's no trouble, really Dave. We're your guests, it's the least we can do.'

At lunchtime, still furious with myself about how badly my meeting went, I run out and buy a couple of CDs for Lydia, to compete with Gail's flowers. As I scurry back to the office I remember we don't have a CD player anymore.

After lunch I have to spend some time in our studio, as our two-person graphic design team calls itself. The senior of them is a Scot called Declan. He's in his fifties and hanging out for an early retirement package, which I happen to know he isn't going to get. He's completely devoid of wit, charm or style and totally unsuited to a creative profession. The only times I've ever seen him laugh are at the news of someone's misfortune. But we get on okay. This isn't because I like him but because Declan's cooperation, or the lack of it, can make or break your project. Whether he'll push himself to meet your deadline depends on his mood and whether he likes you. All he cares about is Scottish football. I always check the weekend's results to see how Hibernian did against Motherwell or Arbroath or Hamilton Academicals or whoever, so we can have a blokey chat before I beg him to do an urgent job or chase up a printer. But today I'm the dour one, moaning about our break-in. I have stumbled on a second topic of interest because he nods his big square head knowingly, as if burglary is something familiar to him. An inevitable part of life even, like traffic or rain.

'How much stuff was lifted?' he asks.

'A fair bit. The usual suspects: TV, stereo, Lydia's jewellery. My bloody computer.'

Declan's white iMac is identical to mine. I see my study desk, its surface bare, the dangling leads and power cords and dust balls all that remain.

'Was there much on your computer?' asks Declan.

'Email addresses. Our photos. Luckily I've got them backed up, and some of them saved on a disc in the car.'

Declan nods his approval to my disaster management plan.

'No, the worst thing is just the bloody hassle of getting a new computer and setting it up,' I say. 'And the mess.'

Again I see my study, the bare desk, and my mind's eye pans back, revealing the chaos on the floor, the emptied drawers, the overturned bookcase, papers and pens and folders scattered everywhere.

'Bit of clearing up to do, eh?' Declan asks with relish.

'You could say that. We're lucky that my brother and his wife are staying. They're tidying up for us.'

Declan grunts and swivels his chair back towards his computer. He's shown enough interest in my problems. So I tell him about how I'm helping pull part of the annual report together, and how important a project it is, what 'milestones' we have to meet. As he grunts and nods and shoots questions through clenched teeth, a tiny ripple of unease sweeps through me like leaves fluttering in an icy breeze. I try to concentrate on paper stock thickness and matt versus gloss finishes and types of booklet bindings. But something is lodged in my brain, an irritant, a little germ of worry. As I half listen to Declan, my mind prods at this germ, probing it, revolving it on its axis. The vision of my desecrated study returns. Now I hardly hear Declan, sensing that I'm close to discovering what this thing is, but knowing there's still a piece missing, that I'm not there yet. The image of my study slides away and for an instant there's nothing, just a blankness, a black funnelling hole that runs through me and beyond, spanning time and place and looping back on itself from long ago and far away. And then an image drops back into place in my head like a slide into a projector, and it's the same one as before, of my study with the mess on the floor. But there's something different this time. Tony crouches on the floor, his hideous bare feet slipping on the piles of papers. He picks through the mess, putting books in one pile, files and folders in another, and meticulously sorts the miscellaneous contents of drawers into a couple of cardboard boxes. Occasionally he unfolds a piece of paper or holds something up to the light.

The ripple of unease becomes a crashing wave of horror.

'Holy shit. Oh, *shit*.' I leap from my chair and rush from the room.

I jump straight in a taxi outside the office and garble our address.

'Which way you wanna go mate?' says the driver. 'Take the tunnel?'

'Jesus, whichever's quickest!' I hate it when they ask this. Whatever I choose always feels like the wrong answer.

The driver shrugs and pulls out from the kerb. I dial our home number, jabbing hard at the keys. It rings four times, then the answer phone comes on. What does this mean? Am I safe? Have they gone out? Or does it just mean that they're still there but didn't get to the phone in time? Lydia's irritatingly calm voice tells me to leave a message after the tone. I try to steady my voice.

'Hi both, it's Dave. Are you there? Anyone there?' My heart rate slows. They must be out. Thank Christ. 'Hope you're having fun at the beach. See you later. Bye.'

A fresh panic sweeps through me. What if they're in the garden and didn't hear the phone? Or maybe they've popped out to the florist and will be back in five minutes.

I rest my head in my hand and try to control my breathing. I'm in the only taxi in Sydney with a law-abiding driver. He doesn't even run amber lights much less the just-turned-red ones. And then we get to within a mile of our house and hit school pick-up time. There mustn't be one kid in our suburb that walks to school. The four-wheel drives jostle for position, doing clumsy u-turns, mums double parking, flicking hazard lights on while they unload huge prams. The cab driver shakes his head.

'Always like this, mate. Worse than bloody peak hour.'

'I know.' I look at my watch and moan.

We grind along a couple more streets until I can take no more. We're half a mile from our house and it's uphill, but I abandon the cab. I force myself to walk. It's as if by running uphill on a hot summer day I would be visibly demonstrating to the world the state of my panic. Making it real. Again I see that clear image of Tony crouching on the floor of the study, holding an object up to the light, turning it over in his hands, reading something on a piece of paper. That gets me running, pushing hard up the hill, my pounding blood almost obscuring my vision, heat bursting in my ears. I swing into the front yard and fumble for my key, head throbbing so I can't hear anything. I almost fall through the door, letting it crash back against the wall of the passageway.

But it doesn't matter that I can't hear anything. There's nothing to hear. I'm too late. They've gone. And in that instant, my breath rasping in our hallway, I know that Tony and I will probably never speak again.

Something still compels me to check the house. A bunch of pale yellow tulips wrapped in blue cellophane lies on the hall table. The bottom ones are crushed, as if hurriedly dropped. I climb the stairs, trailing my sweaty hand along the banister, recreating the scene in my mind. Gail returns from the florist and lets herself in. Tony comes out of the kitchen in a rush, shouting instructions and grabbing her hand, dragging her upstairs. There is almost a faint echo of Tony's cries still in the air. And there's a lingering residual human warmth in the house, something different from the mid-afternoon heat. I must have only just missed them. We must have nearly collided in the street, me pounding up the hill and them scurrying down it, dragging their suitcases, Tony yanking Gail along, ignoring her bewildered questioning. Or, more chillingly, was it the other way around? Was it a sobbing Gail who had to get Tony out of the house, persuade him to come away and cool down, not do anything stupid? In the lounge room there's evidence that the latter is more likely. The elephant lies on the floor, its trunk and tusks snapped off, a dent in the timber flooring. A framed photo from the sideboard of me skiing in New Zealand lies nearby. The glass is smashed and the photo crumpled, as if stamped on by an angry heel.

The guest bedroom is as I expect to find it: evidence of their morning clean up in the piles of books returned to the shelf, clothes no longer strewn over the floor from their rifled cases. Their suitcases are gone, along with any evidence that my brother and his wife were ever here. There's a rectangular indentation on the duvet, where a suitcase would have lain while things were flung into it and the lid jammed shut.

The bathroom is in the same state as last night. Probably Tony was planning to clear it up last, after he'd done the study. My feet crunch on broken glass. I splash some cold water on my face and try to take some deep breaths.

As I near the closed study door, an absurd flush of optimism hits me. Perhaps there's a simple explanation for why their suitcases and clothes are missing. Tony and Gail could yet be down at Bondi, broiling on the sand or browsing in the shops. Right now they could be looking at their watches, feeling the sun-stiffness in the skin of their shoulders, deciding to head back to the house. This new hope creates a fresh urgency and I fling open the door.

The progress of Tony's clean-up operation is clear to see. Three quarters of the floor is bare, the debris that covered it now neatly stacked on the desk or returned to the bookshelves. But the far side of the room is exactly as it was last night. The drawers of the old bedside cabinet I use as an extra cupboard are still upturned on the floor, their contents in a precarious heap. I kneel next to it. On top of the pile, because it was at the back of the bottom drawer, the last one the burglars would have tipped out, are the things from my other life, stashed there long ago by my other self.

The first thing Tony would have done was to leaf through my old scrapbook. A3 size with pages of differently coloured coarse paper. On the front cover he'd have read, in my painstaking handwriting: *My Dad and North Sea Oil. By David Truman, aged 8 ½*. Inside I'd glued magazine clippings and drawn oil rigs, ships fighting huge seas, and scuba divers on sandy sea floors next to giant metal legs. And helicopters. In one picture, a misshapen yellow chopper skims above the waves, with Dad waving from one of the windows. His beard is a ragged black thing like Grizzly Adams's. The chopper's rotor blades are three static arms, like a photograph taken at a fast shutter speed. I never could draw a whirling circle of revolving rotor blades.

Several loose pieces of paper would have fluttered out from between the pages of the scrapbook when Tony opened it. A newspaper cutting from *The Birmingham Post* with a photo of my father and the headline 'Northfield man feared lost in North Sea tragedy'. A beige notelet with a pen and ink print showing a church with a thin pointed steeple and the heading 'St Mary's Parish Church, Selly Oak. In Memoriam. Eric Ronald Truman. 11am, 19 March 1976. Order of Service.' A blurred photograph of a small obelisk made from black granite, shiny with rain, standing in a park in Aberdeen with fresh flowers laid at its base. Dockyard cranes and a churning sea are visible in the far background beyond a jumble of grey roofs.

All these things Tony has placed neatly back inside my scrapbook, each one the right way up on the right hand side of a separate page, facing the reader.

The rest of what is heaped in front of me has spilled from a shoebox in which I had kept some mementos from school and university days.

My old blue and white football scarf that Granny Truman knitted for Dad to give me the first time he took me to St Andrews. So significant then, it seems a scraggly little thing now. I finger the tiny slip of paper bearing my 'A' level results, remembering that dizzily rushing combination of fear, panic and relief. There's the cloth badge with my school emblem, ripped off my blazer; a clipping from *The News of the World* dated Sunday 17 November 1985, showing Jeremy and me and a bunch of university mates with hideous haircuts and wearing nighties in a story called 'Sexy antics of student pyjama party'. There's the orange *Protect and Survive* government leaflet that told us what to do in a nuclear attack. It's amid these items that Tony would have found the things that precipitated his flight from the house.

I push through the pile. They're not here. I haven't opened that box in ten years but I know exactly what was in there. Of course. There's nothing for me to find here. Tony has taken everything. And he's perfectly entitled to. One of them was originally intended for him anyway. They're gone. It's all gone.

But there's a small crumpled ball of greyish paper lying amid the wisps of dust and tangle of computer cables beneath my desk. I smooth it out on the floor between my legs. I imagine Tony unfolding it, reading it, screwing it up and blindly flinging it away. It's a yellowed newspaper clipping showing a black and white photo of a blond teenage girl sitting on the bonnet of a small hatchback car. She's leaning back against the windscreen with one leg raised and one arm held awkwardly behind her head. She wears a one-piece swimsuit and a sash diagonally across her torso. The sash looks too big and has rucked up over her hip. She's smiling directly into the camera. The photo's caption says: *The car to beat the world,* and a sub heading: *Look at those curves! Northfield girl Tracey Downey gets comfortable on the Mini Metro, the new car that will see off foreign competition and restore the fortunes of British Leyland.*

I stand and flex my aching knees. There it is. At eye level, on the bookshelf. The white woollen bobble hat with two pink bands near its bottom edge has been placed carefully on the shelf, the bobble drooping over the edge like the head of a dead swan. I pick it up and slip my hand inside, knowing there's still one thing I won't find. Knowing that Tony has, finally, taken delivery of a thirty-year-old message meant only for him. I stroke the hat and raise it to my face, burying my nose in its softness. Is that scent there? Does any trace of her remain deep within the fibres? There's still mud on it even after my teenage hands had brushed the worst of it off. Tiny grains of grey earth embedded in the wool.

As I turn the hat over there's yet some dumb part of me that hopes both sides will match, and that the side I now reveal will be the same unblemished soft white wool, now aged to the colour of bone. But of course it isn't the same. The side Tony laid downwards on the shelf – deliberately, of that I have no doubt – is the same white wool, but with a nicotine-coloured scorch mark stretching back in an elongated triangle from the hat's lower edge, where the wool is turned back so it's double the thickness, to a tapered point up near the bobble. I run my fingertips over the burnt part, where the wool has a coarser feel to it, the fluffy softness gone forever.

I feel inside the hat again, just to be sure. I look around on the floor in case it's still lying there, fallen from the hat, unnoticed by Tony. But I know it's not. And now a final image of Tony comes to me. He stands where I am now, turning the hat over in his hands. A slip of paper drops soundlessly from inside the hat onto the floor. His red face creases and he frowns and bends to retrieve it. It's a pale pink notelet folded three times in half, so it's about the size of a credit card. He unfolds it, taking care because it's badly worn along the creases and beginning to tear where they meet the edges of the paper. Perhaps he sits at my desk to read the note, smoothing it out on the desktop, angling it into the light to see the faded purple lettering.

Did he have to read the words before he recognised the sender? Or did the memory of that girly teenage handwriting, the cutesy way the i's are dotted with circles, arc across thirty years and hit him like an electrical charge?

> *Dear Tony*
>
> *If you're reading this, it means you haven't come to the fireworks. I really hoped you would.*
>
> *Please don't let's be silly. You and me are meant to be.*
>
> *I'm sorry.*
>
> *Call me soon. Please!*
>
> *Your Tracey xxx*

I pick up my scarf and bury my face in it like I did with the hat. I don't know if it's really there — it surely can't be after three decades

— but the smells of smoke, mingled with the sweet sickly aroma of Southern Comfort, seem as fresh to me now as they were then. I sit like that for a long time, wondering if my tears will cleanse the wool and purge it of those ghastly smells.

BIRMINGHAM

31 OCTOBER 1981

– 6 –

After twenty minutes of slogging through the icy rain the other runners were just ghostly shapes glimpsed through the flickering greyness, like a line of sheep in a moorland fog. I was near the front of the race's main pack, which was perhaps seventy-five strong: a solid panting mass of pink faces, rain-plastered hair, mud-spattered shirts and splashing feet. Ahead was a leading string of around fifteen boys, and behind us were the stragglers, the kids who had been press ganged into a school team to make up numbers and who would have given anything to be spending their Saturday morning watching television or lying in bed instead.

I ran literally in the footsteps of the boy in front as we zigzagged to avoid the deepest pools of water and muddy hollows that looked capable of swallowing a careless runner like quicksand. Conditions underfoot were treacherous, with even the few areas of grass waterlogged and slippery. Several boys had already gone sprawling, dropping from the bobbing heads in the pack as if picked off by snipers, the following runners hurdling their prone forms without slowing. But I was wearing my football boots, a gamble over which I had agonised because their studs made them terrible for running on the concrete pathways and short stretches of roadway along the course, but far better on the grass and through the mud.

Pete appeared at my shoulder and kept pace, splashing alongside. He had been forced to compete in the race as punishment for having been caught smoking during morning break earlier in the week. He thought me insane for liking cross-country running. Privately I suspected that my best friend resented my relative success at it – even though had he wanted to he could have been a good athlete himself.

'Shit, slow down a bit,' he panted. 'I want a word.'

I grimaced, knowing what was coming.

'So Dave, are we going to the fireworks next week or what?'

Pete had been pressuring me for days about the annual bonfire night fireworks show in the park. Even by his standards he was being infuriatingly persistent.

'No, I can't be arsed this year,' I said. 'It's always the same. And there's good telly on Thursday nights.'

'Come on Dave! Don't be boring. It'll be a doss, there'll be girls there.'

'No. Not this year.' I flinched as a raindrop stung my eye.

'I'll persuade you. You know I will.'

'I don't want to bloody go!'

'Of course you do. Look, you know I'm only going to keep asking.'

I knew this was true.

'Oh for god's sake, all right! I'll go to the bloody fireworks.'

'I knew you'd see sense. And you won't regret it. Trust me.' He gave my back a stinging slap. 'I might even have a special surprise for us.'

'Like what?'

'Like something that'll blow your socks off.'

'*What?*'

'You'll have to wait and see, won't you?'

'Yeah, whatever.' I accelerated away from him. I wasn't used to having Pete with me in a race, and I didn't like it. I didn't like giving in to him either, but it was always easier.

'I'm not hanging back any more with you,' I yelled over my shoulder. 'I'll see you afterwards.' I cringed, expecting him to order me back to keep him company for the whole race.

'Fine,' he said, waving me away dismissively. 'I'm stopping for a fag soon anyway.'

Ten minutes later everyone was as wet as it was possible to be, as much from the freezing water splashed up by our pounding feet as from the rain itself. My ears ached badly from the wind chill. But somehow I enjoyed the sensation of being soaked and it no longer mattering how dirty or wet or muddy I got. I liked being part of a huge living entity, each boy fighting alone but also unstoppable. Nothing stood in our way.

My legs were getting heavier but I kept a good rhythm, head down, arms pumping. Adrenaline surged in my chest as the lead runners pounded down the gradient towards the stream in its deep cutting. I'd run this course many times before and knew that we would scramble down, splash across the stream bed, climb the far bank and begin the home stretch. I always got nervous here. Things could go wrong – falls or slips, a clumsy or deliberate shove. And it was easy to turn an ankle on the rocky stream bed. Mark Bennett had once leapt from the bank straight down into the water and broke his leg. It was said that the bone was *sticking through his skin*.

Out in front the stocky figure of race leader Kevin Crump hesitated before dropping into the cutting. It seemed ages before he reappeared, lurching up the far side like an ape. Crump attended Castle Green Boys, a nearby comprehensive school, smaller than ours, and one of the roughest schools in the city. Already well known to the police, he was a psychotic skinhead fifth former whose interest – and talent – in cross country running was a mystery. But it was never questioned, after a fellow runner had once laughed at him about it during a race and the young Crump had calmly elbowed him in the face.

The runners just ahead of me reached the cutting. They paused on the bank, where the turf overhung the edge, and the group of us behind rear-ended them in a pile up of bodies. There were panted mutterings – *fuckin' hell!* – and then boys were dropping into the ravine. It became clear why everyone had stopped. The normally shallow stream was a torrent of filthy brown water. Bodies tumbled down the slope and then paused at the water's edge until pressure backed up from behind and runners were forced out into the water like migrating wildebeest fording a crocodile river. Boys grabbed each other, bodies sprawling, people swearing and panting and laughing. With my boots' superior grip I kept my footing down the slope but took it too fast, my momentum sending me knee deep into the stream, stumbling, the current clutching my legs, but then I was through. Again my studs helped me up the far bank. I grabbed a clump of grass at the edge to pull myself clear, and I was away. Fear and relief pushed me up the incline away from the stream and I was absurdly pleased with myself, for once having made a good decision in wearing my football boots.

With only another half mile to run and the school buildings now in sight I relaxed, thinking about which shops Pete and I would visit in town after lunch. I was jolted from this by the realisation that there was a thirty-metre gap between me and the straggling figures emerging from the stream behind. Second place was possible. Second! My previous best had been eighth. I ignored the nervous fluttering in my guts and kept momentum, determined to at least stay in touch with Crump, use him as a pace setter to make sure I stayed ahead of my pursuers.

But Crump was slowing. He glanced back and there was pain on his face and fatigue in the angle of his huge shoulders. I couldn't believe it. The numbing cold was swept from me in a flush of panicky excitement as I realised what might now be possible.

We entered a thicket of rhododendron bushes where a gravel path wound between the hulking dark plants. Sheltered now from the rain and the vicious wind it was eerily quiet and suddenly Crump and I were alone, as if the only people in the race, in our own world. I followed his snorting breath and crunching footfalls as if they were an echo of my own, keeping my pace but not attacking yet, aware that my best chance of overtaking him was back out on the slippery grass.

I was so absorbed in these thoughts that I didn't notice the sudden silence ahead. I rounded a bend and Crump was only a few yards ahead of me, stationary, squatting on the ground. My momentum carried me forward even as the surprise jerked me back to full awareness. I assumed Crump must have fallen and was about to ask him if he was alright when he sprang to his feet, his right arm swung in a flashing arc and a handful of gravel peppered my face. I staggered, blinded, numb with the shock more than the pain. A burst of fear shot through me in anticipation of what Crump would do to me next but then I vaguely registered the sound of his footsteps thudding into the distance.

I trotted along the path, blundering into the rhododendrons, blinking and rubbing my eyes furiously. From behind came the stamp of multiple feet on gravel as the chasing pack approached, spurring me onwards in a final burst of effort. I emerged from the bushes back out onto the grass with the school now only five or six hundred metres away and the knot of spectators stirring at the sight of the runners. Crump looked over his shoulder again. He was struggling badly now: feet sliding in the mud, head drooping, legs almost plodding, energy spent but dragging himself onwards by sheer muscle power. He was only thirty metres ahead of me. I forced myself into one last effort and was already closing on him, planning to give him a very wide berth when I overtook, when he abruptly slowed until he was virtually walking. He turned and pointed a stubby forefinger at my face, then converted it into a flicked 'V' sign.

'Fuck off!' he snarled. He pointed his finger again and raised his eyebrows as if making sure that I properly understood.

And this time, I did.

Crump turned and powered onwards. I left a good distance between us before I continued, careful to maintain the gap. The boy behind was closing on me but had left it too late and I knew he wouldn't catch me. The final stretch took us down the long school drive to where a small knot of teachers and parents huddled morosely under their umbrellas. My boots clattered and skidded on the tarmac but I kept my feet to the finish. I shuddered to a gasping stop, hands on knees, my body instantly cooling in the wind, and prepared myself to modestly accept the congratulations of Mr McLeish, the history teacher who managed our school cross country team.

'Truman, why the silly grin, boy?' he demanded. 'What's wrong with you? Crump was half dead! You could have easily taken him out at the end there. We were all cheering you on.' He shook his head. Thin streams of water cascaded from the rim of his umbrella.

'But sir, second place isn't bad, is it? Crump always comes first.'

'No Truman, second place is very good. But for god's sake, Crump doesn't always have to win. It isn't preordained, you know.' His mouth twisted into something like a grin. 'Still, well done laddie. Now away and get dry.' He jerked his head towards the changing rooms.

On my way inside I passed Crump, squatting on his haunches, thighs bulging with muscle. He raised his head and gobbed at me.

I dumped my bag on the floor and prised my sodden shoes off but stopped halfway through unwinding my scarf, my arm raised above my head, motionless. The smell of perfume filled our narrow hallway. I closed my eyes and sighed. She was here. My brother's girlfriend was here. Her coat hung next to his donkey jacket and Mum's brown overall from the supermarket. I stroked the grey fur around the coat's hood. A long blond hair was entwined in the fur. I pulled it free and let it go. It spiralled shimmering to the floor. On an impulse I turned back the coat and pressed my face against the inside lining. The same smell, but softer. Was it even still warm? I closed my eyes and breathed in.

'That you Dave?' Tony's voice sounded from behind the lounge door. 'What are you *doing* out there?'

I tossed my door key onto the shelf under the mirror. I was soaked, smelly and covered in cross country mud. Great. The rain had plastered my hair flat so I scraped a rough parting back with my fingers. I prodded the zit on the left side of my jaw and brought my other hand up to deal with it but stopped myself just in time.

My heart jumped as I entered the lounge. Tony's girlfriend sat next to him on the sofa. She wore tight blue jeans and a clingy pink sweater that was fluffy, like a cuddly toy. She sat upright whereas Tony was slumped low with his legs spread and arms folded. The room was hot and his thin cheeks were brick red. She idly twisted her hair in her fingers, making small circular motions against her scalp. The television cast a strange green glow.

'Hi Tracey. Alright, Tone.' I worried that my feet might stink, or that my wet socks might start giving off steam.

'Hello Dave.' Tracey smiled, but quickly dropped her gaze.

'Alright Dave,' grunted Tony.

There was a long silence, which I didn't know how to fill. Neither Tracey nor Tony looked about to say anything. There was in the room what Mum would call 'an atmosphere'. Tracey and Tony must have been having an argument. To leave the room immediately would be too obvious, so I waited another minute or so, pretending to watch television. The hard click of snooker balls and crisp voice of the referee were deafening. The room was too hot, the gas fire turned up too high.

'Who's winning?' I asked.

'Davis of course,' grunted Tony. 'Higgins must be pissed again.'

'Where's Mum?' I blurted.

Of all the things to say in front of Tracey. For god's sake.

Tony jerked his head towards the kitchen. I fled next door to find my mother stirring tomato soup in a pan. She dipped her little finger in, jerked it out and sucked on it.

'Ow, that's done. Hi love, how'd you go?'

'Second.'

'Wow! Well done. That's a bronze medal isn't it? Good for you…'

Raised voices sounded from the lounge room. A hand slamming onto an armrest. A sob. The clacking of footsteps down the hall and the front door crashing shut.

Mum made an 'oh dear' face.

'Maybe eat your soup in here, hey Dave,' she whispered, 'and. leave Tony alone for a minute. He'll probably go out soon anyway.'

That was the first proper lovers' tiff Tony and Tracey had ever had. Usually, coming home and finding Tracey's coat in the hallway meant that another kind of embarrassment awaited me, especially if Mum was still at work and they had had the house to themselves. The lovebirds would be draped over each another on the sofa, smoothing their clothing and pretending to be fascinated by the *Magic Roundabout* or the evening news. My face would sizzle with embarrassment even if I just ran through to the kitchen or up to my room, leaving them to it. Once I came back from town desperate for the toilet after being stuck on a bus for ages. I burst through the front door and legged it into the lounge room, heading for the bathroom at the back of the house. Tony was frantically trying to hide Tracey's bra behind his back, their smirks erupting into unrestrained giggling. A couple of times when Mum was still at work I came home to find Tracey's coat hanging in the hall, the lounge room empty and The Specials blasting out from behind the firmly-closed door of Tony's bedroom upstairs. I sat on the sofa, letting my thoughts allow a somewhat repellent image of Tony to form only so I could dare to imagine what state of undress Tracey was in, and exactly what they were up to.

It was difficult to imagine why any girl found Tony attractive. Tracey Downey could have had her pick of any bloke in the district and was lusted after by every male at our school, some of the staff probably included. But Tony had never had trouble attracting girls. Annoyingly, it seemed the less he tried, the easier it was for him, and now he had a job he was even more sought after. This at least I could understand. I knew from Pete's older sister Susie that a girl wouldn't want to go out with a bloke who had no money to spend. And there were plenty of those around at the moment, with factories closing by the week.

But Tony had never been on the dole. He was an apprentice at the Land Rover plant in Solihull, working mostly on Range Rovers. Many of his friends – those who still had jobs, at least – worked at the British Leyland car factory at Longbridge. They joked that Tony was posh because he built luxury four-wheel drives that only the royal family and rich farmers would ever be stupid enough to want, rather than the hatchbacks and cheap sedans they laboured over.

Tony was eighteen, only three years older than me. But it was as if the gap between us was widening, as he moved deeper into the world of cars and pubs and wages and girlfriends like Tracey Downey. I was still anchored to the schoolboy world of zits and homework and trying to snog girls at discos. Tony didn't have zits any more but you could see where he used to, especially when his face got red or the light caught it at a certain angle, showing the little bumps and hollows in his jaw line and neck. He used to refuse to go to school some days because his acne was so bad, screaming and swearing. Once he inspected himself in the mirror one morning and punched the bathroom door so hard one of the wooden panels broke. Another time he started a fight in a bus queue when three older boys called him 'crater face'.

Tracey was in my class at school, and had been Tony's girlfriend for almost a year. They'd met via her best friend and also my classmate Doreen Greatorex, with whom Tony had gone on a blind date. A year was a long time for any teenage couple to stay together, and even I couldn't ignore that Tony treated Tracey differently from his many previous girlfriends. Tracey was clearly special, and clearly she felt the same way. The passing of their year together had been marked by the milestones of their growing infatuation: Valentine cards and red roses, Easter eggs with fluffy messages, a shirt from Burtons for Tony for his birthday, a trip to Alton Towers theme park for hers. All this seemed bizarrely out of character for Tony, especially things like Valentine cards, which he'd previously scorned as a waste of effort and money. He received several every year without ever sending one himself. It was beyond my comprehension. And before Tracey Downey came along, the idea of Tony buying flowers for a girl would have seemed outlandish. But now we were even hearing rumours of engagement once Tracey was old enough. Admittedly the source of these rumours was Doreen Greatorex, rather than the happy couple themselves. She let it be known that Tracey had confided in her about her planned long-term future with Tony. I dismissed these whispers — it was unthinkable that a girl the same age as me could possibly be contemplating engagement, which led to *marriage*, which was what your parents did.

Pete — and half our school year — also knew via Doreen of the engagement rumours. Pete was fascinated by Tony and Tracey's relationship and constantly pestered me for juicy details. When he'd first heard the news, he spent an entire bus trip home grilling me about it.

'So is it true your brother's shagging Tracey Downey?'

'Dunno. Maybe.'

'The lucky bastard. The tits on her! Don't you reckon Dave?'

'I s'pose.'

'You s'pose. Don't you like Tracey Downey?'

'Well, yeah. Who doesn't.'

I was always careful to keep my voice neutral.

– 8 –

'Right, I'm off out. To the fireworks, with Pete.'

Tony frowned as icy air spilled into the room.

'*Dave*! Are you coming in or going out? Make a bloody decision for once in your life!'

'Sorry.' I stepped fully into the room and pushed the door closed behind me, kicking the draught excluder back into place.

My brother and mother sat slack-faced in the room's warm fug, the blue television light flickering on them in the gloom. Tony's dangling fingers held yet another cigarette. With his other hand he stroked Raquel, our cat, who dozed in his lap. Smoke filled the room, mingling with the smell of gravy and vegetables. Dinner plates lay discarded on the carpet, bearing the cold remains of lamb chops, black and charred but with a few sinews of pale pink meat clinging to the bones. The television news was showing a story about the closure of another local engineering firm. The presenter stood outside the factory gates in a camel hair overcoat and asked tactless questions of the now ex-employees. Most of them looked too stunned to say anything.

I loitered in the doorway, buttoning my school blazer. I wore a thick jumper underneath it and had trouble forcing the buttons through the holes.

'Are you going out as well, Tony?' asked Mum, hopefully.

He shook his head, his eyes not leaving the television.

'Tony love, why don't you just phone her?' she said. 'Say sorry. Make the first move. You'll be glad you did.'

A muscle in his jaw stood out. 'Nah, I'm not going out.'

Abruptly I realised that the only thing I wanted to do tonight was stay at home with Tony and Mum.

'Who's on *Top of the Pops* tonight?' I asked.

'Madness,' said Tony. 'And a bunch of poofs called Duran Duran. One-hit wonders, you'll see.'

I picked up the newspaper from the arm of Tony's chair and flicked through it. I wanted Mum or Tony to tell me I was mad to go out; that I should stay in with them. But they stared at the television as if transfixed.

Then I thought of Pete, and his big surprise. What could it be? With him, anything was possible.

'Right, I'm going. Bye.'

Tony nodded impatiently and Mum waved absently.

'Don't be late. Hey, what about homework?' she said.

'Done it. Come on, it's bonfire night.'

'Alright, love. Wrap up warm.' She turned and smiled. 'Have fun!'

****

Most of the streetlights were out but a full moon cast a bright sheen on the frosty pavement. Pete squatted on the low railing that separated the grassed area in front of the tower blocks from the pavement. He appeared to be wrapped in a shiny blanket, which turned out to be a long black leather coat with wide flapping lapels. It creaked faintly as he moved.

'God, my arse is sore. Frostbitten too, sitting waiting for you,' Pete said. He spat crisply on the pavement and smeared the gob along the concrete with the toe of his shoe.

'Sorry.'

I fingered his lapel as I'd seen Tony do when one of his mates bought a new donkey jacket. The coat gave off a strong bovine smell.

'Quality. How much?' I asked.

'Forty-five. Down the rag market.'

'How come I haven't seen it before?'

'We've not been out anywhere, have we? And I'm not dumb enough to wear this to school, am I? Get it nicked on day one.'

Forty-five pounds? Maybe his Mum had had a bingo win.

'Come on, let's go, it'll be starting soon, and we've got some shopping to do first,' Pete said. He strode away, the coat flapping round his knees.

The shop's windows were plastered with flaking and faded stickers. *Evening Mail, Sports Argus, Benson & Hedges, Carling Black Label.* A thick steel grill inside sectioned off the area that sold alcohol.

'Got any money?' Pete asked.

We huddled under a streetlamp. We had a crumpled blue fiver from Pete, presumably pinched from his mum's handbag, and a few copper coins from me. He rolled his eyes.

'Last of the big spenders, eh? You wait out here.'

'Why? It's freezing.'

'I know, but even Pakis have principles. Patel will sell to schoolkids as long as they're not literally wearing school uniform. Anyway, I look older than you.'

'His name's not Patel, you know. I think it's Mr Minwalla.'

'No, they're all called Patel.'

'What are we buying anyway?'

'Wait and see.'

Pete swaggered out five minutes later, ripping the cellophane wrapper off a packet of ten Players Number Six and letting it spiral to the ground. There was a rounded bulge in his coat over the left side of his chest.

'What's that?' I pointed.

'Remember that surprise I mentioned?'

You could just *feel* it. It was a special night. Across the city, front doors were slamming in terraces and maisonettes and semis and tower blocks. This was happening all over the country too: excited groups heading out into a cold dark night towards lightness and bright excitement. Decorations wouldn't be up along New Street for another fortnight but tonight marked the beginning of the run-up to Christmas; the first sign that the long autumn school term had an end. The promise of a few days off work, or redundancy worries suspended. Christmas specials on television.

The pavements became increasingly crowded as we neared the park, and the kerbsides were jammed with parked cars. Groups of youths smoked and spat and swore; couples dawdled; teenage girls flounced and flirted, their exposed flesh pale like candle wax. Families blocked the pavements with pushchairs and lines of small children skipping along, sick with excitement. The kids clasped their mitten-clad hands two and three and four abreast, forcing those overtaking to spill out sideways off the kerb. Eventually those on foot took over the roads completely, an unstoppable flow of people-power forcing cars to inch their way nervously through the crowds, headlights flashing on darting bodies and dark shapes. Cresting the hill, the glow in the sky became visible like a great orange dome, and the pace of the crowd quickened as one down the incline. People pointed ahead and laughed, collective breath panting in the air in clouds.

I scanned the faces, but careful not to make eye contact. Pete and I needed to watch our backs, this part of the council estate. This was real bandit country, at the far outer reaches of our school's catchment area and bordering very hostile territory. What was I thinking, wearing my school blazer? I hunched and turned the collar up and made sure my Blues scarf covered the crest on the breast pocket. Pete was unfazed, strolling along, greeting people with a thumbs-up or a casual wave. As we passed The Bulldog he even exchanged respectful nods with a group of men spilling out of the pub. I recognised a couple of Tony's drinking mates too — Banger and Juzz, I thought their names were — as they buttoned up their coats and lit cigarettes before moving off with the rest. The one called Juzz stiffened when he realised I was looking at him, but Banger muttered something and they nodded uninterestedly at me and turned away.

Distracted by the group outside the pub I trod on the left forepaw of a dog that was trotting next to me, a lithe grey mongrel with dark eyes prominent in its lean face. It yelped and skipped nimbly along on three legs for a few yards, flexing its injured paw. I looked around in terror, fearing retribution from its owner. But no-one seemed to care. I caught up with the dog and bent to give it an apologetic pat, but it shied away. It stared at me and then trotted off purposefully, back on four legs, weaving nimbly through the surging mass, moving with the people.

Soon we slowed and converged outside the park entrance. People were impatient like cattle, heads craning, raising themselves on tiptoe, bottlenecked through the gates. Finally inside, everyone accelerated and fanned out over the muddy grass, children tugging and straining and breaking free of parental handholds, racing away squealing into the huge black spread of the park, down the slope towards the noise and lights and the silvery sheet of the reservoir beyond.

****

The air was absolutely still. Freezing fog had drifted across from the reservoir and hung in the darkness in wet icy droplets mixed with acrid smoke from the bonfire. The Guy Fawkes effigy had perished an hour earlier, perched in an old armchair on top of the fire. But the flames still reached high into the sky, the rising column of hot air drawing a vortex of glowing embers even higher until they flickered and died in the blackness.

Kids darted round the fire's edge, hurling sticks into it, shielding their faces. Farther back, the vans and stalls selling burgers and baked potatoes were still doing good business. The smell of frying onions drew people in, tempering the odours of mud and smoke. The little fairground was packed. Music blared. The intensity of this throbbing pool of light made the darkness beyond seem deep and impenetrable.

By now I was relaxed and enjoying the atmosphere. Lots of kids from school were there. Kevin Crump and his skinhead gang had been a nuisance early on, threatening a burger vendor in a dispute about change and squirting tomato sauce over him. They took over the kids' playground, swinging like monkeys from the climbing frame, boots flying, gobbing at people. Some gave a few giggly *Sieg Heils* from the top of the slide. Most of the skins were lightly if traditionally garbed in Doc Martens, jeans, white t-shirts and braces and many looked to be in the early stages of hypothermia. They now stayed close to the fire, amusing themselves by trying to wrestle each other into the flames.

I'd been looking for her all night but we hadn't seen Tracey. Probably she was at home, warm in her fluffy pink jumper, watching television in her cosy living room. Or was she perhaps lying on her bed, reading, her blond hair spread on the pillow? I looked at the sky and shivered. The moon had gone and the stars were just a frozen scattering of faint white dots. The cold was intense. I rammed my scarf tighter down the back of my neck.

The first thing I noticed was Tracey's mournful expression. The second was Doreen Greatorex's legs. Her thighs were startlingly white above her long boots and her tight black skirt was very short. Her coat swung open as she and Tracey approached.

'Fucking hell. Look at these two,' said Pete, giving me a not very subtle nudge.

'Hello boys,' pouted Doreen. She thrust her hands into her coat pockets and swivelled her hips.

'Hello ladies,' said Pete.

Tracey wore tight jeans, her pink anorak with the grey fur round the hood, and a white woolly bobble hat. She looked like the blonde singer out of Abba. Both girls looked years older than they did at school.

'Well, look at Mister Sharpe, in that coat,' Doreen giggled. 'I like leather.'

Tracey made a sound a bit like a laugh. Doreen theatrically dragged Pete away. He looked like he had won the pools. I wasn't sure what to do. Or say.

'Is Tony here, Dave?' said Tracey.

'No. He's not coming.'

'I didn't think he would,' she said in a small voice.

I nodded.

'Walk with me?' She was almost pleading. As if I'd say no.

'Where?'

'Anywhere. Let's just go and sit somewhere near the fire until

Doreen and Pete come back.'

Unbelievably, she pushed her arm through mine. At first our heads bobbed awkwardly out of step, but after a while we found a rhythm and she seemed to lean in towards me. We sat on a bench a few yards from the fire, stretching our legs out. The fire's orange glow was mesmerising. Warm. Beautiful. My nose was runny. Shit. I didn't want to pull my wet handkerchief out so I pretended to cough and wiped my nose quickly on my sleeve. The radiating heat seemed to dry my eyeballs and warm the inside of my head, while my back felt colder than ever. I turned my head one way then the other, savouring the alternate sensation of heat and chill on my face. I closed my eyes but kept moving my head in an easy rhythm, lost in my thoughts, relaxed and comfortable. Almost sleepy, half-warm at least for the first time in hours. I opened my eyes. Tracey's face was in front of mine, our noses almost touching. I grinned and began to lean away but she swung her legs sideways towards me and put her arm round my shoulder. She moved in closer, until our noses did touch. The strap of her handbag fell from her shoulder. Her breath smelled of fried onions. I didn't care.

'How about a Christmas kiss, Dave?'

I was about to blurt that it was still ages to Christmas but her mouth was on mine, hot and soft and yielding. Her tongue was in my mouth, not pushing brisk and muscular down my throat like Dawn Skinner's at the last school disco, but just a warm live thing that felt good and made me forget the chill down my back and my stupid brother and everything. I got my breathing right after a while, despite my runny nose. I opened my eyes. Tracey's eyes, just an inch away from mine, were open and shiny blue and beautiful. This unnerved me and I grinned, making our teeth bump, and the kiss was over. I stared at my shoes and tasted her on my lips. She leaned back with her arm still round my shoulders and we listened to the sputtering crackle of the fire and the shrieks from the fairground.

'You're a good kisser, Dave,' she murmured. 'Must run in the family.'

Her reference to Tony made my inner warmth drain away. I was glad to see Pete and Doreen approaching, giggling, with their arms round each other and her free hand inside his coat. Tracey dropped her arm from my shoulders and it was over. It was all over.

We bought tea in polystyrene cups from one of the stalls. The woman serving was stingy with the milk so the tea was too hot and too strong. You could feel it coating your teeth. My hands were shaking and I spilled mine and burnt my thumb. Pete was in top form, doing all the talking, telling the girls how good they looked. But Doreen and Tracey soon said that they were going home. Doreen was complaining sourly about her frozen feet, all her giggly flirting forgotten. Her legs were puckered with little indentations like those on a golf ball. They were now so pale they were almost greenish-white, the colour of the glow-in-the-dark werewolf and Frankenstein model figures that still lined a dusty shelf in my bedroom.

'You can't go yet. You'll miss the fireworks. And I've got a special surprise for us!' Pete pleaded.

The girls glanced at each other, but Doreen sneezed and said something about the cold, and they shook their heads.

'Your loss,' Pete muttered sullenly.

'See you at school tomorrow,' I said.

They walked away through the crowd. Doreen was soon lost from sight. But for a long time Tracey's bobbing white hat remained visible, until eventually it too was swallowed by the darkness.

– 9 –

As soon as Tracey and Doreen left us, Pete launched into an account of how he'd snogged Doreen and got his hand up her skirt, but broke off when he realised I wasn't listening.

'What's the matter, half an hour alone with a girl and you're a tongue-tied twat? So how was Tracey? Just wanted to ask about Tony, Doreen said. Worried he's going to pack her in.'

'Yeah, something like that.'

I was about to tell Pete that I was going home and couldn't be persuaded otherwise when he insisted we climb the steep slope at the edge of the park and watch the fireworks from there. I tried to argue but he was adamant. We had to stay for the fireworks and we had to watch them from the hilltop.

So I trudged up the slope behind him, at one point slipping and getting mud all down my arm. We stopped for a rest halfway. From up here, the fairground's spinning lights looked like the glowing innards of a gigantic machine. Pete insisted we climb right to the top, close to the row of gaunt poplar trees that lined the ridge. In daylight, crows and ravens flapped and cawed and made scrappy nests in the swaying high branches. Now the trees were black and silent. Nothing was visible behind them except a few dim rectangles of light from a couple of distant tower blocks.

At the top we stood and got our breath back, wheezing from the climb and the freezing, tickly air. The exertion gave me my second and final flush of proper warmth that entire night. But the itchy heat on my torso swiftly cooled to a lower level even than before, like my sweat had frozen into a thin icy vest.

Faintly but clearly the shrill screams from the fairground drifted up to us. The slope was at forty-five degrees and flattened out at the top, where we stood. The fire and the crowds were perhaps a hundred yards below and two hundred yards away in linear distance. Pete shivered and wrapped his arms around himself, his palms slapping on his leather coat.

'So, you were saying. Tracey just wanted a shoulder to cry on, did she? Dave?'

'I wasn't saying. But yeah, that was all. Just to talk.'

'Doreen said how Tracey's upset about Tony. What did you tell her?'

'Nothing,' I said. 'It's up to Tony, isn't it. Nothing I can do.'

'True. Is he chasing someone else now? Got a bit on the side? Gone off Tracey?'

'I don't know. Honestly.'

'Imagine if Tracey was chasing someone else. What would your brother do to someone who nicked his bird? Run them over in his car, probably. Or get his psycho mates from the pub to hospitalise them.' Pete laughed grimly. 'He wants his fucking head looking at, your brother. Chasing someone else when you can have Tracey Downey! Imagine.'

He looked at me, and leered encouragingly.

I said nothing.

'No, maybe you can't imagine, can you,' he said sarcastically. 'Come to life, will you Dave? You're a bloody wet weekend tonight. What's up with you?'

'Nothing. I'm sorry. I'm just freezing.'

'Dave, stay and I promise you'll be glad.' He gave a sort of half-wink.

'No, I think I'll head off. I'm not bothered about the fireworks.'

'Oh no you don't! You're not running off on me as well.'

'Pete, I've really had enough.'

'Trust me Dave. You'll be glad you stayed.'

'Fuck, alright. But the fireworks better start soon, or I'm really going.' I pulled my gloves out of my pockets and put them on.

'Here, I've got something to warm us up,' he said, reaching in his pocket. He extracted a flat bottle and fumbled with the cap. It was Southern Comfort, the current spirit of choice among the city's teenagers. I hated the stuff.

'Great,' I said. 'Was that the surprise you had for Doreen and Tracey?'

'Nope. It's much better than that. Just you wait.'

He took a long swig and handed me the bottle. I upended it, nearly gagging as it hit my throat, strong and sickly sweet. Some dribbled onto my scarf. When Pete wasn't looking I tipped some onto the grass. I handed him the bottle back, ostentatiously wiping my lips.

It was only ten minutes until the fireworks began but it seemed like half an hour. My thighs burned from the climb and my back ached. We had been on our feet for hours. I found a bin liner impaled on the spikes of the iron fence than ran behind us and spread it on the grass. I sat and hugged my knees to my chest. But the wet earth was so cold that I quickly stood again. Soon I was shivering uncontrollably. I wrapped my scarf round my neck twice and tucked it down my blazer. I pictured Tony still slumped in his warm armchair; Mum carrying in the tea and chocolate biscuits on a tray; them laughing at the television. Why the hell hadn't I just stayed at home with Tony and Mum when I'd had the choice? Even kissing Tracey wasn't worth this. My lips were cracked and icy, all memory of her warm tongue in my mouth forgotten. Had it even happened?

A ripple pulsed through the crowd below. The fireworks were about to begin at last. There was a brief, delicious stillness when the whole park, perhaps even the whole city, collectively held its breath. Abruptly the sky filled with red and green flares and soft popping explosions. Then the whoosh and muffled crack of the rockets. Gold and silver starbursts exploded high above and slowly died, shimmering sparks cascading in dripping curves through the bitter, still air.

The shifting dark mass of the crowd below us lightened as the upturned smiling faces glowed pale from the lights in the sky. Smoke roiled and plumed above and below us, filling the wide bowl of the park like cannon fire obscuring a battlefield. The later fireworks were no more than dull flashes in the smoke, like a lightning storm on a far, dark horizon. I wasn't about to tell Pete, but this eye-level view, instead of the usual neck-craning upwards aspect, had in the end been worth the effort.

Yet I was still relieved when the last rumble echoed and died amid the tower blocks behind the poplar trees. The sky seemed even blacker than before; the silence more absolute.

'Right, that's it Pete. Let's go.'

'Not yet. Like I said, there's more.'

He imitated the sound of a drum roll, and slowly opened the left side of his coat. With a conjurer's flourish he pulled from inside the lining a rocket with a body the size of a coke can and a long wooden tail.

'What, you've kept that bloody great thing hidden all night, in your coat?' I was awestruck, scared, excited, the cold and my freezing feet forgotten.

'Told you I'd got a surprise for us, didn't I?' Pete cackled. 'Look at its name – Big Boy!'

'Is it safe? Us just setting it off on our own? Is that allowed, just in a park?'

'Yes, you big puff. Come on, it'll be ace.'

'I dunno, Pete. We're under age as well. What if someone sees us? Anyway, look at this smoke in the air. We won't be able to see it go off anyway, it'll be a waste. Why don't we save it for another time?'

Pete shook his head. Later I was to remember his eyes glittering in the cold against the pinched whiteness of his face and the disappointment – or was it disgust? – in his voice.

'I thought you liked fireworks Dave. I thought it would be a laugh, something different. I wish I hadn't fucking bothered now.'

He jammed the rocket's tail into the grass and wandered a few yards away, pulling out the Southern Comfort. He sat with his back to me, shoulders hunched, staring down the slope.

'Alright Pete,' I said with mock weariness. 'Let's do it. Then can we go home?'

He scampered back, all jittery excitement.

'Good man! You won't regret it. Right, I'll get the bastard set up. We need a milk bottle.'

We scoured the ground under the trees and against the spiked iron fence that bordered the park.

'For god's sake!' Pete said. 'Normally there's bottles and shit everywhere, but nothing just when we need one.'

Eventually I found a plastic orange juice bottle with a rain-faded picture of a smiling child on the label. Pete wanted to keep looking for a heavier glass bottle, but the cold was getting to me again.

'Alright, it'll have to do,' Pete said.

He plucked the rocket free and handed me the Southern Comfort. It wouldn't fit in my pocket, and I wanted to keep my hands jammed under my armpits for warmth, so I stood it on the ground. Pete crouched with the plastic bottle and the rocket, his coat splayed out on the grass. The thudding beat of Duran Duran's *Planet Earth* drifted up from the fairground, mingling with the shouts and laughter. I smiled and nodded my head to the music. I loved fireworks, and I also loved, secretly, that Pete did unexpected, fun things like this. I imagined telling everyone at school about it tomorrow. Tracey and Doreen would wish they hadn't gone home.

The air was still thick with fog and smoke. Then the poplar trees creaked and a freezing wind moaned down the hillside. It gathered strength, blowing gaps in the murky air and giving glimpses of stars overhead, before dying again to complete stillness. It was as if a door had been opened and closed behind us. We couldn't believe our luck.

'Is it ready yet?' I hopped from foot to foot, my chest thumping. I wasn't cold now.

'Wait!'

'Come on, what are you doing? How long can it take?'

'Fucking wait, will you, Dave? You can't rush it with a big bastard like this.'

Pete got up at last, rubbing his legs. The rocket stood in the bottle, ready for launch. Waiting to soar vertically into the air, above the trees, above the city, and light up our lives.

'Right,' he said. 'Where are those matches?'

Flat grey light filtered into the room. My mind vaguely reached out for something that swirled away, coming almost into focus and then drifting off in a warm haze. I was curled up in bed, legs drawn up tight to my chest in the messy warmth of the blankets. My thoughts cleared. Great, it was Friday. Double maths this morning but art in the afternoon and a party tonight at Rocky Bishton's because his parents were away skiing. There was a strange smell in the room. My sleep-gummed eyes jerked open and my legs kicked out, my feet shooting free of the bedclothes into the chilly air. I curled up again and pulled the sheet over my head.

The door opened. I rolled to face the wall and coiled my body even tighter, fearing Tony's belligerent voice. The mattress sank as someone sat next to me. A soft warmth and a perfumed bedroom smell. Mum patted me and I turned to face her. I was glad of her touch yet dreaded what was coming. Her hair was pulled back in a messy ponytail. She still wore her nightie, with her anorak draped over it, dotted dark with rainwater across her shoulders. Her hand was icy on my forehead.

'Oooh! Dave love! Thank god you're alright! I've just heard from the milkman! About last night at the park! Were you there? Did you and Pete see what happened?'

'Huh?' I rolled back to the wall.

'A firework exploding in the crowd! That poor dog! And lots of people injured, children trampled, people in intensive care…' Her voice trailed away.

My throat seemed to have closed up again and my tongue was a dry rasp. I gulped water from the glass on my bedside table. Cold rivulets soaked my neck and pyjama collar.

'Yeah, but they'll be alright, won't they? They'll get better?'

'They don't know.' She blew her nose and sniffed a couple of times.

'Have they said who they were, the people who got hurt?'

She shook her head.

'Apparently there's talk it was deliberate,' she said.

She recoiled as I blanched, my eyes wide with shock, nausea rammed up my throat.

'I know love, it's terrible, unbelievable.' She patted my shoulder through the blankets and rocked me.

'How do they know?' My voice was muffled in the pillow.

'People saw a rocket fired from the top of the hill. You're alright, aren't you love? You didn't get hurt or anything?'

'No. We're fine.'

'Oh, thank god. That's the main thing. Did you see what

happened? It must have been terrible.'

I was glad she couldn't see my face.

'Er, no, we just went for a while, saw the bonfire and that. But it was too cold. We left before the fireworks started.'

Her nose wrinkled. 'Did you wet yourself, Dave? I can smell wee.'

'I sort of couldn't get to a toilet in time.' I pushed my face deeper into the pillow. 'Sorry.'

'Love, it doesn't matter.' She rocked me. 'Just wear your other trousers. Tony won't know. He's gone already, he's on earlys.'

I lifted my head. 'What'll happen to them, whoever did it?'

Her tone changed. 'Well, the police will soon find them of course, and then… who knows.' She shuddered. 'Probably best for them if it is the police who find them first.'

Neither Mum nor I ate any breakfast. She just sniffed and dabbed her eyes over a cup of tea and listened to the radio. The BRMB newsreader was breathlessly excited. He talked mostly about the injured dog, which no-one had claimed ownership of. The broadcast switched to a reporter at Selly Oak Hospital who was more sombre. Three people were still in the burns unit, and one had been rushed to the Eye Hospital in the early hours of the morning. Mum tried to give me a hug but I shouldered my bag and ran out of the house.

The excitement was evident even as I slouched down the school drive. Boys and girls whispered in huddles, instead of the usual pre-school chaos of flying footballs and scuffling and movement. I passed a couple of teachers in a corridor. They looked grim. I felt conspicuous in my spare trousers which were dark grey, not the regulation black. My classmates gossiped in groups, Pete in the centre of one. I didn't meet his eye but went and sat on my own and wondered what to do. Part of me still dumbly clung to a belief that accidents and things like this were never as bad as people or the media made out. My blazer reeked of smoke and people came up to me constantly, knowing I'd been at the park, wanting details. I said I hadn't seen anything.

This was almost true, because I couldn't remember what had happened. My mind was a vacant blur of sensations and images: the shivery cold, the mud, the white-hot explosion, the screaming. Above all, I could recall the surprise of Tracey's kiss and the feeling of her mouth on mine. A faint sickly aroma of Southern Comfort reached me. It was from my scarf, so I ripped it off and stuffed it in my bag.

Gossip and ghoulish speculation swirled round the classroom: people had died, been blinded, had limbs blown off, there was a huge crater where the thing had detonated. Girls hugged and sobbed in huddled groups. Those who had been at the park seemed obliged to fill in the gaps in what they knew with creative guesswork that was seized on as fact. Johnny Rose's father was a policeman and a mob surrounded him as if he were somehow responsible. They demanded answers, refusing to accept that he didn't know what had happened. He had to promise to find out. Unpopular pupils who had been at the park thrived on the sudden attention. People put words in their mouths, egged them on, built the story. Almost everyone claimed to know someone who knew something. Mr Preston arrived late, and in the middle of this frenzy, to do the attendance register. A terrible silence greeted the names Downey and Greatorex when he called them out. But my eyes stayed on the door, as if Tracey and Doreen were about to burst into the classroom, breathless and giggling. *Sorry we're late, Sir.*

In assembly half an hour later the whole school sat in open-mouthed silence as the Headmistress told us that about fifteen people had been injured by the firework or from being trampled in the fleeing crowd.

'It particularly saddens me to announce that one of the most seriously hurt is fourth-former Tracey Downey,' she said.

Gasps and mutterings and quiet sobs rippled through our ranks like a shockwave, from the first years crammed cross-legged on the floor in front of the stage to the sixth formers lounging at the back of the hall. Everyone knew, or wished they knew, Tracey Downey. Miss Roberts held up her hand.

'I'm afraid that Doreen Greatorex, also of 4F, has been hurt too. I have no more details, other than I understand Doreen's injuries are not as serious as Tracey's.'

That was it. If Miss Roberts said Tracey and Doreen had been hurt, it must be true. She was the Head, she knew everything. I wanted to be sick.

She led the whole school in prayers for the injured people. At the end, the collective *Amen* dissolved into a fresh outbreak of sniffs and sobbing.

'I know many of you were at the park last night,' she said, leaning forward on the lectern. 'But this is upsetting for everyone. This is a time to be brave, to stay strong, to not let the school down. The best thing will be to concentrate on your schoolwork, and try to keep things as normal as possible.' She cleared her throat. 'Also, I imagine the police will want to talk to people who were there last night, in case anyone saw anything that would help them.'

The sobbing stopped instantly. She peered over the top of her glasses, scanning the open-mouthed rows of children. Absolute silence. Not a cough or scrape of a foot on the floor.

'If any of you *know* anything about what happened' – I fixed my gaze on a point ten feet about her head – 'understand this.' She took a deep breath, and the whole school, pupils and teachers, 1,100 people, leaned forward as if sucked towards her. 'The police will find the culprits. They always do. If anyone knows anything, the only thing to do is to speak up. The only time to do so is now. The longer things go on, the worse it will be if you don't speak up. Unusually, this is one time when selfishness *is* the best course. This is not a time for putting friendships before your own interests. Do you understand? You should talk to a teacher first, or your parents, if you would prefer not to talk directly to the police. That is all.'

The hall erupted with a scraping of chairs and clamour of voices.

I was late for geography. Straight after assembly I had rushed to the toilets. Hoping for privacy, I ran a long way to the boys' bogs near the art and metalwork rooms, well away from where most people would be.

I sat in a cubicle and tried to think clearly. To apply logic. I ignored whatever Pete might think best. In what in the years ahead

I would look back on as a pivotal moment, hunched on a smelly school toilet, blinking away tears, I tried to decide what to do. The accident was barely twelve hours old. It still wasn't too late to confess. But after this it might be. If I did it now, I might even get some credit for having the courage to own up. My remorse would be taken into account. But to own up any later could be perceived as an affirmation of our guilt. It might be regarded as a confession born only of fear and our assumption that we would get caught anyway. Any remorse would be discounted.

Pete was safely in the geography class. Right now I could be knocking on the staff room door. Then talking perhaps to Mr McLeish in an empty classroom, hearing dour Scottish words of calm comfort. Accompanying him to the Head's office to surrender myself and stoically face all consequences. We were only kids. People would surely accept that it had been a horrible accident. The ordeal could have an end.

I washed my hands, dried them on my trousers and headed for geography to learn about the effects of the Ice Age on the Welsh Mountains.

– 11 –

My shoes' scuffed leather was darkly stained and clogged with dirt. We huddled under the trees, sliding on the bare mud. Drizzle whipped through the air like sea spray. Cigarettes were sheltered in cupped hands, smoke swirling away in snatched gusts. Numbly clinging to routine, Pete and I had come for a smoke at morning break, tiptoeing through the mud alongside the flooded tennis courts and down to the woods.

As everyone dropped their dog ends on the ground and headed back to school, Pete motioned to me to wait.

'Dave, we need to talk.'

'About what? When to own up? We might as well. You heard the Head. The police will get us anyway.'

He grabbed my shoulder. 'No they won't! We're fine.'

'Yes they will! Thanks Pete for another one of your stupid ideas! As if the proper fireworks weren't enough!' I shook myself free. I wanted to be angrier, to have the explosive fury to grab him by the throat, to punch him in the face. But my anger was like a sullen, energy-sapping paralysis, just like the night before.

'Why don't we just tell them the truth?' I said. 'That it was an accident?

'Because they won't believe us. We'd be looking at police, borstal, a heap of fucking shit.'

'They'll find out what happened anyway, the police always do! Like the Head said!'

He shook me. 'No they don't! Trust me, they don't! I know what I'm talking about.'

'What, you mean your brother? He's doing two years, isn't he? The police caught him.'

'No, I didn't mean Lee.' Pete flinched as a rain squall hit us. 'Dave, you didn't see *Scum*, did you?'

'The film? No, you said I wouldn't get in, remember. It was an 18. You took Dawn Edwards.'

'Yeah. 'Kin brilliant.' He shook his head in happy recollection. 'She had a black bra… anyway, it's a shame you didn't see it.'

'I know. It was supposed to be great.'

'No Dave. It was fucking scary.'

'You didn't say that! You wouldn't shut up about how you'd got in and I hadn't, and the great bit with the snooker balls in the sock, and the bathroom scene where the bloke bangs someone's head against the taps, and…'

'Dave, you wouldn't last one day in borstal. I'm not sure I would. Think about it. In *Scum*, one of them slits his own throat.' He turned away. 'Come on, we're getting pissed on here.' He led the way up the muddy slope towards school.

'Who says we'd go to borstal?' I shouted at Pete's back.

'What the fuck else do you think would happen? People got hurt… we don't even know how badly yet. It's GBH, isn't it. Grievous Bodily Harm. They won't just take you home and give you a bollocking in front of your mum. It'd be magistrates, court… the works.'

'But not real prison?'

'Borstal's the same as real prison!'

'And what about you-know-who?'

'Huh?'

'Look *who* got injured.'

Pete's face told me he was playing dumb, infuriating me further.

'Say it, Pete! Tracey Downey! And Doreen's hurt too.'

He whirled around.

'Alright! But there's nothing we can do, is there? They'll get better.'

I was close to tears. 'You're not thinking, Pete. Christ, and you go on at me. Tracey Downey is in intensive care!'

'Dave, I know she is. It's bad but we can't change it!' He blinked water from his eyes.

'But what about my brother!'

Pete froze.

'Fucking hell. I hadn't thought about that.' His voice dropped. 'He'll kill us. Literally. He'll kill me, anyway.'

'So what are we going to do?'

Pete drew a breath, seemed to gather himself.

'It's easy. We don't have to *do* anything. We just keep quiet. Say nothing, do nothing, and it'll go away. The fucking pigs don't know what happened. It was dark, there were millions of people around. They're not going to find us. Not unless you do something stupid. Think about it. Think about your brother, and his mad mates. Think about borstal. Prison! We can't change what happened. Okay? This can all go away.' He smiled. 'Come on, let's catch the others up.'

By the start of the next lesson, my thoughts made some sort of sense for the first time since the accident. Maybe Pete was right. It could all go away.

And Pete usually was right. It was easier just to believe him. It always had been, right from when we first met, in the infant class at Manor Farm Junior School. The evening before, Dad had played a joke on me. We shared a bag of reject chocolates that Nana Truman got from the staff-only shop at the Cadbury factory at Bournville. Dad blew up the empty bag and popped it between his hands. I can still smell that cloud of chocolate dust.

Next day at school I blew up a brown paper bag and crept up behind Peter Sharpe, who was playing in the sand pit. I smashed my hands together right in his ear. The bang was so loud he jerked forward and his head thudded on the sand pit's wooden rim. Miss Marsden came running and Peter Sharpe stood, unsteady on his feet, his hand pressed to his pale forehead with bright blood running between his fingers. Everyone looked at me. I scrunched the paper bag, my eyes filling with tears.

'I just tripped, Miss,' Pete said. 'It was an accident.' He blinked from the blood running into his eye, bright red against the stark white of his eyeball.

Miss Marsden pulled out a hanky and dabbed his face. Then she turned paler than him and ran to fetch Mr Carnell from the classroom next door. He'd been in the war and only had one arm but he always knew what to do. Peter went to hospital and returned later that morning with three stitches over his right eye. Miss Marsden asked if he wanted to go home but he said his mum would be at work and anyway he didn't want to.

It was my turn that day to feed the goldfish. As I dusted the surface of the smelly green water with fish flakes, Pete appeared next to me. The two fat goldfish gulped the food. Pete poked one with his finger and it darted away with a plop. I wanted to laugh, but we weren't supposed to touch the fish.

I asked if Peter's eye hurt. He shook his head, and said something I didn't expect.

'You're my best mate now and I'm your best mate.'

It felt good hearing this. Pete poked one of the goldfish again, jabbing into the water harder this time with a bigger splash so a couple of drops of slimy water landed on my arm.

'Cos we're mates, you don't tell on me for doing this, do you?'

I shook my head.

'Right,' Peter went on. 'Like I didn't tell on you about the paper bag.'

When Mum picked me up from school I told her I had a new best friend. She kissed the top of my head and asked who it was. I pointed out Peter, heading for home on his own.

'That's one of those Sharpe boys,' she said quietly.

A few days later I asked Pete what job his dad did.

'He works away from home.'

'So does mine!'

I was so delighted I forgot to probe Pete for more details about his father. Instead I told him how my dad was a cook and had gone away to work on an oil rig about a year ago. I described how he always seemed to be away when the important things happened: when Tony broke his arm falling off a garage roof, when Mum went to hospital with some secret illness and we were looked after by Auntie Sandra, Mum's sister, and when I won the two lengths backstroke at Tiverton Road baths.

I didn't tell Pete any details about my mother's mysterious sudden hospital visit. I remembered little about it anyway except Auntie Sandra crying, which shocked me more than the blood she was cleaning off the bathroom floor. Seeing her in tears made me cry too but thanks to Peter, blood didn't bother me anymore. Auntie Sandra's crying scared me because it made her seem like a girl, not a grown up. I'd never seen Mum cry and assumed she never did.

'Coming in for a cuppa?' Pete grunted.

We had trailed gloomily home from school and now stood outside the maisonette where he and his mother lived. I thought of the hundreds of times Pete had uttered those words and the biggest problem we faced was how to do our maths homework together without making it look like we had.

'Alright. Anything to avoid going home to Mum,' I said. 'And Tony.'

We sat on the vinyl sofa with the sticky tape covering the splits in the cushion and watched *Blue Peter*. We drank strong sugary tea that Pete's mum made and flicked our cigarettes into a heavy glass ashtray.

I liked Pete's mum. She seemed much older than mine. She was weary, chain-smoking and brittle, with grey hair like a kitchen scourer. She even had an old woman's name: Rose. She worked as a dinner lady at a primary school a few streets away. Probably she was only about fifty. Pete was only fifteen, after all. But his elder sister Susie was twenty-nine.

'How was school love?' Rose asked, patting Pete's hand.

'Alright.'

'Did you have a good day too David?'

'Not exactly.'

Pete gave me the stare.

'I just did badly in a test,' I said. 'No big deal.'

'Tests aren't everything, love.' She smiled and nodded encouragement. 'Mind you, school is important, isn't it, Pete? Important to do well. Maybe stay on for A Levels and that, eh?'

'Yes Mum.'

'And wasn't what happened last night terrible! Everyone at school must be talking about it.'

Pete nodded. 'Yeah. All day long.'

'That poor Tracey Downey! She's in your class, isn't she? And she's seeing your brother, isn't she David? Let's hope the police catch whoever did it.'

Pete jumped up, nearly overturning the ashtray. He crossed to the television and turned the sound up. I concentrated on my cigarette and gulped my tea, burning my tongue. Sweat prickled my forehead.

Rose was quiet after that. Perhaps her mention of the police had made her think about Lee, Pete's older brother. My mother once said that Lee had been a bright lad who had 'gone off the rails'. He was serving two years in Winson Green Prison for arson, having set fire to a furniture wholesalers in Small Heath. No-one knew why he'd done it. Probably he'd got involved in some crude insurance fraud. Even with parole he still had at least nine months to serve. I wasn't exactly glad that he was in prison, but neither was I sorry he wasn't around. I was scared of Lee. He was a wilder version of Pete: far more unpredictable and with a frightening temper. From my earliest friendship with Pete I had been wary of Lee and in awe at his disdain for authority.

Pete was more reckless when Lee was around. Once when we were about nine or ten I went up to Pete's bedroom and he was shooting from his bedroom window with Lee's air rifle. It was so heavy Pete could hardly pick it up. I was about to ask for a turn, when Pete pointed.

'Hey! Watch this!'

A poodle was sniffing its way along the pathway in the strip of garden next door. It cocked a leg on a plant pot. It had a white coat with pinkish skin showing through, the fur dirty and clotted around its backside. The gun went *phut* in my ear. The dog jumped and collapsed soundlessly onto its side, its body resting on a line of bricks bordering a flower bed and its face nestled in a clump of pansies. A hind leg twitched, twice.

'It's alright,' Pete said. 'It'll get up again in a minute.'

Pete owned up as soon as his mum came home. She went round to the hysterical Mrs Batty next door and told her. I wondered if I should have owned up as well, because I was there too. But then, it wasn't my idea, and not me who pulled the trigger. But I thought I might feel better in a funny way if Mum and Dad knew what had happened. Pete said that nothing would bring the dog back, but that didn't make me feel any easier about it. For a long time, the image of the poodle sniffing among the flowers, minding its own doggy business, stayed with me.

Pete and Lee had to go to the big new police station on Bournville Lane and stand in a senior policeman's office while he shouted at them for a long time. Rose had to wait outside. Lee made Pete giggle by bending his legs up and down like Dixon of Dock Green even when the policeman was talking about criminal charges and saying that his officers would keep their eye on them in future. Lee thought Pete was dumb to have owned up when he didn't have to. Lee said Mrs Batty was a senile old lady.

'She'd just have thought the stupid dog had had a heart attack or something, and just buried its shitty arse at the bottom of the garden,' he said.

I lingered at Pete's for an hour or so, declining Rose's offer to stay and eat beans and chips with them. I avoided eating anything at

Pete's because although Rose was a good cook, her kitchen — and the whole house — was rather unhygienic, or so it seemed to me. Our house was no museum. But cobwebs and dust covered every surface and corner of Pete's house. Clutter occupied every shelf and tabletop. The kitchen was cramped and grease stained, with only a tiny area of kitchen bench that was not permanently occupied by old jars, bottles, tins, and crockery. How she produced meals from this one foot square cooking surface was a mystery.

My eyes stayed fixed on the pavement on the way home, not registering peripheral movement or traffic noise. I was glad it was the weekend and I would have respite from people at school, with their chatter and questions. But the sight of Tony's car, the racing green Triumph Dolomite Sprint, filled me with dread.

There was a dog turd right outside our gate. Rainwater sluiced over the pavement, dissolving its edges and carrying it into the stream running down the gutter. I scowled at the house next door. One of Mr Hickey's bull terriers, Rocky and Rambo, would have had done it. As I fumbled for my key I pressed myself against the front door to avoid the water that dripped from the eaves in a thin curtain.

Mum was at the stove fretting over the contents of a saucepan. The kitchen was steamy and the window opaque with condensation.

'Dave! Give me a kiss, love.'

I pecked her on the cheek.

'Oh sugar!' she prodded at the pan with a wooden spoon. 'How was school, love? Did you hear any more news about last night?'

'No.' I was glad her back was turned. 'What are you making?'

'A white sauce. But the stupid flour just goes lumpy.'

I leaned in the doorway as she scurried round the kitchen. Rainwater splashed onto the concrete of the yard outside the kitchen window from the overflowing gutter.

'You've been smoking, haven't you?' She spun round, the wooden spoon dripping white sauce onto the lino.

'Huh? I only had one. I've just been round at Pete's.'

'Smells like more than one to me. It won't do your running any good. Bet you Sebastian Coe doesn't smoke.'

I frowned. I hated being reminded about how smoking was bad for the health. It made me feel uncomfortable, and highlighted my constant dilemma about whether to give up smoking to improve my running. I didn't smoke to look big. Smoking in public made me feel less like an adult and conspicuously more like the schoolboy I was. But I couldn't imagine not spending breaks and lunchtimes down the woods with the school smokers. What else was there to do?

'Where's Tony?'

'He's nipped out to get the paper. Listen, Dave.' She looked round conspiratorially. 'Tony's terribly upset. He got the news about Tracey at work, around lunchtime. He dropped everything and rushed straight to the hospital.'

'Is she alright?'

'We still don't know. But it must be bad. Tony couldn't see her. Her dad wouldn't let him. Said Tracey couldn't have visitors.' She shook her head. 'Tony'd taken her a box of Milk Tray and Lucozade and everything.'

****

Tony perched on the sofa with a damp copy of the afternoon edition of the *Evening Mail*. Mum and I read it over his shoulder. His skinny frame twitched as he flicked the pages. His face was flushed, the pale acne scars on his cheeks and neck lividly visible. He shook the newspaper, arms outstretched, as if expecting something to fall out.

'Whoever did this should get the birch! They've got it coming. God help us they have.'

'Tony, calm down love. We don't know yet it wasn't just an accident.' Mum laid her hand on his shoulder.

He shrugged it off. 'Accident or not, someone did this and someone's got to pay!'

'They will, once the police find them,' she said.

'Bollocks will they! They'll get a slap on the wrist and off they'll go.' He tossed the newspaper aside. 'I'm going out.'

'What about your tea?' Mum said. 'The pub's not even open yet, is it?'

'I'll go round Banger's house first, see what he thinks about this. I'll get some chips or something on the way.' He flung his donkey jacket on and patted his pockets, all angry jerking movement. He looked like a scavenging bird, with his skinny legs, bright eyes and bulky black coat.

The front door slammed. Mum sank into the sofa and picked up the loose sheets of the newspaper.

'Let's have a proper look. There.' She smoothed the front page out with her forearm. A black headline covered most of the page: '*Carnage!*' She patted the sofa next to her.

'Sit down, eh love? Let's see what it says. Isn't it terrible about Tracey? No wonder Tony's worried to death. Here, let's look in the paper.'

I couldn't think of any way of stopping her.

'There!' she said, frowning with concentration. 'Tracey Downey, aged 15. And look! One of them is only three years old. Jason Skinner. The poor thing!' She sniffed.

I sat next to her and she smiled and patted my knee.

'I'll make us a nice tea tonight, shall I, since it's just you and me? Your favourite. No lumpy white sauce. That can go in the bin.'

'I'm not that hungry to be honest Mum.'

'Oh, you will be love.'

An hour later the smells of frying meat and the sound of spitting fat drifted in from the kitchen. I tiptoed upstairs to my room. I lay on my bed and tried to read but in the end just watched the Airfix plane hanging from the ceiling revolve slowly on its thread, wisps of dust clinging to its propellers. Why did German planes have black crosses? Pete once said that the baddies always wore black.

I slouched downstairs when Mum called me. My plate was waiting on the side table by the sofa. Two jumbo beef burgers, fat discs blackened at their rims; a neat woodpile of oven bake chips, and a spreading ooze of baked beans, which I knew wouldn't be hot enough. They never were. She was having just one burger, a couple of chips and what she called a side salad consisting of some shreds of lettuce and a quartered tomato. I looked away as she splashed tomato sauce on her chips. I chewed on a chip and forked a burger in half, pressing hard through the spongy sinew. The meat inside was grey-pink and glistening.

'Mum, I'm just not hungry tonight, honestly.'

'Just leave it love. I can put it in the oven for you for later.'

The television national news had headline stories about Princess Diana's latest outfit and a Campaign for Nuclear Disarmament rally in London attended by a quarter of a million people. Then came a round-up of bonfire night parties from across the country in which the newsreader sorrowfully described a shocking accident in Birmingham where at least five people and a dog were seriously injured. I pressed my head back into the sofa cushion so Mum couldn't see my face. The police were appealing for witnesses and putting their full resources into finding the culprits.

'There! I told you the police would find them, Dave. They always do.'

How should I be reacting to this? How would Mum expect me to behave? What would Pete do?

'That's good,' I said. 'Let's hope they catch them soon.'

After the national news, *Midlands Today* devoted its entire programme to the accident. This included coverage of a police press conference at which a man was introduced as the father of one of the victims, fifteen-year-old Tracey Downey, who had suffered a serious eye injury and burns. Mum gasped and raised her hand to her mouth.

'Oh, the poor man.'

I'd never seen Tracey's father before. He was solid with a crew cut and a moustache. His sweatshirt's rolled up sleeves revealed the blue smudge of tattoos on each forearm.

'My little girl.' He took a sip of water. Cameras clicked and whirred. 'My little girl is lying in a hospital bed. Her own mother didn't hardly recognise her. She's too upset to speak.'

Tension showed in his clenched movements and determined monotone.

'And there's other people too, in other hospital beds. Young children.' He stared into the camera. Straight at me.

'There was lots of people at that park last night. And if you weren't there, you might know someone who was. Do the right thing. Give yourself up. Even if it were a silly prank, an accident. You've got to live with yourself.'

Now the anger swelled like a bloom up his neck and cheeks. His voice rose.

'Think of my daughter. Think of Tracey.' He got up to leave amid camera flashes.

A reporter shouted something, inaudible on the television.

'No further questions, Mr Downey has made his statement…' a police officer began to say. Tracey's father sat down and grabbed the microphone.

'*Angry?* Are we *angry?*' The words boomed out in a stuttering rush. 'Damn flipping right we're angry! Our daughter goes out on bonfire night and comes back in an ambulance. All because some blooming nutter fires a rocket at people!'

I was paralysed, not knowing what to say or do. Luckily Mum too was watching transfixed, leaning forward in her seat.

Another question was put to Mr Downey and this time the word 'forgiveness' was audible. He spoke more thoughtfully, and this fierce sincerity chilled me more than his loud fury.

'Look, I used to always think I was a reasonable bloke. I remember when them IRA bombs went off in town, one parent of someone who died said she forgave the bombers and would pray for their souls instead. Well I'll tell you what I'm praying for. That whoever did this gets to suffer in exactly the same way as my Tracey. Or worse. *Forgiveness?* You can stick it.'

Mum sat back, shocked into silence for a while. Eventually she spoke.

'God help whoever did this, Dave. That's all I can say. God help them.'

– 12 –

Mum and I watched television all evening. First was Barbara Woodhouse's dog training show. Happy healthy dogs jumped and frolicked and barked. It was torture. We watched *Brideshead Revisited*, because Mum liked Jeremy Irons. She never got to watch it if Tony was around. He said Jeremy Irons and Anthony Andrews were a right couple of pansies. I thought he had a point.

By 9.30 I could take no more and went to bed where my sleepless mind played flitting scenarios in my head in a frantic loop. Images of flashing police cars. Angry mobs. Being birched. Worse, my mind screened endless footage depicting the sheer embarrassment of it: the incredulous excitement of schoolmates on learning what we had done.

'Pete Sharpe! *And Dave Truman?* Never! Fuck me, they're dead.'

I also imagined being unmasked during assembly: Miss Roberts dramatically pointing to Pete and me; being dragged out in front of everyone, handed to a policeman and whisked off to Winson Green prison.

The green numerals on my clock radio said 23:17 when the front door slammed. Several male voices sounded from downstairs. Tony wasn't alone. This sometimes happened when he went to the pub, although less often now he spent almost the whole weekend with Tracey: one or more of his mates would stop by after closing time to play records and eat chips or a takeaway from the Golden Bowl. Sometimes they'd fall asleep on the sofa until the early hours, sprawled out amid cold cups of tea, overflowing ashtrays, and foil cartons of slimy chop suey. But tonight there was urgent discussion and raised voices.

'Too right! She was your bird, wasn't she Tone?'

'They should be put in them stock things, in The Square, out the front of the shops. Fucking medieval, like.'

'It was probably them stupid boneheads.'

I covered my ears and wondered how long it would be before Tracey returned to school. When would Tony be able to see her in hospital? Shit, would she expect me and Pete to visit her? Would she remember our kiss?

It was only twenty-four hours since the accident but I couldn't remember the feeling of normality, of worrying about nothing more than homework or the life cycle of a zit on my chin. I replayed Pete's warning from yesterday. Prison. It was true he knew something about prison. The most upset I had ever seen him was after he'd been to Redditch Remand Centre to visit his brother when Lee was first arrested for stealing cars. Pete said the place was terrifying.

Bare metal rooms and crashing echoing doors and shouting. He never visited his brother again, saying it was because Lee didn't want to be seen caged up like an animal. Their mother visited Lee every week. Pete said you could smell prison on her when she got home. Winson Green Prison was on the other side of the city, towards Villa Park. I passed it once on a school bus trip to Aston Hall. A group of women were emerging from the gates between the twin castle-like brick towers at its entrance. Many were in tears.

What about the police? They weren't stupid, despite what Tony and Pete said. True, they only caught the Yorkshire Ripper after years of looking. But they arrested the Birmingham pub bombers almost immediately. What little I knew about the police came mostly from television. I preferred the American cop shows to the staid British versions. I liked *Columbo*, *Cannon*, and *Starsky and Hutch*, my current favourite. I liked the exotic landscapes of glass skyscrapers, eight-lane freeways and palm tree-lined beaches. And in the American shows the investigations seemed to always require a visit to a strip club.

After a while I needed a piss. I hated that the only toilet in our terrace house was downstairs at the back past the kitchen, and that the stairs were in the corner of the lounge room. When there were people in the lounge I had to walk through them to get to the bathroom. On one awful occasion those people were Tony and Tracey, entwined on the sofa. It was after midnight and the television was so quiet I hadn't heard it. It was a warm night and I'd dashed down wearing only my old pyjama trousers. They had space rockets on them and two buttons missing on the fly. Tracey never mentioned it of course but Tony cackled about it for weeks afterwards.

The last thing I could stand now was facing Tony and his boozed-up mates. So I writhed in bed for half an hour. I reached critical point and looked around the room for a suitable receptacle when a sleepy, drunken cough and an answering belch sounded from the hallway. They were followed by few slurred farewells and the front door closing. I bolted downstairs, startling Tony, and only just made it to the bathroom. The lino was icy under my bare feet.

Back in the lounge room Tony sat on the edge of the sofa, clearly waiting for me. Shit. The room was a junkyard of foil food containers, overflowing ashtrays and half-full mugs. Tony looked half-pissed. But he sounded alert and purposeful.

'Dave. Sit down a second, will you?'

I sidled towards the stairs.

'Oh Tone, not now. It's late, I was asleep…'

'Just sit will you!'

Act normal. Just act normal.

'What is it?'

'About that firework.' Act normal. 'You and your mate Sharpey were there, weren't you. Did you see anything?'

'Shit Tony, no, we didn't. It was pitch dark. Anyway, we left before the fireworks even started.'

Tony fidgeted with his cigarette lighter, snapping it on, turning the flame up and down. As the flame flared, his face lit up pale against the darkness round his eyes.

'It's just that you seem to be acting strange. You've gone a bit distant, like.' He snapped the lighter off and his face was just shadows again. 'I'm only ever going to ask this once, Dave.'

I needed the toilet again.

'Dave, do you know anything about what happened?'

I tried to act indignant. 'Tony, for fuck's sake, I said no.' He nodded.

'Because you're my brother, I'll rephrase the question, Dave. Does your mate Sharpe know anything about what happened?'

I frowned.

'What do you mean? Like I said…'

Tony leapt up and stood over me. 'I mean does your mate Sharpe, the one who likes fireworks, the one with the firebug brother in the nick, does he know anything?' He slapped my face. Not hard, but it stung. 'Because if he knows something, then he's the one who has to answer for it. The *only* one. D'you understand me Dave?'

I forced myself to look up at him.

'Tony, neither of us knows anything. Promise.'

'Because you left before the fireworks even started.'

I nodded.

'Cross you heart and hope to die, Dave?'

I nodded again.

'Yes Tone. Cross my heart and hope to die.'

****

Tony had blundered upstairs soon after me, and his rasping snores now drifted down the landing. But it wasn't Tony's snoring keeping me awake. I was used to that.

Around three in the morning I clicked my bedside light on. Rain pattered on the window in bursts, like thrown gravel. I reached under my bed and hauled out the Adidas bag I used for my running gear. I propped the bag on my knees and emptied it: trainers, shorts, two odd socks, a pair of once-white underpants, and a ragged towel. The smell was not good.

I cocked my head and listened. I'd made virtually no noise, but had to be sure that Tony or Mum hadn't woken up. I couldn't risk one of them walking in on me. Especially not Tony. The thought made me shudder. But there was just the rhythmic low drone of Tony's snoring and the sound of the rain.

I prised up the bag's rigid base and extracted a plastic bag. From it I removed a white woollen bobble hat with two pale pink bands along its bottom edge. As I pulled it from the bag I wondered which side of Tracey's hat would be revealed: the undamaged side, or the burnt side.

I still didn't know what had made me pick the hat up, because at the time I hadn't properly realised what it was. After the accident Pete and I had managed to rejoin the bonfire night crowd unnoticed, as per his plan. Trapped in the packed mass of bodies shuffling towards the park exit we were forced past the horror of the accident site, with its ghastly smells. Everyone stopped for five minutes while the police cleared a blockage ahead. I squatted on my haunches, tired beyond belief. The grass was littered with the detritus of a big public event: plastic cups, fag packets, sparkler wrappers, beer cans, greasy paper that had once held chips or burgers. Just beyond the man in front of me lay an object of white fabric partially obscured by a torn and trampled sheet of newspaper. I reached through the man's legs and snatched it up. I stuffed it down the front of my blazer just as Pete's icy hand grabbed my collar and hauled me to my feet.

I held the hat up to my bedside lamp. There was no mistaking the triangular scorch mark or the coarser feel to the wool on that side. I flipped it over, and held the other side of the hat against my face. The pure white, unblemished, unaltered, forever perfect side. The memory of Tracey's warm breath returned, and the feeling of her soft mouth on mine. Her wide blue eyes staring into mine. The strap of her handbag falling from her shoulder as we kissed.

I screwed my eyes shut to contain the tears. To cry tears and snot into Tracey's hat would have seemed like an act of desecration.

– 13 –

'Truman! Sharpe! Put a sock in it and get up those ropes! *Move!*'
PE teacher Mr Wilkins was in the Territorial Army, and it
showed. His nickname was Wanker Wilkins. Not subtle, not clever.
But satisfying. Twice a week we had to do an hour of PE. Often this
was a cross-country run, which I relished; sometimes swimming; or
as today, circuit training in the gym: the smells of polished wooden
floor and monkey bars lining the walls, and of sweat and old towels.

Pete and I thrashed and clawed our way up the ropes in the race
to be first to touch the ceiling. I always beat Pete at rope climbing
or things like chin-ups: he was bigger and stronger than me but thus
carried more muscle bulk. He'd also never mastered, as I had, how to
take some weight on the rope with your feet.

'Did Tony ask if we saw Tracey at the fireworks?' he gasped, his
rope spiralling beneath him. His biceps bulged.

'No, thank god. But according to Mum – and you know Tony tells
her everything, don't you, he always has – he's furious that Tracey was

even at the fireworks, when he thought she wasn't going. Fuck, it's high up here, isn't it?'

The floor was a long way down. Boys kicked basketballs at each other or half-heartedly rolled over a vaulting horse. Wilkins's manic screams echoed shrilly round the huge space.

'Well, that's something,' said Pete. 'Let's hope he just worries about Tracey from now on.'

'Maybe. But he's suspicious. Of us. He mentioned your brother.'

'That's crap, just because he doesn't like Lee. Just because Lee once gave him a slap, years ago.'

I didn't say any more. Pete didn't know Tony like I did. How he was like a ferret, he was smart, he could suss things out. I yawned, massively. The rope was fat and bristly in my hands. For a fleeting moment I thought about letting go.

'God, I'm just so tired. I can't keep doing this, Pete.'

'Well, you've fucking got to!'

'I can't! Look at how things are. Tony's going round saying he's going to kill whoever it was... Tracey's still in hospital. Do you even care? How come you're so calm about everything?'

'Yes, I care! But that doesn't matter. It's done, isn't it! We've just got to deal with it.'

His arms and shoulders began to spasm. He hated giving in before me.

'Sod this, I've had enough.'

He dropped away, juddering down the rope.

'But what about Mr Patel?' I hissed down.

'What about him?' Pete's face was puce.

I scanned the gym. There was still no-one within hearing distance of the ropes.

'He sold you the firework! And the booze. What if the police question him? What if he *goes* to the police?'

'Patel won't talk to the pigs. Selling booze and fireworks to underage kids? There's no way the bastard would risk a fine, losing his licence.' He slid down another few feet.

'We don't know that for sure!'

'Yes we do. I'm telling you.'

'I saw him yesterday.'

'*What?* You saw Patel? You better not have been anywhere near his shop Dave, I fucking told you…'

'No! Just in the street. He came out of the post office as I was going past on my bike.'

'And?' Pete's voice was grim.

'It was only a split second, but I think he sort of looked at me funny.'

'I can't believe you've never mentioned this before!'

Wilkins's head swivelled in our direction.

'Right, that's it,' said Pete. 'Patel will have to keep his gob shut, won't he. *Shit!*'

His hands broke from the rope and he dropped the last five feet, landing heavily and nearly banging his forehead on the floor. Wilkins marched towards us, arms swinging high.

'Sharpe! A parachute roll would have saved you there.' He peered up. 'Truman! Get your arse down here. Unless you're planning to stay up there forever?'

****

The final arguments took place in Pete's bedroom, with the volume on his portable television turned full up.

'Dave, we have to do this. You said so yourself.'

Pete was carelessly throwing darts at the board on the back of his door. It was a professional standard board, liberated by Lee via the toilet window of a working men's club and given to Pete one Christmas.

'No I bloody didn't! At least the fucking firework was an accident. This is different. And what's Mr Minwalla ever done to us to deserve this?'

'Patel's done fuck-all to deserve it. But tough shit. It's like you said, we've got to be sure he won't go to the pigs. Otherwise we'll always have that worry. Do you want even more to worry about?'

'Of course not! I want bloody less to worry about! I still think we should just go to the police ourselves, tell them what happened.' I was sitting on Pete's bed, my back against the wall and my knees hugged to my chest.

'Dave, forget it. We're not going to the police. We'd be stupid if we did.' He hurled a dart. It rebounded off the wire and nearly skewered his foot. 'Look, I know this isn't going to be fun. But we have to do it. It'll be quick, it'll be easy, no-one will get hurt. His insurance will cover it all.'

'Can't you do it on your own? I might stuff it up or something.'

Pete froze in the act of throwing his next dart, his arm outstretched.

'You're fucking unbelievable sometimes. We're in this together Dave. As you well know.'

'And what if we get caught?'

'Well, even if we did get caught it would just be a slap on the wrist from the pigs. It'd only be vandalism. But we won't. There'll be no one around there to see us, there isn't a pub or takeaway or anything nearby.'

'And we don't even know if it'll work! Maybe it'll make him more likely to go to the police. What then?'

Pete's voice had an edge to it now. 'Dave, for the last time. There's three good reasons why Patel won't go to the police, and probably would never have done anyway. One, his kind don't ever talk to the police. Two…'

'What do you mean, his kind?'

'Pakis. They keep to themselves, don't they? Sort things out their own way. I suppose they know the pigs are never much interested in helping them. So. Two, like I said, he wouldn't risk getting a fine for selling booze or fireworks to underage kids.' He took more careful aim, imitating Eric Bristow's grip, with his little finger sticking out. Treble twenty. 'And third, think about this. Suppose Patel went the pigs. And suppose, from that, they found us and we got arrested and charged with letting off the firework. I've already told you what would happen to us, though it doesn't seem to have sunk in with you properly. But think about what would happen to Patel. Fucking nutters like your brother's mates would have his bollocks just for selling the firework that did the damage.' He groaned as his second dart thudded into the five. 'So Dave, you have to make a choice. You have to decide, I can't make you. But I'm telling you, we have to do this thing tonight. It'll just be a gentle reminder to him of what might otherwise happen. And then, Dave, we'll be able to relax. Everything will go away. Yeesss!' Another treble twenty.

'Will his insurance really cover everything for him?'

'Definitely. He'll even get nice new stuff for what gets damaged. I bet he'll be glad this has happened, in the long run.'

We left Pete's house at 11:45pm. Rose was still up watching television, and I was worried that she would challenge us.

'Just going out, Mum,' Pete called as we ran past the lounge room door.

'Okay love,' she replied over the sound of gunfire and thudding horses' hooves.

The night was moonless and quiet, the streetlamps reflecting in shiny pools on the wet pavements and a spray of rain still in the air. We paused for final preparations in a pedestrian walkway a hundred yards from the row of shops. I was already agitated simply about being out this late, with people still on their way home from the pubs and potential trouble everywhere. Pete insisted we tie our scarves round our faces, which only made me more nervous. My breathing was heavy and moist through the wool. The half brick in my right hand was rough and heavy, tucked against my chest Napoleon-style. Pete did the same, hiding his arm inside the old donkey jacket he wore. He hadn't worn his leather coat since bonfire night. We had found the half bricks in a pile of builder's rubble in a front garden.

Pete issued final instructions and we were away, walking fast, heads down. My mouth was dry and my breath rasped in my chest. What the hell was I doing? Why was I trusting Pete? Why did I never learn? Then I became conscious of passing a point of no return, of things speeding up and out of my control, of stepping away so my body became an independent being under the influence of Pete alone, mimicking his movements, treading in his footsteps. Snatches of Pete's instructions flashed in my mind. Throw hard. Slow down, but don't stop. Then keep running, fast. No talking.

And then Pete's fast walk became a trot and there was no time for rational thought. There was only the percussion of our soft footfalls on the wet pavement – Pete had insisted we wear trainers – and my panting breath loud in my ears. Pete glanced back to check I was with him and we wheeled into the pedestrian strip with the row of five shops on each side and the graffiti-covered benches down the middle. My heart pumped and I couldn't feel the weight of the brick anymore. Pete's black figure accelerated towards Mr Minwalla's shopfront, third down on the left and then he hesitated for a second. The shop window was protected by a metal security shutter. How stupid of us! But Pete's right arm cocked back and with his left he pointed at the shop doorway, set in a recess to the right of the shuttered front. He took a running leap high in the air, his hair whirling round his ears, and I gripped my fingers round my half brick and hurled it at the glass panel in the top half of the door just as Pete's arm flashed towards the upstairs windows. There were two simultaneous crashes of broken glass: hard, jagged, perfect blinding sounds that echoed out over the silent concrete roadway. Instantly a dog barked somewhere close but we were sprinting away, me into my racing stride, stretching it out, overtaking Pete in a burst of pure energy as we turned the far corner and were gone into the night. We slowed to a jog and stopped behind a row of garages down near the flats. Hands on hips, bent over, we panted and spat and recovered our breath. Pete looked up at me.

'There! Told you it'd be easy. That was a right laugh, wasn't it?'

'No it bloody wasn't a laugh. It was stupid.'

'So why are you laughing, Dave?'

'Am not!'

'Yes you are.' Pete reached out and pulled my face round by my chin.

'Gerroff!'

But I couldn't stop myself, knowing Pete had seen the smile on my face. We laughed together for a long time in the heart-pumping wind-down until the midnight cold bit deeper and we turned for home.

****

The pavement in front of the shop was a mess of broken glass. Mr Minwalla was knocking some of the loose pieces out of the front door with a broom handle. The proprietor of the adjacent video hire shop lounged in his doorway, smoking a cigarette, watching. A woman in a bright blue and gold sari was talking to Mr Minwalla. She blew on her cupped hands and glanced up and down the street. A boy poked his head from an upstairs window. Mr Minwalla shouted at him and brandished the broom, and the boy slowly withdrew his head. He had poked it through a jagged hole in the window pane.

An icy wind chilled my face, ballooning out the hood of my parka and scouring tears from my tired eyes. But I was still glad to be out of the over-warm stuffiness of the house. It was stupid, and in contravention of Pete's stern order that we stay well away from Mr Minwalla's shop, but I had to come and take a look. It was different in daylight: stark and confronting and ugly.

Mrs Minwalla noticed me peering from behind the post box. I clutched my hood round my face and hurried away. I told myself that maybe Mr Minwalla wouldn't be too troubled. As Pete had said, he would have insurance that would reimburse him. And such events, after all, weren't unusual in the area. I had heard things, at school, about what the skinheads got up to sometimes, and a few times on the way to the football I'd seen a few National Front supporters mingling with the ordinary football fans outside St Andrews: older-looking skins and a couple of fat, piggy-eyed middle aged men in suits and beige raincoats. Some boys at school wore Anti-Nazi league badges on their blazer lapels along with the usual badges everyone wore with the names of bands. I thought about Mr and Mrs Singh, two doors up from our house. Not long after the Singhs had moved in Mrs Singh had brought round a tray of samosas that she'd cooked because it was a feast day in their religion. Tony and I enjoyed them but Mum was wary, explaining repeatedly that she had nothing against foreign food but how Dad always said that in his job he knew about food hygiene and wouldn't eat something if he didn't know the kitchen it had come from. Mum and I said hello to the Singhs if we saw them but this was less often now because Mrs

Singh and her two children always crossed the street before passing our house. Mum said she thought this was something to do with Mr Hickey.

****

'Ooh, it says here that stray dog's had its leg amputated. Hoppy, they're calling it. The poor thing.'

'Front or back leg?'

'Hind. That's back, isn't it? There's an appeal, they want someone to give it a home.'

'Here, look. "Curvy teenager Tracey Downey is still being treated in Birmingham Eye Hospital." Curvy teenager! Just 'cos she once did them photos.'

'Maybe someone should organise a get well card for her.'

'Why bother, she won't be able to read it now she's blind.'

'Piss off Quigley, you sick twat.'

'Make me.'

My classmates clustered round copies of *The Sun*, some of the girls trying to appear sniffy and reluctant to look at Tracey's swimsuit picture, but crowding round just the same. I hovered on the edge of the group, trying not to appear too desperate for news. *Act normal.* A whirl of images flashed past my inward eye: me treading on the dog's paw; the blue five pound note crumpled in Pete's hand outside Mr Minwalla's shop; and Tracey's eyes, shining into mine.

Neil Quigley's challenge provoked a scuffle which was followed by yet another round of speculation as to how badly Tracey was hurt. No-one knew with any authority. Anne Withers claimed to know one of the small children who'd been hurt, a boy from her street. His hair had been burnt and his ear and neck were bandaged up, but he was out of hospital, bless him, the little mite.

Doreen, the one person who would know about Tracey, still hadn't returned to school. Their two desks stood three rows back in the middle. They were ugly and bare, the usual chipped wood and worn seats. The room was as full of noise and movement as always. But the empty desks were like a void in our midst, a dark thing that you couldn't ignore, like a freshly dug grave.

Pete insisted on coming home with me after school. He said vaguely that he needed help with his English homework, but once there he made no move to get his schoolbooks out of his bag. I can see, now, that he probably wanted to keep an eye on me. See how I behaved in front of my mother. Make sure I was 'acting normal'.

He left as soon as Tony got home. I saw Pete out and lingered at the front door, glad of the fresh air. To my left, through the side pane of the front room's bay window, Mum stood at the ironing board. Her mouth moved and her head bobbed. She always sang when she ironed. Neil Diamond, usually. I leaned against the doorframe, not minding the rain dripping from the gutter, cold and sharp on my head, icy fingers running through my hair. Mum pulled from the laundry basket my school trousers that she had washed the day after the accident. She held them up in front of her, and her face changed. She stopped singing and appeared lost in thought, holding the trousers up until her arms trembled. She bit her lip, lowered them, and began ironing. She kept rhythmically pushing the iron over the same place, her face now blank.

Later she came up to my room, where I was trying to care about my maths homework. She closed the door and leaned against it.

'Dave love, are you alright?'

I pretended to concentrate on the properties of an isosceles triangle.

'Why wouldn't I be?'

'Because of what's happened to Tracey, that's why. Because Tony's upset. Because you don't seem yourself at all.' She advanced into the room and sat on my bed.

'Mum, can you go please? I've got homework to do.'

'Alright, Mister Suddenly-keen-on-his-schoolwork.' She stood. 'But if ever you need to talk about anything, remember I'm your mother. I'll understand. I'll help you.'

I nodded, and ostentatiously turned the page of my exercise book.

My mother picked up the framed photograph that stood on my bedside table. It showed my father and me grinning with our arms in the air in the manner of footballers celebrating a goal.

'I always liked this photo,' she said. 'You both look so happy.'

Now she had my attention.

'When was it taken?'

Our house was littered with photos of Dad — wedding pictures, holiday snaps, even one of him playing football for a work team, when he was still at Longbridge.

'It was when he'd just got home one time. I can't remember exactly. But look at you – you must be about eight. So let's see, that must be around 1974. Look at his haircut!'

'Look at my haircut. Looks like you let Tony do it.'

Mum held the photo at arm's length. Her eyes were half closed.

'It's funny,' she said. 'I've got no photos of Tony and your Dad, together like that, except when Tony was very small. Not a single one.'

****

You could tell by the buzz coming from the assembly hall as we neared it that something unusual was happening. Inside, the level of noise was fearsome: an electrically charged whispering and muttering and stifled, panicky laughter. Our class arrived last and the whole school turned to look at us: ranks of angry pale faces turning and frowning and, as I imagined, all focussed on me. I stared at the floor and literally pushed Pete to get him to hurry up and sit down. Only when we were seated did I properly look up. Pete muttered 'Oh, shit,' and when I saw who sat on the stage, the tired numbness of the last few days was obliterated in an invigorating spark of sheer terror.

Sitting next to the deputy head was a policeman in an immaculate dark blue uniform. The bright lights made his badge and buttons glow with an unearthly silvery whiteness. It was the officer who had introduced Tracey's father at the press conference. He and Miss Roberts were talking, heads close, intense. She pointed at the ranks of pupils, and he nodded gravely.

Miss Roberts rose and walked to the lectern. The noise in the hall died as if a mute button had been flicked. No-one even coughed or scuffed their feet. Everyone craned forward. The loudest sound was the rain splashing from the roof of the covered walkway alongside the hall.

She took her time, letting the full dramatic impact sink in. We could not have been more attentive if her arrival at the lectern had been preceded by a drum roll, and she seemed to be absorbing that knowledge, taking careful note, remembering. I was stifled and fidgety and was now finding it hard to breathe. I tried to take long slow deep breaths but felt that I was being slowly starved of oxygen, so I sighed and breathed in sharp puffs. Before Pete could nudge me the girl in front turned around, irritated by me blowing on the back of her hair. Pete kicked my ankle, hard. He sat with his arms crossed, legs spread. His face was expressionless but I could tell by the line of his jaw that he was tense too. In a strange way this made me feel better.

Miss Roberts pointed to the policeman.

'This is Superintendent Bannerman.'

With the whole school looking at him, Bannerman seemed to swell. He was a vision of absolute authority made real. His buttons and braid glowed even brighter, as if illuminated from within. He rose abruptly and the whole school, including a couple of teachers, instinctively leant back. He joined the Headmistress at the lectern, which barely reached his waist. He cleared his throat.

'Good morning,' he boomed. 'I need your help. My officers need your help. The people affected by the firework tragedy need your help.' Pete's breath whistled out of his nostrils and I sensed some of the tension leaving him. I too felt less terrified.

'We would like to talk to everyone who was at the park last Thursday night, or anyone who was in the surrounding streets. It doesn't matter if you think you didn't see anything useful. We want to talk to you.'

'Stuff that,' Pete muttered.

'My officers will be here, in the school, this afternoon. We are asking that everyone who was at the park give their name to their form teacher, and we will talk to them each in turn. There is no need for your parents to be involved: Miss Roberts will remain present throughout.'

I felt that things were spinning away, my life no longer my own, that I was a character in a game. Fucking Pete. Fucking Tony. Fucking Tracey and Doreen. It shouldn't have happened! The firework shouldn't have gone off in the crowd! Why was this happening to me? Why couldn't everyone just leave me alone?

Bannerman adopted a softer tone. 'There's nothing to worry about. Remember, you're not helping the police.' He tried to smile. 'You're helping the people who were hurt. Including Tracey Downey.'

Sympathetic murmurs rippled back through the hall.

He stood back, and Mrs Roberts spoke again. She reiterated 'for the avoidance of doubt' that the police wanted to speak to everyone who was there, not just anyone who thought they saw something.

'Everybody who was there.'

****

I had never wanted a cigarette more but the rain was so heavy that going for a fag was impossible. The playground was a shallow lake frothy with wind gusts and the playing fields resembled a vast paddy field.

Finding solitude at break time in a building containing 1,100 people was difficult. Pete and I were in an upstairs corridor in the science block.

'Talk to the pigs? No way.'

'Pete, we have to. Never mind what Lee might think of you. We have to.'

'Bollocks! Remember what I said. We keep our heads down.'

'No! Too many people from school know we were there.' I was close to tears. 'I don't fucking want to talk to them either! But everyone knows we were there. We have to do it.' A thought occurred to me. 'You choose, Pete. If you won't agree to owning up, then we have to do this.'

'Shit, maybe.' He rolled his eyes and sighed. 'But can you do it, Dave? Talk to them? Remember: we watched the fireworks, the accident happened, we saw nothing, we went home. Forget about what you told your mum and Tony.'

'So, we went home just after it happened, right?'

'Yes. Well, not immediately after. We were stuck in the crowd for ages, like everyone else.'

'Right.'

Pete jabbed a finger. 'Dave, have you got this in your head? This is important.' He stopped. 'Let's think. It was probably only five or ten minutes between the fireworks display ending, and our firework… well, you know.'

'Your firework.'

'Whatever, Dave. Don't start with that now, for fuck's sake.' He raised his finger again. 'Have you got it? Keep it simple, answer their questions, but don't tell them about something unless they particularly ask. Don't be over-helpful. The pigs get suspicious of people who seem too keen to help them.'

I leaned against the wall, shuffling onto my other leg. The parquet floor in the anteroom outside the Head's office was shiny and worn from decades of nervous teenage feet. Miss Parker, the school secretary, sat at a desk that filled half the room. Framed photographs of her two poodles sat on the desktop next to the phone. I had hoped that Pete's turn would come first but a random list had been drawn up of pupils who had been at the park. My name was first.

Miss Parker usually smiled nervously and said hello but today she kept her head down, pecking at her typewriter. The tight scraped bun on top of her narrow head and the tip of her sharp red nose were all that were visible. She gave a watery sniff every few seconds and reached for the twisted hankie next to her on the desk. There were three plastic coloured lights above the door to the Head's office: red for 'busy, do not disturb'; amber for 'wait'; and green for 'enter'. The amber light was on. My tired gaze blurred and lost focus so the yellow light and even the whole room became a vague fluttery image, like a dream. The glowing green light jolted me awake. Big thumps in my chest. I waited, unsure if I should go straight in, until an irritated shout came from behind the door.

'Enter!'

I didn't know where to put my hands. I shoved them in my pockets at first but they were now folded hard across my chest. The detective and Miss Roberts sat side by side behind her desk in front of the window. Even with the sky dark grey with rain, the light behind them made it difficult to properly see their faces. The detective was in plain clothes. He had dark greasy hair with long sideburns and a thick moustache. The sour reek of stale cigarette smoke clung to him.

Fatigue dulled his movements and speech as he explained that the police were going round the local schools to interview teenagers who had been at the park that night. I tried to pull myself together. What had Pete said? Stick to the story. We saw nothing. We know nothing.

'We didn't see anything,' I blurted.

'David, just wait for the officer's questions,' Miss Roberts said, shaking her head.

The detective doodled in his notebook. Strong hands, nicotine fingers. He spoke without looking up.

'Son, do you like Southern Comfort?'

'Huh?' My heart made clutching jolts up into my throat. I tightened my arms round my chest.

'Do you like Southern Comfort? It's a simple question.' Now he looked right at me.

'No, not much.'

'You know what it is then? You've drunk it before?'

I shook my head vaguely. 'Once or twice.'

'It's just that we found a bottle on the hillside near where the firework was launched from. It's gone for fingerprinting.'

I tried to think back, to focus. The memory of the sickly taste flooded my mouth.

'Who were you with, on bonfire night?'

'Pete. Peter Sharpe.'

'He's a mate of yours, is he?' The detective's eyes narrowed. 'Has he got an older brother?'

I nodded. 'Lee.'

The corners of the detective's mouth flicked upward briefly. 'Were you with anyone else?'

I squirmed and clenched my buttocks. Pete hadn't prepared me for this.

'We were with Tracey and Doreen for a while.'

'Tracey Downey? So did you see Tracey get injured?'

Miss Roberts was nodding eagerly, as interested in my responses as the policeman.

'No. They left us before the firework display. Said they were going home.'

'So where did you watch the fireworks from?'

'Just with everyone else, around near the bonfire.'

'That's where Doreen says she and Tracey were. Funny you didn't see them again.' He rubbed his eyes. 'Still, it was dark I suppose.' He looked keenly at me. 'Do you think that's why you didn't bump into them again?'

'Why didn't they go home?' I blurted. 'They told us they were cold, they were going straight home!' Hot tears poured into my eyes and my shoulders heaved with sobs.

And now Miss Roberts leaned across, holding out a tissue.

'Alright David, it's alright. Come on, pull yourself together, for goodness sake.'

As I blew my nose, my eyes caught the policeman's. Did the man seem more alert, more thoughtful than he had been when I had first walked into the room? Or was my vision distorted by the blurred veil of tears?

I rushed straight into the nearest bogs, praying I wouldn't meet anyone on the way. I had cried! A fourth former, crying! If anyone found out, I would never ever be allowed to forget it. I sat in a cubicle and tried to calm down. The windows were closed against the rain but I hardly noticed the foul atmosphere. After twenty minutes I felt no better but knew I would be missed soon. I was supposed to be in double history. I emerged and checked myself in the mirror. I splashed my face with cold water and slapped my cheeks hard, both to rouse myself and also because if my whole face was red, maybe my bloodshot eyes might be less obvious. No-one could know I'd been crying. It could not happen.

My next worry was how to communicate with Pete before it was his turn in the Head's office. Maybe I could whisper to him during what remained of the history lesson. But he wasn't there. There were urgent whispers from others – what did the pigs want? – but

I ignored them. I almost didn't care anymore about what happened. Maybe a part of me even wanted it to end today, and whatever happened tomorrow could take care of itself. This was crazy but I let my thoughts stay with the idea, and after a while felt a tiny degree of tired peace. It could be over soon.

Pete and I couldn't talk alone until we got off the bus after school. I was desperate for the two of us to go off together as soon as the final bell rang, but Pete insisted we travel home as normal with everyone else. Not to do so would be suspicious, he said. He was right, of course. But it was torture to sit sullenly as the bus whined along the rain-drenched roads listening to Pete compare notes with a couple of other boys who had been questioned. Pete mostly ranted about how the detective was a pig who knew fuck all, and only girls or puffs drank Southern Comfort. There was talk about why the police were suspicious that teenagers were somehow involved. Pete pointed out that there had been a vast number of teenage children at the fireworks and hence it wasn't surprising that the pigs were questioning as many as possible. Jeremy Whitlam said it showed that the police were no nearer catching the culprits.

None of this lessened the worry that had been with me since the incident. Why were the police interested in teenagers? Had someone seen something? What about Pete's stupid coat? It was so distinctive. But I couldn't rationally consider this risk because my memories of the night itself were no more than an incoherent jumble of images and sensations: kissing Tracey, the white flash of the explosion, the hot urine on my leg, and the hideous smell around the accident zone.

At last we jumped off the bus.

'Pete, what are we going to do? They're onto us.'

'Bollocks! Police always act like everyone's guilty. They are not onto us, unless you said anything stupid to them today.' He stopped. 'You didn't, did you?'

'I don't think so. They kept asking me where we watched the fireworks from and I just said near the bonfire. And I said we were with Doreen and Tracey.' I cringed, waiting for Pete's reaction.

'Good, Dave. They asked me that too – we had to be truthful there, since they'll have spoken to Doreen. And where did you say we watched the fireworks?'

'Oh, from just in the crowd, near the bonfire.'

Pete nodded in satisfaction. 'Our stories match! Well done Dave, you handled yourself well. We're in the clear.'

'But the Southern Comfort! They've got your fingerprints!'

'And yours.'

'No, I had my gloves on.'

'No you didn't. You took them off. Definitely.'

Had I? I had no idea, but had to assume Pete was right.

'So, we should own up. It's only a matter of time, isn't it?'

'Get this in your head: we are not going to the police to own up! What are they going to do, fingerprint the whole fucking city?'

'Then let's go to my mum, or your mum. Or a teacher. Mr McLeish is alright, we could tell him…'

Pete lunged at me and jabbed his finger.

'Don't be stupid! If you tell them, it's the same as telling the police!'

'No it isn't! My mum wouldn't go to the police if we told her.'

'She would, she'd have to — or you'd be making her part of it, like us.'

I hadn't thought of that.

'Dave, listen to me.' Pete kept his finger up, pointing. 'Don't you go telling anyone. That's how people get found out, get in trouble. Like Guy Fawkes and his mates, like we've been doing in history. Remember? They only got caught because they told too many people what they were doing. Their families. And look what happened to them.'

I shuddered. Mr McLeish had included in his account of the gunpowder plotters' fate a detailed description of what being hung, drawn and quartered involved. The thought so sickened me I didn't entirely believe him.

Pete punched my shoulder. 'Dave, I know things are bad. I do. But just hang in there a bit longer. Things will die down. The police will go away. Christmas is coming up, no more school, everyone will forget about a few fireworks injuries.'

- 14 -

The five boys and two girls formed a tight semicircle. At first Pete and I couldn't see what was going on. But from the tension of their movements and grim set of their faces it was clear someone was in trouble. The figure inside the semicircle was thrown back against the garage doors with a metallic boom. The attackers closed in and there was a flurry of shouting and angry movement.

The bus had been early and there was just time for a smoke before school. Pete, Terry Hart and I hurried round the back of the garages, pulling out our fags and matches. The mob was twenty yards away. Straightaway we recognised Neil Quigley's bony freckled face and ginger hair. The rest were in the year above us, the fifth year, including Quigley's brother Paul. The two girls were also fifth years, a couple of skinhead groupies called Sharon Burns and Dawn Clutter. The victim was visible through a gap in the scrum of bodies, his back against the garage doors and his arms outstretched, pleading.

'Fucking hell, that's Johnny Rose,' said Terry.

'What's he ever done?' said Pete, and shrugged. 'There's nothing we can do to help him.'

The mob wasn't fully laying into Rose but there was the occasional kick, and a couple of times Paul Quigley cuffed him hard across the back of the head as if playing a forehand tennis shot with maximum topspin. Neil strutted over to us.

'Anyone crash us a fag?'

No-one responded, and he shrugged and pulled a battered pack of ten Bensons from his pocket. He grabbed Hart's cigarette from his mouth and lit his from its tip.

'Fucking duck-arsed.' He looked disgustedly at the wet filter of the donor cigarette. 'Here, catch.' He tossed it back, Hart having to step smartly aside and let it drop to the ground.

'Funny, Neil. What's the deal with Rose? Think there's enough of you?'

'His old man's a pig, we was just asking Rosie when they're gonna catch those wankers what set off that firework.'

'Why do they care?'

'Shazza knows one of the kids that got hurt. Her little cousin.'

'But Rose's dad's a traffic cop,' I said. 'He's not a detective. It'll be nothing to do with him.'

'Yeah, well, they're all pigs.' Quigley hawked and gobbed onto a garage door. The blob of mucus slid down a couple of feet and came to rest wedged against a peeling flake of paint. 'They need to pull their fingers out. It's been a week and they've done fuck all.'

'I heard everyone reckons it was them skinheads that did it,' muttered Hart. 'They were there that night, Crump and those other nutters, being prats as usual.'

Quigley sneered. 'Don't you boys know anything? Our brother's told me, definitely not. It wasn't them. Think about it. Those two' – he nodded in the direction of Dawn Clutter and Sharon Burns – 'would hardly be putting the frighteners on Johnny Rose to get the pigs to get off their arses, would they, if their own mates had done it?'

Before he took the register Mr Preston announced that Doreen Greatorex would be back at school the following day. He asked that everyone respect that she had gone through a traumatic time and not press her for details about bonfire night. He also said that Tracey Downey was out of danger but still in hospital. She was not ready yet for visitors, and it would be a long time before she came back to school.

'Sir, is it true she's blind?' asked Neil Quigley.

There was tutting and shaking of heads, although everyone listened keenly to Mr Preston's answer.

'As we understand it, Tracey may have lost sight in one eye. And she's suffered severe burns. She's not blind, though. That's all I know.'

'So sir, will she have to wear a glass eye?'

'For god's sake Quigley, I don't know.'

'Will she have a white stick?'

There were some giggles from Quigley's cronies.

'Or a guide dog?' he added.

This time most of the class rounded on him angrily.

'Shut up Quigley, you psycho.'

'You sick twat!'

'Wanker.'

Rocky Bishton reached forward and calmly hacked Quigley on the crown of his head with the edge of his metal ruler. He was the only boy in our year who would dare do that. Mr Preston stepped in to deal with the chaos just as the bell rang for assembly.

'Right, everyone go,' he shouted, 'except you, Truman.'

I shot Pete a panicky look. Pete loitered as everyone surged out of the room, trying to get a word to me, but Preston waved him away.

'Go on, Sharpe, you can be separated from Truman for a few minutes, for pity's sake.'

Pete made a sarcastic face and backed away, making surreptitious calming motions to me with his hands. It didn't work.

Preston perched on the edge of his desk and I stood in front of him, looking at the floor, trying to get my thought processes to work. What could this be about? I'd spent the night replaying the police interview, and my later conversations with Pete, over and over in my mind. Now, anything out of the ordinary, like this, spooked me badly.

'Truman, how are things?'

'Fine, sir.'

'I doubt that, after what happened last week. It's affected us all.' He cleared his throat. 'A few teachers have said to me that you seem to be taking this particularly badly. I know it's only been a week, but everyone is saying you seem completely unable to concentrate in class. Are you having trouble sleeping or something?'

'No sir.'

'I know you were there that night, but so were quite a few boys and girls from this school. Is Tracey a particular friend of yours?'

'She's my brother's girlfriend.'

'Ah, that explains why you're more upset than most. I imagine things aren't easy at home. Look, try to concentrate on your work. It'll be a good distraction, like a sort of therapy, eh? Don't fall behind. These are 'O' Levels you're doing now, remember. This is about your future.' He stood up and flicked some dandruff from his shoulder. 'Off you go to assembly.'

****

'I don't want a chop, thanks Mum,' I said. 'I'll just have potatoes and carrots.'

The kitchen was full of meaty smoke. I had no appetite anyway but the sight of the fat pink slabs under the grill and the smell made me feel sick.

'Don't tell me you're becoming one of them weird vegetarians Dave,' she said, waggling a fork at me. 'You'll go hungry in this house if you are.'

'Maybe I am,' I said, glad she had given me an opening but knowing what was to come.

'You great puff,' said Tony. 'Are you turning into a homo or something?'

The carrots tasted aromatic and sickly and I gulped one down, gagging. Tony gnawed on a chop, his hands glistening with grease, a strip of sinewy meat stretching and snapping into his mouth as he pulled the chop away. The sick feeling dissolved into anger as my brother chomped wetly on his food.

'How's Tracey, Tony?'

'I was gonna ask you what you'd heard at school.'

'But she's your *bird*, isn't she. Don't you know how she is?' My anger made me reckless.

Tony's eyes narrowed and he pointed his knife at me. 'Watch it, Dave. It's none of your business.'

Mum cut in. 'Look, everyone's upset about Tracey and everything…'

'Have you sent her a get well card?' My blood pumped hot in my ears.

'Dave, I'm fucking warning you. It's none of your business.' Tony's neck was flushed. I went on, feeling dizzy.

'You didn't care about her before the accident, but now she's "your bird", just so's you can go round pretending to care…'

Tony shoved his plate aside, his knife and fork sliding off onto the floor, and jumped to his feet in a rush of movement. He leaned over me, jabbing his finger in my chest, his teeth bared, lips curled back.

'Last warning, Dave. Fucking leave it!' he hissed. And now I was silent. Tony wiped his greasy hands on his thighs. 'I'm off out.' He snatched his coat and slammed the door behind him.

'Dave! What's the matter with you?' asked Mum, aghast.

'Well, it's true! He doesn't care about Tracey.'

I'd never seen my mother so angry.

'David Truman, you take that back! Your poor brother is absolutely sick with worry about Tracey. He's tried to go and see her. She still won't see him. He doesn't know why. He's extremely upset. Tracey's father had words with Tony. He says he doesn't want Tony bothering Tracey anymore.'

'Sorry Mum.'

'Don't say sorry to me. It's poor Tony you should be sorry for.'

Poor Tony. Of course. I was tired again now, drained and numb. The room was hot and smelly with food.

'I'm going out too, Mum. I might go round to Pete's.'

She nodded, reaching for a tissue.

I had no intention of going to Pete's. I started walking, choosing my route randomly. The rain had stopped but the dark streets were lacquered with water. I pushed my parka hood back, glad of the cooling wind on my face. Thoughts generated by Neil Quigley's stupid comments that morning zoomed in and out of my consciousness. What if Tracey was blind? What would a glass eye look like? Were they really made of glass, like marbles with their twist of colour in the centre? At primary school we'd had a music teacher called Mrs Stevens who was supposed to have had a glass eye. Both her eyes were pale and watery, so it was hard to tell. She was old, or seemed so to us kids. There was a story that her glass eye had once fallen out of its socket while she was giving a piano lesson and the girl she was teaching had been sick over the keys.

I tried to push these thoughts away. But thinking about primary school days, in what seemed a long ago happy time when Dad was alive, calmed me. My thoughts flowed back to my time at our primary school. Games of football and rounders in the summer when the weather seemed to always be hot and sunny. Pete and me working on art projects together with me often taking underserved credit. Pete drinking five bottles of milk for a dare and being sick in the sand pit. It was only three and a half years since we had left but it felt like ten or more. My old school was only a couple of streets away. I walked past it. It was dark and silent and looked tiny, the playground a little concrete square and the low set buildings like models.

I walked on down quiet backstreets of terrace houses with flickering blue television lights in every window. I crossed the dual carriageway into the council estate beyond. Brick semis and squat tower blocks with dented low white metal railings protecting the strips of soggy grass. Decrepit cars in colours like beige and lime green and chocolate brown lined the access roads and kerbsides.

I passed almost no-one. Rain fell again, slanting flecks in the glow of the streetlights. This area was not a place to be after dark – or even during the day. Here it was unwise to make eye contact with anyone, and even young children would hurl things off the high balconies of the tower blocks onto people below. But I just didn't care about what might happen. Not in a reckless sense, but almost as if I felt detached from my surroundings. The rain was icy cold, but I scarcely felt it. It was as if the activity was in my head, and the streets were quiet corridors of dark, wet calm.

Only as I neared it did I realise that I had always intended to return to the park. That my aimless wandering had a purpose. I sat in the bus shelter opposite the park entrance, hunched with my elbows on my knees. My hair dripped and my shoes were sodden. To my right, the road curved along the ridge where the line of poplar trees disappeared into the darkness. The tower blocks were black rectangles against the dark sky. Hardly a light shone in their windows. Windblown leaves and scraps of paper were caught in the park's steel entrance gates. Eventually I got up and crossed the road. It wasn't leaves and litter. The gates were hung with bunches of flowers and scraps of sodden paper and cards covered in plastic, flapping wetly. Most of the flowers were limp and half-rotten, stalks drooping and their petals gone. A teddy bear was tied to the railings by a blue ribbon round its neck, leaning forwards in an upright position with its arms open.

I tried to read some of the messages. But it was too dark, and rain had penetrated the plastic coverings so that most were just slimy pulp. A few words were still legible. They were fragments of phrases like 'pray for you', 'get well', and 'in our thoughts'. Most of them would have been put there the day after the accident, when several people were in intensive care and rumours were circulating about people fighting for their lives. It seemed like weeks ago. For the first time, I thought about the other people who had been injured. It wasn't just Tracey. There were a lot of others too. I thought back to that list of names in the newspaper. The three-year-old boy. Another child of seven. The teddy bear looked sad and lonely, staring out from its meadow of rotting flowers and scraps of soggy paper. I shivered, realising how far I was from home.

There was more writing on the wide square concrete columns that supported the gates. It was sprayed on in dark red paint. The lettering had run and was bleeding down the concrete in pink trails. On the left hand gate was written: OWN UP OR DIE. The lettering on the other gate read: OWN UP AND DIE.

I was still absorbing the impact of this when there was movement away to my right. A group of people came into view fifty yards away along the road on the same side as me. The park side, where it was dark and shadowy under the overhanging trees. Cigarettes glowed red like angry eyes. A panicky fear hit me. From the group's loose, jostling movement it was obviously a gang of youths. Probably skinheads. That meant trouble. Maybe serious trouble. I tried to think, to be decisive. To run was stupid, as it would guarantee they chase me. I had one slim chance. I walked away briskly but nonchalantly, without looking back, praying they couldn't be bothered with a chase.

'*Oi!*' A rough shout split the night, followed by the splashing clatter of boots on the pavement. I ran, accelerating as a bottle smashed at my heels. The fear kept me head down in a long sprint, feet pounding on the concrete. My heart thumped hotly. My unzipped parka flapped infuriatingly, hampering my speed. After two hundred yards I slowed and risked a glance over my shoulder. The ragged line of figures in the middle of the road was still pursuing. They gesticulated and shouted.

'Fuck *offffff*!'

I glanced back again. One of the skins was well ahead of the pack, only thirty yards behind me: a stocky figure with a powerful, hunched, ape-like running style, his arms swinging wide and low. My pursuer flashed beneath a streetlamp and I glimpsed, in an instant of shock and pure terror, the snarling pale face of Kevin Crump. Fleetingly I wondered if I should slow, make myself known to him, plead for mercy as one fellow cross-country runner to another. But at the same time recognition flared on Crump's face and then he was head down and after me, fast, rallying his flagging troops with a wave of encouragement. Panic leapt in my chest and pushed me into a faster sprint. This was my only hope of escape, since Crump was an endurance runner and never much of a flat-out sprinter. I turned left at a T-junction and raced across a wide grass verge to cut the corner off, exhilaration and hope flooding through me. I could do this. I could *do* Crump.

My right foot skidded on the wet grass and I did the splits, my leg sliding away like a wishbone and a hot stab of pain in my knee. I crashed down onto my front. The left side of my face hit the ground, hard, and my momentum carried me sliding along on the grass and slime. I tried to get up but my left knee was twisted and weak. I hobbled a couple of steps, hunched over, terror now hammering in my chest. Then he was on me.

Crump let his momentum crash into me from behind. His rigid leg and raised boot hit me at the base of the spine and sent me sprawling in an explosion of pain. Before I could plead with him or even register what was happening I was face down in the mud. Boots thudded into my ribs and legs. Everything went even darker as the pack surrounded me in a solid ring of frenzied violence. I coiled into a tight ball with my hands over my head. The stomping continued, the mob uttering guttural shouts and panting laughs, jostling each other to get at me. There was surprisingly little pain. I heard as much as felt their blows: rapid-fire solid thuds, like fast-pounding jungle drums. They made throaty flicking noises too. They were spitting on me and on each other, while their boots were swinging. It went on for a long time. The blows kept coming until I couldn't hear or sense the individual kicks. It was simply as if my whole body was being pounded by a hammer. My arms weakened, my interlocking fingers slipping apart. A boot stomped down onto my hand where it covered the side of my head. White lights exploded in my eyeballs. It felt like my thumb was broken.

'I've called the police!' An old woman's voice: wavering, high-pitched, but piercing in the night. A front door slammed.

It stopped. I stayed down with my eyes screwed shut. I became conscious of my breathing. A loud rushing noise filled my ears like a waterfall, hot and throbbing, and spread through my whole body. I could almost feel the blood pumping out from my chest, hurtling into the blood vessels in my ears and fingers and legs and trying to explode out of my skin in a pulsing high pressure jet. Something told me to stay down, to play dead.

The skinheads were gone. I uncoiled and flopped onto my back, letting my heart slow and my rate of breathing return to near normal. The sky was a dirty blend of black and brown and orange. I was sweaty and itchy in my parka, but quickly cooled. It hurt even to breathe, so I just lay numbly with the stinging raindrops washing my face.

My freezing wet clothes made me shiver in a long spasm. I

staggered to my feet and tried to assess how badly I was hurt. My body throbbed and there were sharper pains in my thumb and left knee. My head was tender on the left side from when I first fell and the boot stomping me. My clothes were soaked and stained with mud and filth. But I could walk, just about. The old lady who had saved me was probably lying about calling the police. But I didn't want to risk still being here if they turned up. The cold and my desire to get away helped me ignore the stabbing pain in my knee. The skins had probably gone back in the direction from which they had chased me, so I set off the other way, homeward.

The streets were deserted again. I felt like the only person in the whole city out in the cold and rain, while everyone else was in the cosy warmth of living rooms or pubs. I wanted to be home. I thought of Mum, on her own, watching *Top of the Pops* and the new sitcom we all liked, *Only Fools and Horses*. Would she laugh as much, sitting there on her own? It was exactly one week since the accident. I wiped the beads of water from my watch: 8:09. The fireworks display had started at 7:45. It must have been about now that our firework had exploded. I shivered. I couldn't stop myself trying to guess exactly what the time must have been. But the details were too vague. The evening was still mostly a blank memory, except for those few startlingly vivid images: the kiss, the explosion, the wailing woman. I tried to piece it together, to guess what exactly Pete and I had done, but it was like projecting myself into a fictional scene, as if watching myself in a play: it just wasn't real. I lifted my face into the rain so that the icy stinging pinpoints mingled with the tears.

I wiped my nose on my sleeve and plotted the fastest way home. I broke into a shambling trot. Half a mile farther, I stopped at a street leading off to the right. Brindley Close was a typical cul-de-sac of modern brick houses. Except that this was where Tracey lived, at number 11. I'd never been there. I dithered on the corner, and then limped up towards her house. It was just like the others: a rain-stained brick semi with a driveway and oblong of front lawn shiny with water. What was going on inside? A pinkish glow shone from behind purple curtains in an upstairs room. It looked sort of feminine. Perhaps that was Tracey's room. I wondered how she looked right now, lying in a hospital bed. I felt again her warm mouth, soft curves and blue eyes staring into mine. That image, at least, was vivid. In the last day or so it had begun to alternate with another image, where I couldn't see one side of her face. It was just black.

A curtain moved in one of the downstairs rooms. A dog barked. I felt vulnerable, exposed in the glare of the streetlights, a lone youth in a quiet cul-de-sac at night. I jogged home, each step shooting pain up my legs and back and jarred my head, worse than before.

****

Doreen Greatorex was pale and her dark wedge of hair flat and greasy. Perhaps mindful of Mr Preston, the class, including even her close friends, went to such lengths during the morning not to talk about Tracey and the accident that they virtually ignored her, not knowing what else to talk about. Following Pete's lead and his stern look that I now recognised as meaning 'act normal', I said hello to her, but nothing more. She smiled and said 'Hi Dave'. She didn't seem to notice the grotesque red swelling around my left eye.

But by lunchtime people wanted information. Like sparrows trying to summon the courage to take bread from an outstretched hand, people milled around her until finally someone dared ask about Tracey. When she didn't explode with anger everyone surged in, shouting questions.

'So what happened?'

'What did Tracey's eye look like?'

'Was there lots of blood?'

'How come you didn't get hurt?'

'Why didn't you see the firework coming?'

Pete and I glumly watched the scrum around Doreen. Pete had eaten a Mars bar for his lunch but I had no appetite. I flexed my bad leg and prodded the side of my head where it was tender. My whole body ached and my ribs hurt when I breathed. Pete was alert and twitchy beside me, drumming his fingers on the desktop.

'I don't know, alright!' Doreen erupted, screaming. People backed away. 'I can't remember anything. Leave me alone!' Her shoulders heaved with sobs.

Pete leapt up and waded in, elbowing people aside.

'Fucking vultures! Fuck off, leave her alone.'

I had rarely seen Pete so instinctively angry; at least, not in a protective sense.

'Or what, Sharpie?' snarled Neil Quigley.

'Ooh, alright, we was only asking,' said a couple of the girls.

But everyone backed away sheepishly. Pete sat next to Doreen and put his arm round her. I wished I had the nerve to hug Doreen in front of the whole class. He talked to her and eventually she lifted her head, her eyes red and wet, and laughed. He had made her laugh! If I had tried to comfort her I would probably have ended up crying too.

At the end of the last lesson, Doreen walked back down the aisle to our desk. Her eyes were still red and puffy, and she looked flat and grey, nothing like her usual thrusting, sparkling self.

'Hey boys, walk me home?' she said.

She was pleading, rather than making what would otherwise have been a typical Doreen flirty offer. I waited for Pete to make an excuse, as he surely would. As sorry as I felt for Doreen, I didn't want to talk to her, in case the accident came up. I'd been waiting all week for this moment, too: the beginning of the weekend and a break from the chatter and speculation at school. Time when I could be alone and not have to pretend.

''Course we will, Doreen,' said Pete. 'Right, Dave?'

Doreen lived a ten minute walk from school. For the last two hundred yards, she linked arms with us both. I felt strange and awkward at this sudden rush of affection. We had known each other since primary school and had always got on, but had never been particularly close. But now she seemed changed, as if she regarded Pete and me differently. I wasn't sure why but sensed it had something to do with bonfire night.

Doreen invited us in, saying her parents were out. I tried to catch

Pete's eye, for guidance, but couldn't with Doreen stuck between us, pulling us by the arms. Would he even want me there? One of the few things I could recall from the firework night was that Pete and Doreen had been all over each other.

Once inside, even Pete seemed unsure of himself, perching on the edge of the sofa instead of lounging back, arms spread, like he usually did. Perhaps he too was wary, knowing that Doreen was upset by the trauma of the past week. She put a Spandau Ballet record on with the volume low and offered us a cup of tea. Her eyes brightened.

'I know, let's have a proper drink. It's Friday night after all.' She was trying to sound cheerful. 'You both like Southern Comfort, don't you?'

'It's okay,' said Pete. 'I'd sooner have whisky.'

'No thanks, Doreen. I don't like it.' I just wanted to go home.

Pete snorted. 'Dave got chased by some nasty boys last night, didn't you, Dave? Got a bit of a kicking.'

Doreen looked at my swollen eye and shuddered.

'You can have sherry, Dave,' she said. 'It's only our Gran ever drinks it, so no-one will notice if the bottle goes down. Dad'll know if we steal his whisky. So Pete, you're on the Southern Comfort with me.'

An hour later, the colour had returned to Doreen's cheeks, and the room was hazy with cigarette smoke. I was on my fourth glass of Harvey's Bristol Cream and Pete was struggling less with the Southern Comfort. He had gagged on the first glass. I had rarely seen him so uncomfortable. The sherry was making me feel better, less tense, deadening the pain in my ribs.

'Thanks for not pestering me about Tracey,' said Doreen, slurring. 'But you must be dying to know how she is.'

My stomach growled. I felt a dizzy swirl of sherry, the heavy sweet taste. I slammed my glass down. Doreen's words came out in a rush.

'Tracey's really bad. It was horrible.' Her shoulders shook. 'She doesn't want to see anyone else. Her face is bandaged up. They've had to shave half her hair off.' Her voice was choked and snotty. 'But I don't think even she knows yet how bad she is. That's the worst part, having to lie to her.'

I expected Pete to leap up again and comfort Doreen. But he just sat, stricken, his face pale.

'*Why didn't you go home?*' I shouted. I couldn't stop myself. Doreen looked stunned.

'Sorry,' I said. 'It's just we thought you were going straight home before the fireworks. Why didn't you?'

'Tracey got it in her head again that your stupid brother might turn up, after all, and decided to hang around longer. We got something to eat, then the fireworks started anyway…'

She trailed off, crying properly now. Her voice was clogged and snotty. Her head was in her hands. 'Oh god, I wish we'd just gone home!' she wailed.

Now Pete jumped up. He sat on the arm of the chair, patted her shoulder. He looked at me, horrified.

'Is there anything we can do to help Tracey?' asked Pete.

I thought this a stupid question. The only thing that would help her would be for us to travel back in time and not do what we had done that night.

'No,' Doreen sniffed. 'She doesn't want to see anyone.' She leaned her head against Pete's thigh, and tried to smile. 'I think the only thing that could make her feel better would be to know what happened.' The nervous look returned to her face. 'Not like her dad, though. He just wants to kill whoever did it. He's scary, Mr Downey. He used to be in the army. He's been in Northern Ireland and everything.'

I had never seen Pete look so terrible.

'What do you two think?' Doreen asked. 'What should happen to whoever did this, when they catch them?'

****

For once I was glad the streets were so dark. And that the phone box was set back from the pavement in a recess surrounded on three sides by a straggly privet hedge nearly six feet high. Luckily, the phone still worked. The dim plastic light globe set into the domed ceiling emitted only a guttering yellowish light and the window panels were cracked and filthy. Nonetheless I felt scared and vulnerable.

The phone was heavy, the cord thick and inflexible. Although it was icy cold inside the phone box the receiver was warm and clammy. A solid, greasy feel in my palm. How many mouths had breathed into it, warm and moist and stinking? What words had passed into its maw, whether whispered, hissed, screamed? What promises? What threats, pleas, ultimatums?

I had planned to dial 999. I couldn't think of an alternative. But incredibly, the phone directory was intact. It must have just been replaced. I hefted it out from the shelf and flicked through the pages, cursing the poor light. I had to hold the heavy book right up to my eyes and tilt it towards the ceiling light. Eventually I found what I was looking for.

My head was still reeling from the alcohol. I belched, tasting sherry thickly in my mouth. Cloying and sweet. I lit a cigarette, not because I wanted one but because filling the booth with smoke might make me even less visible. The flare of the match illuminated a foil condom wrapper amid the cigarette ends and other litter on the floor. I stretched my handkerchief over the mouthpiece and dialled the number. Seven slow arcs of the wheel. Heavy, cold metal.

Someone answered the phone. The frantic hungry beeps were loud. I dropped ten pence into the slot and shoved it down hard with my thumb. There was a metallic clunk.

'Yeah, Desk Sergeant.'

I had a sudden panic that the handkerchief trick might only work in television crime shows. Too late. I tried to affect a deep voice and a brisk, decisive tone.

'Oh hi. Is that Bournville Lane Police Station?'

'It was last time I looked. What d'you want, son?'

Son? Shit. Slam the receiver down? Walk away into the night? I took a deep breath.

Do it.

'I might know something about who set off that firework.'

- 15 -

‘A re you sure you’re alright to go into town?’ Pete asked. ‘You look fucking awful.’

‘I’m never drinking sherry again,’ I replied. ‘Ever.’

I had awoken sick and depressed after our evening at Doreen’s house, and planned to lie on the sofa all afternoon watching *Grandstand*. But as yet more snooker came on and pale sunshine brightened the room, I became desperate to get out. I limped round to Pete’s, assuming we would head into the city centre to mooch round the shops, our usual Saturday routine. His mother was smearing too much lipstick on her face in front of the mirror in the hall.

‘Hello, Dave love. Peter’s still in bed. You see if you can wake him. I’ve given up.’

She would be going to the prison to see Lee. I didn’t know what to say to her. I trudged up to Pete’s room. Lee was due to be released in only a couple of months. I felt a rush of envy. Lee had nearly served his time, done his punishment. For him, it was almost over.

Pete was propped up in bed, morose and irritable, watching his black and white portable with the curtains still closed. He eventually admitted that no, he didn't intend to lie in bed all day and yes, he supposed we may as well go into town.

On the bus neither of us mentioned the horrible evening with Doreen. But being in the city centre was at least a diversion, a change of scene. We did the usual Saturday things: flipping through the racks of vinyl in Cyclops Records for as long as we could before the owner, a fat man with the apparent ability to see around blind corners, threw us out. He threw every teenager out of his shop even if a boy genuinely intended to make a purchase, although admittedly this was a rare event. Shoplifting was the current craze among many of our schoolmates, their bags always full of football diaries and pens from WH Smith and lockers overflowing with chocolate bars from the local newsagent. But no-one had ever stolen an LP from Cyclops Records, even the likes of Neil Benson, who had once nicked a Sham 69 single from HMV.

It was 2pm on a Saturday but all the stores in the shopping centre above New Street Station were closing. Shopkeepers herded customers out and grimly pulled down their security shutters. There was an atmosphere of fearful anticipation, like a Wild West town awaiting an outlaw gang's arrival. Nervous-looking policemen were assembling at the top of the pedestrian ramp down to New Street and where the escalators ascended from the station platforms.

'What's happening mate?' Pete asked the proprietor of a furniture shop who was fiddling with the padlock on his steel roller shutter.

'Man United are playing at the Villa this afternoon.'

'So?'

'So the Red Army's coming. Thousands of them.' He snapped the padlock shut. 'That's it, I'm off.'

As always we avoided the bleak concrete of the Bull Ring shopping centre. Pete's mum was the only person I knew who shopped there because she liked the bargain clothes and cheap homewares stores. I was terrified of the place, largely through fear and ignorance, I now realise. It was said to be the exclusive domain of black youths from the city's inner and northern suburbs: places which to us might as well have been the moon. Even Tony's mates wouldn't go into the Bull Ring. An ugly rhyme was doing the rounds at school, an adaptation of an advertising jingle on BRMB radio:

At the Bull Ring Shopping Centre, there's a smile on every face;

From the moment that you enter, you'll get mugged by another race.

I enjoyed the afternoon, and Pete perked up too. The decorations weren't up but there was an atmosphere of pre-Christmas anticipation about the shopping streets. We wandered round the usual stores – Rackhams, Oasis, Reddington's Rare Records. I liked seeing people's surprise when they saw my damaged face. I imagined myself as cutting a dangerous figure, someone not to be messed with, someone even the Red Army might steer clear of. We had a burger in the Wimpy on New Street and shared a couple of fags and some banter with schoolmates Stu Taylor and Ian O'Hara. Taylor's father ran a Victoria Wines off licence and Stu had a bottle of Mann's Brown Ale in his bag. We passed it round, giggling, until the manager threw us out and threatened to call the police.

By late afternoon we were exhausted and my legs were aching. We headed back to the bus stop on Navigation Street, the grey buildings darkening in the dusk, pigeons wheeling in to roost.

'Mail. Evening Mail…' The newspaper vendor was the typical ash-faced man of indeterminate age wearing a donkey jacket and with a cigarette stub glued to his lower lip, hunched in his booth on the pavement, his mournful cries rising above the din of the street. When we saw the wording on the board propped next to the booth, we stopped instantly.

ARREST MADE IN FIREWORKS ATROCITY

People crowded round or stood close by, reading the paper, open mouthed. Pete fumbled in his pocket for some change.

Firework youth in custody

By Carl Woodbine, Crime Correspondent

Police today questioned a 16-year-old youth for several hours in relation to the bonfire night tragedy in Castle Park. He was arrested at his Northfield home at 7am and taken to Bournville Lane Police Station. A police spokesman disclosed only that a youth was helping them with their enquiries, and that at this stage, no formal charges had been laid.

By early this afternoon an angry crowd had gathered outside the police station and a tense three-way standoff developed between local residents, the police, and a heavy media contingent. Mounted police in full riot gear were required to bring the situation under control.

Local people have waited over a week for police to make an arrest in this case that has shocked the city and made headlines nationally. The Mail understands that the police investigation was hampered from the start by a heavy flow of false information and by the vigilante atmosphere that has been building in the area since the accident.

Nine people and a dog were injured when a firework exploded in a crowd of bystanders in Castle Park on 5 November. Among them was schoolgirl Tracey Downey, a teen beauty queen and (cont on Page 3, with photos).

We sat on the bus, smoking, as it barrelled down the Bristol Road in the deepening twilight gloom of the afternoon. We had stood in the street and read the story and the newspaper now lay between us on the seat, neither of us wanting to touch it, as if it were an object of evil. The bus was crowded, so we couldn't talk about it. I was glad in a way. I tried not to even think about what this meant; about what would happen now, about what I might have to do.

As I came through the front door Mum ran from the living room and crushed me in a hug, babbling about how wonderful it was that they had caught the person who let off the firework. Warmth from the living room flooded the cold hallway. I squirmed to get away, knowing I reeked of cigarette smoke and brown ale, but she didn't seem to care. She gave a sob and tried to turn it into a laugh, but only choked some more and sniffed.

'Oh love, maybe you'll start to feel better now. We can move on.'

She was still half crying, half laughing from joy and relief. I relaxed against her warmth and let my head slump to her shoulder and gave a shuddering sob.

'Is Tony here?' I croaked.

'No love, it's all right,' she said.

Then it all welled up and I was crying too, looking down the hall into the familiar comfort of the living room through a hot watery blur. She hugged me tighter.

'I've been so worried about you, Dave. I've been wondering, I've been thinking dreadful things. But it's over now, isn't it.'

I realised what she meant. And then I knew that this was the right time, now, and the words formed in my mouth, they were there, all ready to go. *Mum, it's not him. He deserved punishing. But he didn't let off the firework. It was us. It was me and Pete.* But my mind wouldn't let me do it. I couldn't tell her, not now.

It was too late.

****

I tossed the book onto the kitchen table. *Twelfth Night, Or What You Will*. What a joke. How could I care about English homework? Mr Lacey had given us a stern pep talk earlier in the week about next year's 'O' levels. But I couldn't think ahead two days, let alone a year and a half. What did 'O' levels matter now? I felt utterly, crushingly depressed. I hated winter Sundays at the best of times: dark by 4pm, anxiety about the forthcoming school week, a dreary Midlands derby on *Star Soccer*, nothing but religious programmes on television at teatime, all the shops closed.

Mum was out. Most Sunday mornings she went to visit her Auntie Ethel, who lived alone in Tipton. It was an hour and a half and three buses each way. Sometimes I went too. She usually stayed to cook Auntie Ethel's lunch and didn't get home until late afternoon.

Tony bounced into the room and slapped me playfully across the back of the head.

'Ow! Piss off, Tone.'

'God, I thought I was bad after last night, but you look like death warmed up.' Tony crashed into the chair opposite. 'Here, turn it up, I like this one.' He reached for the radio.

I winced. 'I'm sick of Christmas songs already.'

The prospect of Christmas, with presents and family and the forced happiness, Mum getting teary remembering Dad, was awful.

The song faded in a jingle of electronic reindeer bells, and was followed by a news bulletin. Tony's eyes narrowed as the newsreader spoke.

'There's been another shocking twist in the search for the perpetrator of the fireworks atrocity. A youth believed to have been the individual questioned and released by police late yesterday without being charged has been hospitalised after a brutal street attack. The incident took place around ten o'clock last night outside The Bulldog pub in Weoley Castle. Police have appealed for witnesses.'

'They won't fucking find any,' said Tony. He laughed grimly. 'Did you hear? Lack of firm evidence, my arse. That psycho had been in trouble with the pigs before over fireworks. Apparently he let off loads of bangers on a bus once. Twat. You know him, don't you? From cross country running?'

'Yeah. Tony, how badly is he hurt?'

My brother eyeballed me, his head cocked.

'Dave, I would think he'll be alright, eventually. Probably he got a couple of taps on the head, some sore ribs, a few bruises. A fright mostly. He'll live.'

I nodded. 'Thanks Tone.' I reached for the Frosties, suddenly hungry.

****

An icy white fog obscured the end of the street as if the roadway disappeared into nothingness, the lines of feeble yellow streetlights merging into blurred oblivion. Pete was not surprised to see me.

'Heard the news this morning?' I asked.

'Yeah. Of course, Crump getting his head kicked in could have just been coincidence. Happens all the time, after all.'

'I don't think so.'

I told him about my conversation with Tony.

'He does have some psycho mates, your brother,' said Pete. 'I suppose he arranged it because of Tracey, her being his bird.'

'She's not his fucking bird anymore! He doesn't give a shit about Tracey!'

'Alright Dave, calm down.' He grinned slyly.

'Get lost.'

'Pretty incredible of the pigs to arrest Crump, though. Typical of them to get it wrong. Not that I'm sorry. Maybe they got a tip-off or something.' He whistled. 'I wouldn't want to be the person who did that, if the family Crump ever found out.'

I was desperate to change the subject.

'Pete, I still think we should just tell the truth. Maybe I could go to the police on my own. I could just say it was me, not mention you.'

Did I mean it? I wasn't sure myself.

'Bollocks, Dave. You'd crack straightaway if they asked you if you were alone. You'd end up grassing me up.'

I said nothing. He was right.

'Anyway,' Pete continued, 'the fact that the pigs arrested Crump yesterday only proves they don't have a fucking clue what happened. We're as good as in the clear now.'

'But it's not just about will we get away with it, is it? It's about, I don't know, doing the right thing. Christ, maybe we'd even feel better!'

Pete looked at me incredulously. Then his face changed. 'Dave, you know my mum's sick, don't you?'

'She's always been a bit ropey, hasn't she?'

'The doctor's said she has to take it easy, like, because of her heart. Any shocks could kill her. She needs looking after. Lee's away, our Susie's in London now.'

'So?'

'So she's only got me. And if I'm away in borstal, if *you* put us in borstal by doing something stupid and going to the police, well… I don't know. She'd probably… well, die.'

I said nothing. Pete's mum would probably die soon anyway, by the look of her.

We stood on the footbridge over the dual carriageway, leaning on the wet railings, watching the cars and double-decker buses slide past beneath. Many happy times we had stood here, gobbing onto the passing traffic. The clearance between the roofs of the buses and the deck of the bridge was so small it seemed you could just step off the bridge onto them. I imagined myself doing so and falling to the roadway, injured, crippled for life. Or worse. So what? What then?

I no longer had the ability to think ahead, to apply logic to a situation. My thoughts were based on instinct: fear of Tony and the police, the constant, nagging, sick guilt that I had to drag around everywhere, slowing me down, making me tired. It had to end.

Pete's arms were on the railing, his head on his arms, bent nearly double at the waist. Now his voice was muffled, crushed. I sensed a change in him.

'Jesus, Dave, I don't know. I just don't know anymore. I didn't know it would be this hard. I hadn't thought about it all.'

'About what?'

'About how it's not just about us. It's not even just about Tracey, or the other people who got injured. Until we saw Doreen the other day, I hadn't realised that there's loads of people affected… family of people who got hurt, friends, and what about people who weren't hurt, but were right there when it happened? Seeing people burnt, screaming… fucking hell.' His voice was immensely tired. 'You may be right, Dave. Maybe we would feel better if we owned up.'

'So let's do it! Together! We can tell my mum first, and she'll help us decide who to tell next…'

'No, Dave. It's too late.' He sounded desperately sad. 'Maybe we should have told someone, that first morning, before things got completely mental. It's too late now.' He spoke as if I wasn't there.

My ears burned red.

'*I fucking said, didn't I?* But you wouldn't let me!' I banged my fist on the railing next to Pete's head. 'I knew it was the right thing to do, but you wouldn't let me!'

I felt weak and stupid, hating myself. Why hadn't I been more forceful? Why hadn't I just done it, fuck Pete, maybe the whole thing would have been half over by now, after more than a week. We might already have been able to see the end of the ordeal.

'Dave, if we'd owned up we'd be either in borstal now, or hospital, or both. You can't have it both ways. You think now you'd feel better, that you wouldn't have this fear, but you'd only have another kind of fear. Look what your brother did to Crump last night. Imagine that, every single night. That's what borstal would be like. And we'd be there right now.' His voice was still flat, emotionless, unlike I had ever heard before. 'And by the way Dave, we wouldn't be together either. We'd be in different borstals, on our own. That's what they always do. Could be miles away as well. Down south, or fucking Yorkshire or somewhere.'

I was silent again, my thoughts a jumbled mess. Why did Pete always seem to make sense, to make me agree with him, see his point of view?

'Dave, what happened with the firework?'

'Huh?'

'What happened? Why did it go off sideways, instead of straight up? I was so careful. I was. For once, I was careful.'

Pete's voice sounded strange. I tried to remember the last time I'd seen him cry. Had I *ever* seen him cry? I'd seen him get punched in the nose at a disco and there'd been tears, but not proper crying. I thought of yesterday, and hugging Mum, and felt ashamed.

'I don't know Pete. I can't remember.'

We took the shorter route home along the canal towpath, past the glassy black water and the frost-shattered red bricks lining the banks. The fog hung over the canal and turned from white to grey in the dusk, a few streetlamps showing through in haloes of dull yellow light. I tried to focus, to worry about the homework I hadn't done, but all I could think about was that Mum would be home and she would know that the police had released Kevin Crump. I thought about drowning. Once Pete and I had pulled a dead cat out of the canal, hooking it with a tree branch. Its fur was plastered dark and flat but it looked like cats always do: smug and peaceful. Pete said that with drowning, you didn't feel a thing. Next time we went swimming with the school at Northfield baths I pretended to drown, to see what it would be like. But I decided it wouldn't be so painless, spluttering water up my nose and hanging onto the rail, coughing my guts up.

****

Mum watched me listlessly cut up my fish fingers. She put her tray down, pushed herself out of her chair, walked over to the television and turned it off.

'Dave love, is there anything you want to tell me?'

'Huh? Like what?' I couldn't look at her.

'Dave, I can tell something's not right with you. I'm your mother, remember. I can tell. Ever since bonfire night.'

I concentrated on spearing a pea onto each prong of my fork.

'Everyone's upset by everything that's happened,' she said. 'But you seem to be taking it worse. Much worse. It's nearly two weeks ago now, but you're still not eating, you're half asleep all the time, you look miserable.' She took a deep breath. 'So, if there's anything you want to tell me, remember I'll support you. Love, however bad some things seem, it's always better to get them off your chest.'

My fish fingers were a shredded orange and white pulp. I put my knife and fork down, but still couldn't look at her.

'Mum, there is something I need to tell you.'

'Oh, what, Dave? What is it? Just tell me!'

I remembered Pete's mum, pale and drawn that morning, off to Winson Green to see Lee. Pete's warning about being in separate borstals rang in my mind. I couldn't think properly now.

'I just wanted to tell you that I'm going to get in trouble at school tomorrow. I haven't done my homework, and we've got a test. I'll get another detention.'

'Well you're silly then, aren't you?'

'Well I don't fucking care!'

'You watch your language in this house, young man!'

I stared down at my plate. My face was burning.

'Is that all you wanted to tell me, Dave? About your homework?' Her voice was hard.

I nodded.

'Then you'd better go and do it, hadn't you.'

I scraped back my chair.

'Dave, did you hurt those people with that firework?'

I shook my head. I hadn't, had I? Pete had bought the stupid thing, it was his idea. I had just wanted to go home.

'Dave, did you?'

'Piss off with all the questions will you!' I kicked the chair back into place. It banged against the table. 'Just piss off!'

I braced myself, but Mum just sat down. She looked tired and her voice was flat.

'Go and do your homework.'

LONDON

DECEMBER 1987

My mother was avoiding telling me something. The higher pitch of her voice and her nervous laughter alerted me. When the conversation stalled I said nothing, to make her break the silence. I sensed her shifting the phone in her hands.

'You'll never guess who came into the shop the other day, love.'

I tensed. 'Oh yeah? Who?'

'An old friend of yours. From school.'

I kicked the spokes on Jeremy's bike which was propped against the wall, my toe bouncing back with the give in the metal. From the way she'd said 'came into the shop', I knew there was more. That she had spoken to this person.

'Go on Mum, who was it? Pete Sharpe?'

'No, he's never around anymore. No, it was Doreen Greatorex.'

'Doreen? God, I haven't seen her for years. Not since school.'

'Well, we had quite a chat.'

Another silence, which I broke irritably. 'Well, what did she say?'

'She's keen to see you for a Christmas drink, when you're home for the holidays.'

'And?' I knew there was more.

'She said Tracey Downey is coming back to Birmingham for a visit this Christmas, and would love to see you.'

I phoned home every fortnight to have a chat with Mum, sitting in my overcoat in the freezing hallway of our rented terrace house, spinning the pedals on Jeremy's bike. Typically the conversation was about the mundane things of university life: what I was eating, how were my housemates, had I found a nice girlfriend yet. She worried about me living in the East End of London, imagining that the streets teemed with modern day Jack the Rippers or 1960s-style gangsters or hardcore football thugs.

On this late October Sunday I made my phone call home following an afternoon playing football in the park to work off the effects of three pints of lager and an all-you-can-eat curry banquet at the Star of India. The hallway smelled of muddy shoes and damp socks. From the living room came crashes and shouts as my housemates played cricket to the backdrop of the theme tune to *Ski Sunday*.

After hanging up I sat for a minute in the hallway's deepening gloom. The noises from the living room intensified. Andy was doing the Richie Benaud impression he always did when playing cricket with Jeremy. In our indoor cricket games I was always made an honorary Aussie so that the four of us could play the Ashes, me and Jeremy against Steve and Andy.

Instead of joining them I opened the front door and went outside.

The sky beyond the row of chimney pots in the terraces opposite was yellowing into the usual autumn London murk. A flock of starlings peeled and weaved above, a dark moving smudge in the sky. The shape dissolved as the birds dispersed and a flurry of them swooped into the plane tree outside our house. They always roosted there and shat all over Jeremy's Mini.

The evening air had a sharp edge to it for the first time that year. Tired yellow leaves still clung to the plane tree's branches, but its skeleton showed beneath. The sky had a greyness to it that spoke of winter chills and icy mornings. From somewhere a few streets away drifted the faintest hint of smoke from a backyard bonfire.

I leaned against the doorframe and wrinkled my nose at the smoke. Soon I would have to go through it again. I hadn't been in a newsagent's or corner shop for three weeks now, just to be safe, buying my fags and newspapers from the shop in the university union building. I imagined the fireworks in their little oblong boxes, and the bigger fireworks sold loose in neat trays in the shop's counters – the bigger roman candles, the more elaborate Catherine wheels. And the rockets. I closed my eyes and the inside of my eyelids exploded into a flash of silvery brightness. I opened them again, and the sky was just a flat grey sheet, but an imprint remained in my vision. I blinked a few times to clear it. Far off a siren wailed, rising and falling mournfully above the constant drone of the city of London. All I could see now was a white woollen bobble hat, scorched on one side. I clenched my fists and shook my head violently to rouse myself. This time of year was bad. This was the worst. And now Tracey coming home at Christmas. Wanting to see me.

****

'Pappadums?' asked the waiter.

I looked at Doreen for guidance.

'Definitely,' she said. 'And some of that mint sauce stuff. Then I'll have a chicken korma.'

'Prawn jalfrezi for me please. And rice for us both.'

The waiter disappeared and we sat back with our lagers.

'So, how's Tracey?' I asked.

'Same old same old. One step forward and two steps back. Anyway, you'll find out next week, won't you?'

This wasn't the answer I hoped for. What I wanted was for Doreen, preferably in her usual unadorned way, to tell me what Tracey looked like. Prepare me for what to expect.

'Yeah. Thanks for arranging for the three of us to get together. Have you seen her much, since school?'

'No. It's hard, with her being in Wales. Early on, I went down a few times with her mum and dad, sitting in the back of his car listening to them carrying on. Him ranting on about vengeance. Like he was demented. And Tracey's mum sort of in denial. She was in la-la land. Going on about how Tracey was sure to be looking more her usual self after the latest operation. She went all Catholic, too. Twirling rosary beads all the way down the M5. In the end I couldn't stand it, the arguments on the way down and the tears on the way back. So I stopped going.'

The waiter slid a basket of poppadums onto the table and set down a tray with dishes of mint chutney and onion and tomato.

The poppadums had a light sheen of oil. I eyed them hungrily. I was tired of Mum's cooking; it was too much like a more hygienic version of the rubbish we ate in London, except with lots of meat: burgers, chops, bacon. Tony, eating at Mum's on Sunday lunchtime as was his habit, had lambasted me for my continued dedication to quasi-vegetarianism. My feeble protests about still eating seafood were swept aside.

'So why didn't Tracey ever come back to school?' I asked Doreen, careful to moderate my voice. The memory of those fearful days, awaiting news of Tracey's return, was still vivid.

'I don't know. God, that was hard. Everyone at school constantly asking me when she was coming back, why she buggered off to Wales.' Doreen picked up her knife and held it by the tip of the blade, suspended over the stack of poppadums, swinging like a pendulum. 'She was seeing a burns specialist in Cardiff but that didn't mean she had to move down there permanently.' She released the knife and it speared the stack, shattering them and clattering sideways in the wire basket. 'I dunno, Dave. Maybe she kind of didn't know who she was anymore. I mean, going from the pin-up girl everyone knew and raved about to… well, you know what I mean. Losing her looks. No, I reckon she just couldn't face coming back to school. She probably couldn't stand the thought of everyone staring at her, laughing behind her back.'

'Oh, surely no-one would have laughed at her? Were we so awful?'

'Not everyone. You weren't, Dave. Nor Pete Sharpe. But remember some of them – Nigel Quigley, he was a right little bastard, all them elephant woman jokes. But the girls were the worst. Sandra Gleeson, Jacqui Butcher, some of them others – I know they was half glad about Tracey's face getting ruined. I know they was dead jealous of Tracey, having her photo in the paper that time, getting all the boys. Like your brother.' Doreen rolled her eyes and shook her head.

She loaded a heap of tomato and onion mix onto a generous shard of sauce-laden pappadum and manoeuvred it between her lips. I watched fascinated as she flattened and widened her mouth to get it into her maw.

'Tony? Was he really such a big deal?'

She shrugged. 'Beats me. But they thought so. Tracey too. Him being older, and having a car and a job and all.' A drop of mint sauce stood out as an off-white viscous blob against her scarlet lipstick.

'Funny, isn't it,' I said, 'nowadays everyone's got a job, whereas back then, only a few years ago, just having a job apparently made girls fancy you.'

Doreen crunched another mouthful. 'Our Kevin hasn't got a job.'

'Well, true, not everyone's got work. Sorry Doreen.'

'It's okay Dave, I know you didn't mean nothing by it. It's true, I know there's lots of jobs, and all these people making pots of money. But it's like you always have to have qualifications. Can't do nothing any more without *qualifications*.' She emphasised the word with loathing. 'O levels, A levels, CSEs, polytechnics, college, god knows what.'

'So Tony was a big deal just because he had a crap car and a job?'

'Well yes, he was. Like I said, god knows why – no offence Dave – but he was. He was her first, if you get my meaning.' Doreen raised her eyebrows and tried to look innocent, in case I had failed to understand. 'And now she half wants to know what he's doing nowadays and half hates his guts.'

'Hates his guts? Why?'

'Because of that stupid row they had. Because he didn't show up at the fireworks. She wouldn't even have gone were it not for the hope of seeing him.'

'Shit. So she blames Tony for what happened?'

'I think so. She needs someone or something to blame, since the stupid police never caught who did it.'

'But, didn't Tony try to see her in hospital? To make up? To see how she was? I know what Tony could be like but he was devastated, as far as I could see.'

'Well, yes, he did, in fairness. But the thing was, Tracey was really screwed up. She would hardly let her own mum see her. She wouldn't even see me for ages.'

She took a long gurgling swig of lager.

'It must be hard for you, Doreen. You were there too, that night.'

'I know. People forgot that, in the fuss over Tracey.' She tossed her head back, huffily. 'I have the nightmares too. And I even got hurt. Here.' She pushed her hair up off her forehead. 'Those are burns.' There was a trail of shiny pockmarks along Doreen's hairline, where the skin was bone white. 'And here.' She tilted the back of her left hand so it caught the light. 'The blast got me there, too.' More tiny flecks of scarring across the back of her fingers.

'You were lucky, weren't you, Doreen? Given how badly Tracey got hurt.'

'Well, I s'pose so.' She glanced away, annoyed that I'd brought the discussion back to Tracey's injuries.

I couldn't stop myself. I had to know.

'How many operations did Tracey have?'

Doreen looked impatiently to see if our main courses were on their way. She turned back frowning.

'I dunno exactly. Loads, though. She had some ages afterwards – a year or more. They were the skin grafts.'

'Skin grafts?'

'Yeah, the burn was so bad they had to take bits of skin from her leg and stick them on her face.'

A waiter pushed a laden trolley past our table. A plate of shish kebabs sizzled as if alive, tandoori-red in a white dish. I turned away. It was hot in the restaurant.

'I always wondered how they got the skin graft to stay on,' she said. 'Where's our bloody food?'

A vision floated past my inward eye of the photo of the teenage Tracey that had been in the paper, the Miss British Leyland beauty queen picture. The perfect creamy smoothness of her thigh, unblemished by even the tiniest mole. The tight fabric of her swimsuit. The angle of her raised leg as she reclined on the car bonnet. I'd looked at that photo clipping many times when it had come out in the colour pages of the *Birmingham Post* – often while lying on my bed, with predictable outcome. As had most of the boys at school. And now I imagined a raw, bloody flap being cut out from

Tracey's beautiful thigh and stitched onto her face.

'The worst thing was the eye, though,' Doreen said. 'The actual eye is plastic, but Tracey has to take it out almost every day to wash behind it. Wonder how she prises it out? God, about bloody time!'

Two waiters parked a trolley next to us and unloaded dishes and plates, fussing around, flashing smiles, rearranging the table to make space. I eyed my prawn jalfrezi with dismay. A gleaming moat of yellowish oil floated around the edges of the dish, suggestive of the fluid inside a blister. Doreen's korma was pale and creamy and made me think of pus weeping from a wound. I tried to forget I'd had the thought but could only more clearly see images of hospitals and gore and Tracey's raw face, flesh stripped away, revealing sinew and muscle and white bone. I shut my eyes and saw an empty eye socket, a deep fleshy crater, moist from being wiped with a damp tissue.

'Shit.' I sat back and took a gulp of lager. It was warm and flat and made me gag. Doreen was oblivious, slopping her korma onto a mound of rice.

'Have some of mine too, if you want Doreen.'

'What's up? God, you look hot.'

I wiped a hand over my forehead, slick with sweat.

'I'm just feeling full. Too many poppadums.'

'Ha! Classic mistake: you've overdone the starters,' she chortled.

I pushed my food around my plate and watched Doreen eat and order herself another pint of lager. After a glass of iced water I felt less nauseated. Without thinking, I asked a question I had wanted to ask for six years.

'Why did you stay?'

'Wha?' Her voice was muffled with food.

'When Pete asked you and Tracey to stay with us to watch the fireworks, you said you'd had enough. You were going straight home. But you didn't. Why not?'

Doreen frowned. 'Your stupid brother again. As we were leaving we saw those two retard mates of his from the pub. Banger, he was called, and that other dipstick. They were buying hot dogs. Tracey became convinced that if they were there, Tony might be too. But she didn't want to go and ask them. So we trailed around after them on the off chance they'd lead her to Tony. We sort of lost them in the crowd as the fireworks started. And, well, you know the rest.'

I still can't believe what I said next. Why I gave her the prompt.

'I don't know the rest. I just remember at school you saying you couldn't recall the accident.'

'That's right. God's truth. For a long time, the first few years, I couldn't remember anything at all. Didn't want to neither.'

I didn't prompt her further. Stupid of me to have asked. I was about to ask something inane about *Neighbours* when she put down her fork and took a deep breath.

'Look, like I said, it was Tracey who changed her mind and wanted to stay, not me. So it was only because of her that we were still there. I know it sounds bad me saying that, but it's the truth, so there's no point me not saying so, is there. I was so desperate to go home. I'm sure my flipping toes had frostbite, that's why we didn't stay with you boys and watch the fireworks. I don't know why you two were so keen to stay just for a few fireworks. Well, Pete Sharpe was. You weren't so bothered. You were away with the fairies, like you always used to be. No offence, Dave.'

I shook my head. But Doreen was already into her stride again.

'I'd never wanted to even go to stupid bonfire night in the first place. It was for Tracey, to be there in case she couldn't find bloody Tony, which of course she couldn't because he wasn't there, like I knew he wouldn't be. Then she insisted she needed to be alone with you. So I agreed that if we bumped into you, that I'd drag Pete away, leave you two on your own. And that's what happened, wasn't it?

'But after that, I was very pissed off. I'd done my bit – although I quite fancied Pete Sharpe to be honest, that part wasn't hard. But then more trailing round trying to find your stupid brother. I was freezing and fed up. Anyway, it was impossible. It was just so dark and there were so many people.

Doreen wasn't looking at me anymore.

'And then the fireworks display was about to start, and we got stuck in the crowd so we couldn't go anywhere anyway. I was really, really pissed off by then, knowing we were stuck for another twenty minutes or whatever. Who wouldn't have been? I didn't even like fireworks. Why didn't they have Guy Fawkes' night in summer, when it was warm?

'So we had to stand there while the stupid fireworks went off. It seemed like hours but I suppose it can only have lasted ten or fifteen minutes. I didn't complain to Tracey – I'm not one to complain – but I didn't watch the fireworks. I was hunched down with my coat round my ears, trying not to freeze to death. God, other people were excited though, like you wouldn't believe. All that oohing and ahhing. Like it didn't happen every year, just the same. Like it was flipping Las Vegas or somewhere.

'So at last, the fireworks stopped. But everybody just hung around, still gazing up at the sky with their mouths hanging open, like they were expecting an encore. Finally they seemed to realise it was over. People were moaning, kids whining, but gradually the crowd started moving, just at the edges at first, and we were still stuck right in the middle of the crush. And so I was fuming by now. I feel guilty saying this now, but I admit it, I was cross with Tracey. I was just waiting until we started moving before I said stuff it, I was going home right then with or without her. It was horrible and smoky now as well, tickling your throat, people coughing and spitting on the ground, it was disgusting.

'This wind began blowing, even colder. It was like a knife in your face, I couldn't believe it. Only good thing was it cleared the smoke. I sort of pushed Tracey -- only gently of course — so I could use her as a shield from the wind. I knew she wouldn't mind. She was taller than me and I got behind her and hunched up. I rested my forehead on her back. Then she turned round and gave me a hug, so my face was on her shoulder.

'"Thanks, Dor," Tracey said. Then she smiled and said, "Let's go home. This is stupid." I think that's what happened. I know she smiled, but I'm also sure I had my eyes closed. And I had my jacket jammed tight over my ears, I must have done.'

I wondered how to interrupt Doreen's outpouring. Too slow. She started talking again. Gradually, her words came faster and faster.

'So like I said, I've got my head resting on Tracey's shoulder. And then I've sensed that people around us are moving, that some gaps are at last opening up in the crush. I can remember hearing someone yawn. I'm thinking thank Christ, now we can get going. So I opened my eyes, and looked up, over her shoulder.

'I didn't know what it was. It looked like a little dart low in the sky far away so at first I thought someone had just thrown a sparkler into the air but it kept getting bigger and bigger like a fireball shooting down towards us ever so fast it was blasting out these huge golden sparks and there was this kind of whooshing noise god it was so fast and loud and Tracey must have realised something was wrong from the look on my face and she twisted her head round to look and I buried my whole head in her boobs.

'The first thing was this massive bang. Even with my eyes shut I was blinded by the flash, it seemed to light my eyes up but as if from the inside of my head and then it was like Tracey had been hit by a car and she knocked me over with her, I remember the shock of the cold wet mud on my hands and back of my bare legs but at the same time this burning suffocating wave of heat on my front like when you open an oven door with your face too close. I was winded and I couldn't hear properly, everything was black and silent, it was like I was underwater at night. It felt like the bloody world just vanished. I didn't know if it was black smoke or if I was unconscious. My head was pounding, my ears were ringing. I didn't have a clue what was happening. Then the silence turned into a sort of rushing noise in my head and odd muffled sounds and then I could clearly hear screaming and that must have sort of woke me up and then I could see, though my eyes were sore and watering and a couple of people's clothes were on fire, and there were three or four shapes crumpled on the ground amid this smoke and some people were running away, pushing and fighting and trampling over each other and I thought god are there more coming, whatever it was, I just couldn't register what had happened, god knows why people didn't just think straight away it was a firework since there we were at bloody bonfire night but probably everyone's first thoughts were the IRA and it was a bomb but anyway the worst thing were the smells it was like this stink of fire and people were coughing and what I now know was the smell of burning hair, it's a smell like nothing else on this earth but the worst was this kind of meat smell like a barbeque and around me there were people trying to scoop water up off the ground and throwing it onto people but I think it was mostly just mud but of course they were trying to help the burns. And Tracey's face, right next to me lying on the ground, she was sort of crumpled on her side and her face was wet, shining in the light of the flames on the back of her jacket, then someone pushed her over onto her back, to put the fire out I suppose and I know now that the wetness on her face wasn't water it was blood and god knows what else too. Thank god it was dark, that's all I can say now, the smells and the noise were terrible enough but thank Christ it was so dark nobody could see properly.'

It was as if I wasn't there anymore. Doreen certainly wasn't talking to me. Her words came faster. And louder. A fierce unbroken monotone.

'They say that adversity brings out the best in people, don't they?

Well that's bollocks. The St John's Ambulance people got there fast, I'll give them that. But it was just this fat old bloke and a dozy girl who turned out to be his daughter, just a trainee, not properly qualified. And so they were useless. But you couldn't blame them really. The worst thing they must have ever seen before would have been a kiddie with a burnt finger or some dumb skinhead who'd sniffed too much glue. And now they had to deal with something far worse than even a bad car accident. Burns, kids trampled and crushed, god knows what. People got angry with them, some parents fighting over which of the kids needed treatment first. And people were screaming, not saying proper words, just screaming. Most of the noise was being made by that stupid dog, howling and carrying on. I didn't know then that the people making the most noise after an accident aren't the ones you should worry about first, it's the people who are lying there, quiet. Like Tracey was. I knew she must be hurt, but I assumed no worse than me, so I suppose I just kind of worried about myself. It's what anyone would have done, isn't it. I got to my feet and sort of stumbled away. I didn't know what I was doing. If I'd known how badly she was hurt, I would have tried to help her. I was her best friend after all.'

The whole restaurant was listening. A group of customers stood by the door, delaying their exit. The phone behind the counter rang unanswered. Doreen was practically shouting. I didn't know that anyone could speak so quickly yet so clearly.

'It was the police who finally got things under control. Never thought I'd hear myself praising the pigs but there were two of them and they knew exactly what to do. They radioed for the fire brigade and ambulances and they were much better at looking after the people who were injured, making decisions, shouting instructions. Their biggest problem was the crowd closing in again, people coming to gawp at what had happened, some getting angry about who had done it, shouting and pushing and shoving. By now everyone had realised it was a firework, not a bomb. Someone found what was left of this rocket just near where Tracey had been lying, a great big bloody thing it was too. The police took it away.

'I tried to get in one of the first ambulances, but then realised that other people were hurt worse than me, so I gladly said I'd wait. I looked for Tracey but she must have gone in one of the first ones. After patiently waiting for ages, eventually I got put in an ambulance. For the first time in hours, I was warm, lying under a blanket in the back. The driver was a bit of alright, too.'

– 17 –

I had told Mum of my forthcoming evening with Tracey and Doreen, but now realised that something about it was troubling her. Several times I had to repeat the date of our planned meeting, and affirm that Tracey was going to be there — or at least, as far as I knew. It was only when, at teatime two days beforehand and in a state of severe agitation, she mentioned that Tony might telephone that night that I finally understood.

'I think it's probably best,' I said, 'if Tony doesn't know I'm meeting Tracey for a drink on Friday, don't you?'

My mother gnawed her knuckles and looked out of the window.

'Mum, it's not lying, is it, if we simply don't tell him? It isn't like he's going to ask you, "Oh by the way, is Dave going for a drink with Tracey?" Ignorance is bliss, and all that.'

'I suppose so.'

She sounded unconvinced.

'Look,' I said. 'Doreen hasn't said that Tracey will absolutely one hundred per cent be there. So I'm only *definitely* going for a drink with Doreen. So there's no need whatsoever for you to mention you-know-who to Tony.'

'Perhaps you're right, love.' She sounded happier.

'Anyway,' I said. 'Tony and Clare have got their minds full at the moment with their own problems, haven't they?'

'That's true. Poor Tony.'

****

I didn't like The Gun Barrels. I never had. It was a squat modern brick place, the reincarnation of an older pub that had been demolished when the road was widened back when I was doing my 'A' levels. We used to come here as teenagers.

It was usually a ten-minute walk from home but took me twice as long this evening because the pavements were treacherously sheeted with ice. I still arrived half an hour early. I sat alone in a booth, reading the paper, listening to the beep of the fruit machines above the rumble of traffic. The bar had an empty, echoing feeling. Just me and an old man. He sat alone with half a pint of mild, staring into space, chain smoking. One of the bar staff, a woman stuffed into a black pencil skirt, was listlessly winding tinsel around a pitiful Christmas tree that occupied the space between the bar and the juke box. I bought a second pint and sat at a different table, so as not to be directly facing the girls when they came in. I skimmed the newspaper, wondering what they'd think of me, reading *The Independent* instead of one of the tabloids. We'd been told at university that we should read a good broadsheet newspaper every day. I'd come to enjoy it, liking the more detailed coverage of the stock market crash and the October hurricane.

It was nearly time. My hands trembled, fluttering the newspaper's pages. I tensed my arm muscles, trying to slowly relax them, breathing out through my nose, doing the technique Jeremy's naturopath sister had taught me. I leaned my head back on the velour seat and closed my eyes. My breath whistled faintly in my nose.

'Hey, Dave.'

An icy explosion in my chest and my eyes jerked open.

'Hi Doreen. Hi Tracey.'

Doreen gave me a kiss and a hug.

'Hi Dave. Hope your curry didn't give you trouble the other day. I was up half the night.' She patted her stomach and giggled.

I forced a smile. What little I had eaten of my Indian meal hadn't stayed down long after I'd got home. The evening with Doreen had ended with me kneeling on the bathroom floor with what little food I'd eaten splashing into the bowl and the gory images of Tracey's injuries flitting through my mind.

Tracey stayed where she was, with the table between us. I raised my arm briefly, sensing that she didn't want to be touched.

'It's great to see you,' I said.

I dared a glance at her face. Her left eye, partly obscured by her fringe, hadn't moved. The effect was disconcerting. I dropped my gaze.

'It's good to see you too, Dave.'

I flicked my gaze back for a second and there was a lopsided smile turning up the right corner of her mouth, but her voice didn't sound like she was smiling.

Her appearance shocked me. Her neat wedge of shiny blond hair was gone. There was now an untidy frizz, like dirty straw, cascading over the left side of her face. Most of all, Tracey was so much bigger than I remembered. Her neck had thickened so that in profile she'd lost the delicate jaw line and become almost chinless. Her fingers bulged as if drawn tight at the joints with fishing line.

I bought drinks and sat down with Doreen to my left and Tracey opposite, across the table. I didn't know what to say to Tracey. 'So how are you?' would clearly not be the best opener. Finally I asked how she liked living in Wales.

'It's okay.' She shrugged. 'Rains a lot.' Her voice was unchanged. Soft and quiet.

I filled the silence that followed by drinking half my beer.

'So what are you up to, Dave?' she finally asked.

'Dave lives in London now, don't you Dave?' Doreen chipped in. It could have been Rio de Janeiro from the awe in her voice.

'Yeah you know, just at uni,' I said.

'Uni? Tracey asked. 'University, you mean?'

'Yes. Sorry, uni's an Australian expression. I share a house with Jeremy Whitlam. Remember him? He was in our class at school.'

'Was he from Australia? Funny, you ending up friends with him. Is he like the people off *Neighbours*?'

'I suppose.' I laughed. 'Some of them anyway.'

'I like *Neighbours*,' said Tracey. She made it sound like *Neighbours* was the only thing in the world that she liked.

'Me too,' I said. 'We all watch it, in our house.'

Doreen tutted. 'Alright for some, isn't it. Wish I could watch telly during the day too.'

'Are you still friends with Pete Sharpe?' Tracey asked.

'No, I haven't really seen him since we left school.'

'He's an estate agent now, out past Solihull way,' said Doreen. 'One of those posh towns.'

'How do you know?' I asked. I imagined Pete in his Ford Escort XR3i, leggy girlfriend next to him, burning up the green laneways of Warwickshire, his wallet fat with sales commissions.

'Neil Quigley told me. He came in the shop. I sold him some brogues. He said Pete Sharpe's turned into one of those yuppies, like you see on telly. To be honest, I thought Quigley looked like one himself. Smart suit and everything.'

'And how about your brother, Dave?' asked Tracey.

Was this why she had wanted to see me? To ask about Tony? But she didn't sound like she cared. It was more like a polite question.

'He's in sales too. Cars. A VW dealership out Bromsgrove way.'

'So is he married or anything?'

'He is, as it happens. About two years ago.'

'Anyone I know?'

'Nope, I don't think so. He met her through work.'

'What's she like?'

'She's okay.'

Tracey nodded a couple of times, and kept nodding, rocking her whole body backwards and forwards.

'Kids?'

'No, not yet, but I'm sure it won't be long. Do you want me to say hi from you, when I see him?'

She stopped rocking, and shrugged. 'Up to you, Dave.'

As we talked, the curtain of hair hiding the left side of Tracey's head occasionally shifted, giving glimpses of her damaged face. But all that was visible in the pub's dim lighting was an area of cheek caked with makeup.

An hour later the pub had filled up and there was noise and chatter everywhere and a vaguely festive feel. *Do They Know It's Christmas* was playing on the jukebox for the third time.

Doreen was drinking her fourth snakebite. Her face was flushed and her voice loud. Tracey hadn't said much after our initial exchange. She seemed happy to let Doreen chatter about her job and the funny people that came into the shop, and how she'd been devastated when *Wham!* split up. Tracey was drinking steadily too and had switched to double vodkas after her third half of cider.

'*Tonight thank god it's them, instead of you,*' screamed Bono.

I risked yet another glance at Tracey. Her left eyelid sagged slightly, giving her a mildly dopey, lopsided look. Was this the same girl, the warm soft beautiful creature from six years ago that I'd held in my arms, whose tongue had been in my mouth? *Kiss me, Dave.*

We talked about schooldays and Tracey became more animated. She and Doreen reminisced about clothes, music, discos, teachers liked and loathed. Doreen could recall every boy she had danced with at every disco from the age of twelve upwards. I chipped in occasionally but was happy to listen. It was funny to now hear the girls' perspective on those critical adolescent events like school discos where at the time the only thing that mattered to us boys was the one thing we never knew: what the girls were thinking. I commented on this, saying something about the benefit of hindsight. They laughed.

'Yeah,' slurred Doreen. 'If only we could all turn the clock back to when we were fifteen and change things!'

I couldn't look at Tracey. I hoped Doreen would keep chattering on, not realising the mistake she had made. But she put down her drink and put a hand on Tracey's arm.

'Trace, I'm sorry, I didn't mean nothing by that, me and my big mouth…'

But Tracey was already sobbing quietly, her hands at her face.

Doreen rushed round the table and put her arm round Tracey's shoulders.

'Come on, let's go to the ladies', eh, get cleaned up. Maybe Dave will get us another drink.'

I managed a tight nod.

'What could I change, anyway, if I could go back in time?' Tracey's voice was choked and bitter. 'I didn't *do* anything. Someone did this to me.' She burst into a fresh wave of crying. People at surrounding tables went quiet, staring.

I felt that I should be crying too, that this was the right response, that my eyes should be welling with tears. I willed it to happen. For Tracey to see that I felt her pain. But my eyes had never felt more dry and scraped, and I felt only desiccated, hollow and sick.

'I know, Tracey. I know.' I said. It was all I could manage.

As Doreen led Tracey unsteadily to the toilets, a final, awful thought came to me. What must it feel like to cry out of only one eye?

The girls were gone a long time. Perhaps they had stepped outside for some fresh air. It was 9pm now and the pub was full: every table occupied and a crush at the bar. The old man was long gone. Sitting alone I felt self-conscious and was becoming agitated. People pestered me, wanting to take Tracey's chair. I was beginning to wonder if Tracey and Doreen had gone home.

I don't know what Doreen did or said to her while they were gone, but it was a more cheerful Tracey who returned. She even managed a smile as she sat back down. And this time, even though the smile was still lopsided, I made proper eye contact with her for the first time and had a glimpse into the past. To that old beautiful Tracey Downey smile. It gave me a jolt. Warmth flushed through me, boosted by the alcohol.

'Sorry about that, Dave,' Tracey said. 'I just lost it for a minute. Talking about the old days. Old faces. It's fun, but I just got emotional.'

'It's okay,' I said. 'Doreen says you're living with your Gran. Are you working, or studying or anything?'

She shook her head, her mane of frizzy hair quivering. 'I started doing 'O' levels at an HE college, but...' her voice trailed off.

'But you were working, weren't you, Trace?' Doreen gave her a drunken nudge.

'What were you doing?' I asked.

'I was a teacher's assistant, two mornings a week. I sat with a little disabled girl in class and helped her.'

'What was she, Trace,' said Doreen, 'artistic?'

Tracey caught my eye and there was the hint of that old smile again.

'Autistic, Doreen.'

'That's great,' I said. 'So are you doing more teaching now, or other work?'

'No.'

Two drinks later, in the middle of a slurred but detail-rich monologue about how she and Kevin were trying to have a baby, Doreen emitted a vigorous belch and her head shot back against the seat as if propelled by the blast. She was pale.

'Are you alright?' I said.

She didn't reply but toppled sideways until her cheekbone clunked onto my shoulder. She grunted and lunged sideways to get comfortable.

I raised my hands in a mock 'help me' gesture. Tracey laughed and again I experienced the weird sensation of looking at her damaged face as if looking at a mask but seeing straight through it to the old Tracey's features I remembered. The perfect smooth hollowed curve of her cheeks. The clear, shining blue eyes. The almost imperceptible upward tilt of her chin. The gleaming symmetry of her teeth beyond parted lips. Those same lips pressed onto mine in a freezing park six years ago.

Tracey was on her feet, hauling Doreen off me.

'Come on Dor, time to go home. You'll be fine out in the fresh air.'

I jumped to my feet.

'Shall we find her a cab?'

'How about you go and put her on the bus. She'll be okay once she's in the fresh air. It's only three stops to her house. I'll stay here and keep the seats.'

'Alright, if you're sure. I won't be long. Hey, that's assuming you don't want to go home too?'

'I'd like to stay longer Dave, if you do.'

The bus stop was opposite the pub and Doreen's bus arrived within ten minutes, but we were frozen. As the bus approached she hugged me and aimed a slobbering kiss at my mouth which I managed to deflect onto my cheek.

'You two behave yourselves now.' Her breath formed a heady alcohol-laden cloud around us.

I grinned. 'Yes, Mum.'

Doreen waved an unsteady forefinger in my face.

'I mean it, Dave. You look after Tracey. What she needs right now is someone to be nice to her.'

The bus doors hissed shut. She weaved down the aisle and slumped into a seat. The bus pulled away and I hurried back to the pub, blowing on my hands and trying not to slip on the icy pavement.

Be nice to Tracey? Why wouldn't I be?

Nowhere had ever seemed so welcoming as the Gun Barrels pub

that night as I came skating back from the Bristol Road bus stop with five pints of lager and two rum and cokes inside me. The lounge was dimly lit and beautifully warm and smoky. I weaved my way back to Tracey through a crush of beaming faces and coloured lights to a soundtrack of nostalgic Christmas songs. *Super Trouper. Don't Stop the Cavalry.* The cold air had made me feel more pissed but had kick-started my senses, so that I felt less drowsy, more alive. Why had I ever been nervous about meeting Tracey again? It was fine. But as I neared our table my happiness died. Tracey was gone. Her chair was gone.

I turned to leave and a girl next to me, dancing on her own, her piled-up hair shimmering with every gyration, dug me in the ribs and pointed. Tracey waved from the bench seat next to where I'd been sitting, held up her empty glass and mimed 'please'.

'How's your mum, Dave?'

'She's fine. Still working at Sainsbury's.'

'She was always nice to me, your mum.'

'That's because she thought you were the best thing ever. Like everyone did.'

'Including you?'

I didn't answer, but swivelled my eyes to look at her without moving my head. She looked at me. We held the gaze for a few seconds, grinning.

'How about a Christmas kiss, Dave?'

The smile died on my face. The years fell away. This was not a good idea.

'Please? Just one? Just for me?'

My head spun. The pub was hot, the music was loud. She tasted of vodka and orange juice. Sweet and sour. Her body was soft in my arms. Her satin blouse slid over her skin as I held her.

Tracey's parent's house was a ten-minute walk from the pub, in the opposite direction from mine. No bus went past her door, as with Doreen. And at pub closing time on a Friday night I couldn't leave her to walk home alone.

The pavements were so treacherously icy that we had to cling to each other, giggling. Still pleasantly pissed though I was, my mind was now in damage control. So, another Christmas kiss with Tracey. One more secret. What the hell.

We reached the corner of Tracey's parents' street. Brindley Close.

'I'll watch you to the house from here,' I said.

'No way!' She tugged my arm and laughed. 'I want door to door service.'

So we stumbled the last fifty yards, locked together. The house was quiet, the windows dark. I felt more uneasy. At the door I extricated myself from her grasp and stepped back.

'Night Tracey. It's been great to see you.'

She took a stride towards me so our bodies crashed together. Her face was two inches from mine. Her arms locked around the small of my back. She stood on tiptoe, clutching me for balance.

I looked directly into her eyes. She didn't flinch. The dark disc of the dilated pupil in her right eye was much bigger than the one in her left.

'Mum and Dad are away for the weekend. Do you want to come

in for a coffee?'

'Tracey, thanks, but I think I'd better be going.' Something like panic must have shown on my face.

Her tone changed. Her voice became quiet, and uncertain, and needy, and utterly compelling. She pulled my head down to whisper in my ear.

'*Please*, Dave. I'd love it if you did.'

BIRMINGHAM

JULY 2013

– 18 –

The arrivals hall at Birmingham airport is a milling mass of sunburnt holidaymakers and unhappy families, kids running amok. I'm tired and gritty after 24 hours on a plane and still feeling sick after eating a dodgy sandwich during the two-hour stopover in Dubai. I barge through the crowd and get a taxi to Mum's house.

I don't know what I expect to achieve, coming back to England. Probably I'm wasting my time. But I had to come. I've had no more than four or five nights of uninterrupted sleep in the six months since Tony and Gail left. Too often I'd wake, jaw stiff and head pounding, to find the other half of the bed empty, Lydia having fled to the spare room.

I've started dreaming about it. After almost thirty years. Images and sequences and even smells have begun to spool through my sleeping mind in crystal threads of corrupted memory. The rankness of wet mud. Mushrooming white lights, like nuclear explosions. Dark cindery fragments fall from these explosions and disappear hissing into an icy stormy sea. Hospitals, with more bright white lights and silence and hushed whispers. Sometimes the dreams get weird and involve people I know. Or once knew. Doreen, wearing a silver swimming costume, lies on the bonnet of a car that bursts into flames. Johnny Rose, whom I haven't thought about in three decades, rushes in and sprays her with water. But he's too slow and I scream and rush out from the sidelines to attack him, but he runs away and my leaden legs won't move fast enough, and I can't decide what to do: chase Johnny or rescue Doreen. Too often my dreams are full of fire and smoke. In one, my father nails a Catherine wheel to the fence and lights it but as always it won't spin properly but just hangs sputtering, rotating a few degrees on its axis but unable to complete a full turn. Mr Minwalla, wearing a butcher's apron red down the front, goes up and spins it hard and off it goes, round and round but getting bigger until it is six feet in diameter, a gigantic flaming wheel, whose heat I can feel pressing onto my eyes.

As the weeks went by, I did not know what to do. I only knew that I couldn't continue like that. But I stuck to my routines. I tried to concentrate on work. I went running a lot, although I felt dull and sluggish. I fought the numbing tiredness by drinking too much coffee during the day and too much wine at night.

Eventually Lydia told me what I needed to do. Too tired, too depressed to even think about work, I'd phoned in sick one morning. Lydia arrived home to find me pouring my first glass of Shiraz of the night.

'Want one?'

She nodded.

We took our drinks and slumped onto the living room sofa.

'Dave, why don't you go back to England?'

For a second I thought she meant permanently. The fact that I could even think this hit me hard, like a slap on the back of the head.

'Have a holiday,' she said. 'See your mum. Maybe try to clear the air with Tony.'

I exhaled gloomily at her last comment.

'I know you haven't told me everything about why Tony and Gail left.' She sniffed. 'You haven't really told me anything. Tony's a stubborn idiot… but he wouldn't cut short a dream holiday after a row about nothing. I know there's more to it. I'm not stupid, Dave. I know you've got your secrets. Stuff you've never told me. You didn't move to Australia just because of the lifestyle. You don't even like the beach.'

I said nothing, forcing her to continue. To tell me what to do, what I need.

'Go and see your mother at least,' Lydia said. 'How long is it since she was last here? Five years?'

'Six.'

'So think how much she'd love to see you. She's not getting any younger.'

'Maybe.'

'Dave, you have to do something. We both know it. You've been useless in every way since Tony and Gail were here. You know it. I know it.'

I looked away, knowing that she includes our love life, or recent lack of it, in my overall uselessness. But she was right. She always is.

And so it was agreed. I briefly and half-heartedly tried to persuade Lydia to come too, but she dismissed the idea.

'I can't take the time off work, Dave. Anyway, you don't need me trailing round. Go and hang out in Birmingham. Spend time with your mum. Look up your old friends, eat lots of curries, whatever. And try to make peace with Tony. Apologise for whatever it is he thinks you did to him. Even if he won't talk to you at least you'll have done the right thing. You'll feel better in yourself and can move on. *We* can move on.'

Even I couldn't mistake the emphasis she put on her last sentence. And in that moment I saw that she was right. Even if it meant I'd get arrested for a crime I was involved in over thirty years ago. And this risk is real, because Tony could have gone to the police as soon as he and Gail got home. But I had to go despite this possibility. Or perhaps even because of it.

****

Even after being at my mother's house for a week, a place I called home for twenty-five years, I still feel like a stranger. An intruder even. Yet there are some things so alarmingly familiar it is as if I have never been away. And that's what's strange: it's the things that have remained the same that surprise me more than the things that have changed. Is this some memory trick, where your mind automatically expects things to be different just because a long time has elapsed, so that it isn't change that is alarming, but constancy?

The red brick terrace house where I grew up is unaltered.

There's the same furniture, the same brands of baked beans and soup in the pantry, the same sliced white loaf in the bread bin I made in third year woodwork and whose lid never properly closed. On its underside is still a rust-coloured smear where blood from my thirteen-year-old thumb impregnated the wood after a slip with the chisel. The fluffy toilet seat cover is still in the bathroom, and Mum is still overdoing the toilet hygiene, with two blue flush cleaners hanging from the rim and an air freshener on the cistern, so that the combined floral, pine and citrus scents make your eyes water.

The house is still full of things Tony and I made at school – an ugly metal towel rail in the kitchen, a wooden chess board that no one ever used because only I knew how to play, and a bird feeding platform swinging forlornly from the back fence. Everything Tony made was of a high-quality, whereas my efforts were not. It was my towel rail in the kitchen where the movable arms had an unintended downward angle so that the tea towels slowly slid off and collected on the floor.

The same photos in the same frames jostle for space on the sideboard in the living room. The first thing I do on arrival is to look at them all. I'm still grimy and sticky-mouthed from my journey, my suitcase not yet carried upstairs. Mum is in the kitchen making us tea, getting the proper cups and saucers out in honour of my homecoming. Most of the photos I remember: Jeremy and me grinning in our graduation gowns; Mum and Auntie Sandra as teenagers on a seaside pier; Mum with Warwick Castle behind her, an arm round each of Sandra's two daughters, crinkling their eyes in the sun; even the picture of me and Lydia on a yacht on our

Whitsundays honeymoon.

There's one of Mum and Dad's wedding: the pair of them outside the ancient church at Frankley, looking incredibly young. Beyond is the crumbling churchyard and the white marble angel with the spreading wings, the one that's supposed to be haunted. Tony used to terrify me by swearing that every time you drive past it faces a different direction.

There are recent pictures as well, including several of Tony and Gail's Caribbean wedding. One is from the reception, with Tony red faced and beaming with his arm round Mum. She looks happy too, in a nervous kind of way.

Tony appears on this sideboard eleven times, and me five times.

And there are lots of photos of my father. Many more than I remember. One shows Dad aged about thirty with a man who looks vaguely familiar. They're in fancy dress like heavy rockers from Black Sabbath with ridiculous flares, skin-tight shirts with big collars, cardboard guitars and wigs cascading over their shoulders. Dad's beard is real and he looks very convincing. But instead of looking mean, they're holding back giggles.

Mum brings the tea in and sets the tray down on the nest of tables by the sofa. She slowly straightens her back. I hold the Black Sabbath photo up.

'Who's that?'

'That's your dad, and that's Uncle Brian.'

'Yes Mum, I know it's Dad,' I say, rolling my eyes. 'I meant the other bloke.' I study the photo again. 'Uncle Brian. He was Dad's best friend, wasn't he? I remember. He was here a lot. They used to take us out, didn't they. And babysit and stuff?'

She nods. 'That's right. He and your dad were old schoolfriends, from years back.'

I collapse on the sofa opposite Mum, still with the picture in my hand.

'So what happened?' I ask. 'I know Dad went away, but I can't remember Brian being around, except when I was very young.'

She takes her time pouring the tea, fussing with the biscuits.

'Well, they had some kind of falling out. Silly, they were grown men.'

I wait, but there's no more.

'What about?'

'I don't know, love.' She shakes her head, and passes my tea across. The cup rattles in the saucer. 'It was a shame. Brian and Sheila's little girl was my goddaughter. Janice.'

'Was?' I put emphasis on the word.

'No, she's not dead. She still lives round here. She works at Tesco, just down the road.'

Janice. That name again. My mind flashes back to my nocturnal conversation with Tony at Port Stephens.

'I think I remember her,' I say carefully. 'Didn't she have some kind of accident? When she was very little?'

'Yes. It was a terrible thing.'

Mum clearly doesn't want to talk about it anymore. And neither, I realise, do I.

She lowers herself back into her seat and rummages for a biscuit.

'So what's the reason for the visit, love? Is everything alright with you and Lydia?'

'Fine, Mum, fine. Lydia would have come but she's got no holiday saved up.'

I rouse myself, conscious of the need to sound convincing. Act normal.

'I just felt like a break. Maybe I'm homesick. Maybe I'm having a belated mid-life crisis.'

This is supposed to be a joke, but she doesn't laugh.

'I'm not sure when you'll get to see poor Tony,' she says. 'He's so busy at the moment. He works too hard.'

I'm needled by this, as I always was, by the 'Poor Tony' of old.

'*How* hard does he work?'

'Ooh, he works such long hours. Sometimes he doesn't finish until after six. And all that travel. Some days he has to go to London and back just for one meeting!'

It's pointless talking to Mum about this. Let her keep thinking that everyone in Sydney finishes work at three o'clock and goes to the beach. So I just nod.

'Oh dear. Poor Tony,' I say.

'Is everything alright between you and him?' she says.

'Why do you ask?' I am unprepared for this question, but I am not surprised it has come up.

'Well, he's practically said he's going to be too busy to see you. He's away on a management training course this week. I don't see why he couldn't have got out of it.'

She takes a careful sip of her tea.

'I don't know,' she continues, frowning. 'He and Gail didn't talk about their holiday. As soon as they got back I wanted to see the photos, hear how you were getting on… but it was as if they didn't want to talk about it.'

She waits, wanting something from me. But I just shrug.

'Anyway, I've invited them over here for Sunday lunch, next weekend. Tony said he'll see. He might have to work. But I so want us to have at least one family meal together.'

I never told Mum anything about Tony and Gail's sudden departure from our house. For a long time afterwards I dreaded her asking me was it true what Tony was saying about what happened all those years ago. But our phone conversations stayed on her usual topics: the drought, the recession, the riots, how too few of the beggars on the streets speak English.

I'm unsure why Tony hasn't told Mum about why he won't speak to me. Could it be that some lingering doubt exists in his mind about the part I played? Or is he just sparing my mother the anguish?

Over the next few days I do no more than sleep off my jetlag and let Mum spoil me. I go for walks round the local streets, or borrow Mum's hatchback to go further afield. Sometimes she comes with me, and we stroll round Cannon Hill Park or go into town.

My mother's house may be in a time-warp, but elsewhere much has changed. The row of crummy shops where Mr Minwalla's newsagent once stood has been replaced by a mini supermarket with a fat security guard at the door. The community hall where we dodged the skinheads at neighbourhood discos has been rebuilt with lots of steel and smoked glass after the original was burnt down a few years ago. Mr Hickey is long gone and a Bosnian family now lives next door to Mum.

My mother has changed too. She's turning into an old woman — which is what she now is. She's consciously altered nothing about herself: she still wears her hair in the same once-blond ponytail and wears the same clothes. But her body's components are failing. Her age shows in the angle of her back, in the twist of her finger joints, in the way a frailty has corroded the timbre of her speech, and in the battalion of pill bottles in the bathroom. But most prominently failed are her eyes. She had cataract operations a couple of years ago. In a dim light, her eyes reflect lamplight in an unnatural way. It makes me think of robots and bionic eyes and stirs memories I don't want to know about.

– 19 –

It is humid and the mid-morning sky is the colour of porridge but there is still no hint of rain after six weeks of drought across most of England and Wales. I take the old familiar route from Mum's house, retracing the steps I made to and from school every weekday for seven years. I walked this route in high excitement over school disco nights and Valentine's Day promises; in concern about the poor quality of my French homework or the overnight appearance of a zit on my chin; in nervous excitement on cross country race days; in the grey depression of winter Monday mornings, the week stretching ahead, crammed with unendurable demands. And I walked it in such extremes of fear and guilt that it seemed at times impossible that some passer-by didn't look at me and yell out, *It was him! He did it!*

Today the streets of my childhood are quiet, just a few prams being pushed around, tradesmen repairing roofs and roads, a council gardening crew desultorily planting frail-looking saplings along the main road's median strip. Unless it rains soon the trees have no chance. The grass everywhere is dusty, cropped and yellow, the biscuit-coloured earth showing through.

The shrill echoing din of 1,100 teenagers at play is audible long before I reach my old secondary school. The school's new name is on a shiny sign board set into the wall at the street entrance. A neat row of two-storey buildings now stands in what was the lower football fields, and the muddy route we smokers used to take down to the woods is blocked by two lurid blue tennis courts. Pupils — or students, I suppose — swarm everywhere, chasing each other and playing football and huddling in groups around electronic gadgets and mobile phones. They wear the same old grey and white school uniform, although the girls' skirts are now unfeasibly short. I pull out my camera. I already know I will never come this way again, and feel an urge to take something of my old self back with me, perhaps to show Lydia. But as I'm framing my first shot of the school buildings, looking down the driveway, I notice the security camera winking at me from a light pole. I move on.

The tall ironwork park gates and fencing are no longer rusted and flaking but have been re-galvanised with a gritty powder-grey coating, and the concrete pillars supporting the gates have been re-rendered and painted beige. The horse chestnut trees that line the fence are massive now, their thick branches overhanging the road and their roots splitting cracks in the wall and pushing up spreading ridges in the pavement. I step through the gates and a wide downward slope of parched grass opens up. A ride-on lawnmower roars up the slope towards me, its blades banging and clicking on twigs and litter, throwing up a cloud of pale dust. As it turns there's a whiff of cut grass and dog shit.

I walk down towards the pond in the hollow at the bottom of the slope. The trees' limbs hang listlessly, heavy with their fat green foliage. I won't allow myself to look to my right, where the slope curves round like a bowl and rises further, ending in a ridge with a row of poplar trees and a jumble of tower blocks beyond.

When I get to the flat ground, will there be a trace? If not a patch of scorched earth or a scattering of thirty-year-old cinders then perhaps at least a richness in the green of the grass, nourished by fire and ash each November. But there's just dead mown grass piled in untidy ridges. And now I turn and look back, and then trudge up the slope. My right knee aches badly and I stop just below the top. The poplar trees and tower blocks are gone. The park's boundary is now marked by a yellow sandstone wall beyond which sits a close-packed row of detached houses, their roofs bristling with satellite dishes. The safety net around a child's trampoline is visible in one back garden. Some homeowners have strung barbed wire across the tops of their walls in dense rusting coils.

I sit facing down the slope. Ground that once was wet and soft enough for a plastic bottle to be pushed into it is now like cracked concrete. In the distance is a high gritstone wall and beyond that the reservoir, or what remains of it. The water has receded in the drought to the demands of a thirsty city so that swathes of dark brown rocks and pebbly beaches, stained and dusty, are exposed.

The sheet of grey water that remains is shaped like an hourglass, perhaps five hundred metres long but only about thirty at its neck. It looks shallow enough to wade across. As kids we thought the reservoir was bottomless, like Loch Ness. A place where crimes and secrets could be swallowed forever. I close my left eye and squint down my extended forefinger, moving it like a gun barrel, tracing the route Pete and I took that terrible night: along the slope to my right and all the way down in the lee of the wall and along it where it borders the reservoir, and out into the open, skirting the pond and back to the flat area in the heart of the park.

And then I'm back on this same hillside in the dark, thirty years ago. I breathe the smell of wet mud and slimy autumn leaves, my feet numb and my fingers stiff and aching with cold. Or is it pure excitement, schoolboy adrenaline, that makes my fingers stiff and clumsy and my arms shudder in wild spasms? I jump from foot to foot, burying my hands in my armpits. Yet again I reach into my inside blazer pocket and finger the square of paper that Tracey gave me an hour earlier, as we sat by the bonfire. Sealed with a kiss. But the note wasn't meant for me, and neither was the kiss, although it took me years to admit it.

'Tell you what Dave,' says Pete. 'I'll even let you light it. How's that?'

'No way! I'll leave that to you.'

'No, I owe you a favour. Dragging you up here. It is bloody freezing.'

'I'd rather not, Pete.'

'Why, are you scared?'

****

There's no icy wind sweeping across the park today. Just the still, cloudy warmth of a July afternoon. I jump up, brushing dust and twigs from my jeans, and trot back down the slope.

The playground where we used to come as kids is still here, although much changed. The clutch of rusty swings, ponderous roundabout, shiny steel slide and climbing frame set into a square grey concrete slab, are gone. A fence surrounds the playground bearing a council sign listing the usual disclaimer and prohibited activities and substances. Underfoot is a dark green rubbery compound designed to absorb the impact of a falling child's body. As well as modern incarnations of the usual swings, slide and see-saw there are cubby houses with moveable numbers and letters and funky climbing frames from which sprout curved tubular slides of red and yellow plastic, like ripped-out intestines.

A handful of toddlers run around laughing, weaving in and out of the obstacles. Their mothers sit on the benches, chatting and sharing a family bag of cheese and onion crisps. Cigarette smoke swirls above them. Four or five prams stand in a tight cluster, like a parking lot for moon vehicles. Two little girls bounce up and down on the seesaw with what looks like spine-jarring force. One of them abruptly jumps off, propelling the other girl upwards and sideways. She sprawls flat on her face on the ground, motionless. For a horrible moment I wait for one of the adults to do something, but the girl raises her head. She shrieks with laughter and jumps to her feet. For the briefest of moments, watching the little girl, something in my deep consciousness stirs almost imperceptibly, like a few grains of silt drifting up off a dark lake bed. I try to clarify this thought, this memory, but it swirls and settles, and is gone.

I watch the happy kids for a while. Then one of the mothers nudges her neighbour and hisses something and jerks her head in my direction. I leave before they've even turned and looked at me properly.

****

I make a real effort cooking dinner tonight, despite the limited equipment in my mother's kitchen. The only frying pan, a shallow thing with a half-melted plastic handle and chipped orange coating, I remember from when we were kids. Probably it was a wedding present. How many fish fingers, beef burgers and bacon rashers have slid out of that pan and onto our hungry plates? Surprisingly my pan-fried salmon fishcakes taste okay, their seasoning perhaps even enriched by a fifty-year residue of carbon and grease.

Afterwards we chat in the back garden with cups of tea and a packet of Jaffa cakes. Mum's ability to remember things has shifted. It's diminished in some ways but become enhanced in others. A few times she calls me Tony. Once, more disturbingly, she calls me Eric. It's as if her short-term memory functions are short-circuiting themselves. Or perhaps the energy needed to maintain them is diverting to her long-term memory. She mentions schoolmates or teachers from my primary school days, people who weren't significant in my life even then and whom I'd long forgotten. We laugh about her recollection of people and things from forty years ago.

'You watch it, Dave,' she says, mock serious. 'It happens to everyone. You'll start remembering things you thought you'd forgotten about.'

'I'm not that old,' I laugh. But I'm not laughing inside.

'You wait,' she says. 'One day you'll forget where you put your keys but remember what you ate for lunch on your first day of school. Things you never even knew you'd taken in at the time, they're all buried in your head.'

'I know.'

'There's also things you wish you could remember better,' she says. 'People and things you did that you wish could stay with you forever.'

'Like Dad?'

She nods. 'I think about him all the time, love,' she says. 'But I can't remember him properly anymore.'

I think about the growing collection of photos of Dad on the sideboard, the walls, the bookshelves. When did her memories of him begin slipping? How she must have tried to keep them real: the sound of his voice, the feel of his beard against her cheek, what it was like having sex with him. I'm old enough now that I can think about this without shuddering, even if it's not an image I want to dwell on. But she was only in her early thirties when she was widowed.

'Can *you* remember your dad?' she asks.

'Of course I can.'

'What do you remember most?'

'Lots of things. Taking me to the football and putting me up on his shoulders so I could see. That time he accidentally hit Uncle Brian in the mouth with the cricket bat. Him dressing as Elvis for that party.' I smile. 'Listening to the shipping forecast.'

'He used to love sitting with you and listening to that.'

When Dad was home from the North Sea, he'd often sit me down at the kitchen table – Tony was never interested – and we'd listen to the shipping forecast on Radio 4. I would swing my legs and drink cocoa until the announcer would say, 'Forth, Forties, Cromarty'.

'Forties!' Dad would say. 'That's where the rig is. Forties Field.'

Often the announcer would say in her calming, melancholy voice something like 'Forties: cyclonic six to gale eight, decreasing four or five for a time, perhaps severe gale nine later. Rough or very rough'. Dad described working in the canteen or lying in his bunk while gales roared around him in the dark of the night and waves pounded the flimsy platform. I would sit open mouthed and ask how high the waves were and how far from land the rig was and what would happen if someone fell from it into the water.

What I really remember most about my father is probably the same as Mum does: his absences. How the weeks he spent at sea seemed like months, marking our lives like alternate light and dark: his presence for a few happy days and then everything empty, cold and quiet, just the three of us and the television. I remember his departures. I'd stand in the pre-dawn kitchen after a sleepless night, my feet freezing on the linoleum, clinging to his legs until he pried me off when the taxi arrived. I remember Mum leaning over me to hug him, me sandwiched warmly between them, Tony snoring upstairs.

And I remember his biggest absence of all. The terrible endless blur that began with a phone call one November evening when Mum, Tony and I were eating tea. Auntie Sandra coming to stay and taking charge, she and Tony constantly arguing. Mum a hysterical, different version of herself, hugging Tony constantly, always in her nightie or dressing gown. Learning what a Chinook was and having the phrase 'no survivors' ingrained into my ten-year-old consciousness. Of the funeral – or remembrance service, since only three of the bodies were found, Dad's not among them – I remember almost nothing beyond being forced to wear a pair of smart trousers in a scratchy tweed-like material that I hated then and still do.

Mum and I sit in silence for a long time, listening to the evening sounds of the neighbourhood: barking dogs, the shrieks of children, the engine revs of cars manoeuvring over the speed bumps. She shivers and pulls her cardigan round her, but makes no move to go inside.

'Want me to get you a coat?' I ask.

'No thanks love. Talking of memories, I sometimes see an old classmate of yours.'

'Oh yeah?'

'Doreen Greatorex. Well, she's married now, got a different name. Got two grandkids. She still lives in the same street.'

'Does she still work in a shoe shop?'

'Yes, a posh one in the Bull Ring. You'll never guess who came into her shop recently.' She brushes crumbs from her lap.

'Well go on, who?'

'Peter Sharpe.'

'God… I honestly can't even imagine what he looks like now. I haven't seen him in years.'

That had been an awkward last meeting. A chance encounter in a pub in town when I was home from a university vacation. Christmas music blaring, three deep at the bar. Pete in his suit: wide lapels and big shoulders, his wedge of jet-black hair falling trendily over his eyes. Me the scruffy student. He said, laughing, that the bouncers should never have let me in but he was only half joking. We chatted for ten minutes, going through the motions, but there was nothing between us, no connection, the chemistry that had once made us inseparable now completely inert. That was a quarter of a century ago.

'He was back here for his mother's funeral,' Mum says.

'God, I'm surprised she lasted so long. She seemed so old and frail even when we were kids. So what's he doing now?'

Mum frowns, and flaps her hands. 'Well, Doreen tried to explain. Something about buying and renovating houses and leasing them to students and other people, as sort of hostels. It doesn't sound like a proper job at all, does it?'

I feel a stab of jealousy. Pete Sharpe the real estate mogul.

'What about his jailbird brother? Lee?'

'Well, he came good. He took a photography course in prison, and now he's got his own business. He takes pictures for glossy brochures. Cars, furniture. Things like that. Tony bumped into him once through work. They were doing a new car launch.' She lowered her voice. 'I think they still didn't get on.'

'You say Pete was back here. So where does he live now? Still out Warwick way?'

'Oh no. He lives somewhere near London now.'

I fall silent. What else is there to know? A pigeon zooms past, its wing beats punching the air. It lands on a television aerial, making it sway precariously.

'Peter Sharpe never forgave you for becoming friends with Jeremy, did he love?'

I shrug. 'No, he didn't.'

My mother smiles and looks down into her empty teacup.

'It's nice love, having someone to talk to about your dad. I know Sandra's sick of me going on about him. And Tony just cuts me dead whenever I mention him. He always has.'

For the first time in my life I realise that my mother probably still thinks about my father virtually all the time. Right now she's probably remembering the many nights he occupied the chair I'm sitting in, when the two of them relaxed outside on warm summer nights while Tony and I slumbered upstairs. Their laughter would have drifted up into my bedroom. If I closed my eyes now, I could still hear it.

She reaches across and pats my bare arm.

'You've got goose bumps,' she says. 'It has got chilly, hasn't it? You can't always go round in just a t-shirt, like in Australia.'

She pushes herself up and gathers our cups.

'Come on, let's go inside and see what's on telly.'

– 20 –

I wake early next morning. My body is tired but my mind is buzzing. I think about yesterday, the park and the playground, my father. I find myself thinking about another day, long ago. A day I've never forgotten but have not had the ability to see as clearly as I do now, lying in Tony's old bedroom in the lilac pre-dawn stillness.

It was a cold day. A Saturday. Dad and Tony watching *Grandstand*. Tony snuggled up to him on the sofa until the horse racing came on and we got ready to go to the park. This was our Saturday routine, weather permitting: to the park with Dad and Mr Dawson, then they dropped us home and went for a pint at the Dog and Partridge. Mum fussed over Tony, kissing him as she buttoned his coat, trying to pull his woolly hat over his ears, tickling him so he squealed and wriggled away.

'Tony! You'll freeze without your hat!' she said, grabbing him from behind.

'You ready, Big Davey? said Dad, ruffling my hair.

I hugged his leg. I loved him calling me Big Davey or Big Man. Mum crumbled some bread into a bag which Dad stuffed into the pocket of his donkey jacket. The doorbell rang and Tony and I ran squealing to greet Mr Dawson. We were always excited to see him. He knew lots of games and jokes. I loved the trick where he pretended to have a mouse in his hands but really it was his thumb poking through his fingers. We called him Uncle Brian, although he wasn't our uncle. He and Dad were best friends from schooldays. Now they worked together at the car factory. Brian made Mum laugh too. Often Mum and Dad and Mr and Mrs Dawson went out and Nana Truman babysat me and Tony.

'Alright Bri,' said Dad. 'Chuffing cold, isn't it?'

'Ar. Brass monkeys today,' said Brian, rubbing his hands together. 'Freeze your whatsits off.'

They laughed, and Brian came into the hallway while Mum finished fussing with Tony. Brian's little daughter, Janice, tried to hide between his legs. She was the same age as me. Women were always stopping Brian in the street or in a shop to say how cute she was. I can only recall huge blue eyes and a mass of dark curly hair. I felt sorry for her because she wore glasses with the left lens covered with pinkish-brown sticking plaster, although she wasn't wearing them that day. I assumed she'd hurt her eye, and thus couldn't understand why the sticking plaster was on the glass, not on her actual eye. She was Mum's goddaughter. Mum would often joke about swapping Tony and me for Janice and sending us to live with Brian and Sheila.

'Where's Tony?' whispered Janice, peeping round Brian's leg, her eyes wide and hopeful.

Janice adored Tony. Far too young for it to be a proper crush, she had nonetheless developed a real infatuation. She trailed after him and always wanted to sit with him. One of Tony's classmates teased him about having a girlfriend and Tony got in trouble for fighting with him about it.

Eventually Mum finished getting Tony ready, and the five of us stepped out of the house into a biting, gritty wind.

'Put Dave's gloves on!' called Mum.

But Dad was laughing with Brian and didn't hear, so the gloves just dangled from my sleeves on their elastic cords. I remember walking along our street windmilling them like propellers. They were chunky knit mittens, red and white, a sort of zigzag Aztec design. Tony was wearing his Blues bobble hat, the one Nana Truman knitted. I can still see it. The blue wasn't the right colour. It was a touch too navy.

I loved going to the park with Dad and Brian. Sometimes I went there just with Tony, but without adults such trips were fraught with danger. There were often bigger kids from the flats there. They wouldn't let us go on the swings or the seesaw unless we paid a forfeit. This might be sharing sweets or lending them our bikes. We always feared of ever getting them back. Worse, there might be kids from a children's home a few streets away. These boys and girls knew no fear nor understood the concepts of consequences or adult authority. But there were none of those worries that Saturday with Dad and Brian as we dribbled a football along the pavement. At the park, we headed straight for the playground, we three children running on ahead, yelling and hooting. The men played keepy-uppy, the ball flying everywhere. I can still see my father's bearded face, split wide with laughter, his breath panting in clouds.

My mittens stayed off all that terrible afternoon. I can still feel the icy metal edge of the slide under my bare hand. I was usually careful to avoid the muddy streaks left on the slide by kids' feet. But this time I got bird shit on my fingers and had a screaming fit. Dad and Brian were sitting smoking, one on each end of the seesaw, rocking up and down. They told me to go and wash my fingers in the pond. So I ran down the hill to the pond – more a little lake – and dipped my fingers in the water. It was so cold it burned. I wiped my hand on the grass. The ducks and geese were coming, fighting and flapping and churning the water. Even a few seagulls wheeled in and landed nearby. They stood in a group watching me with their keen red eyes, flexing their wings. The Canada Geese were particularly scary. Once Tony threw some sticks at one that was lying on the bank and it jumped up hissing and snapped at him. I was getting scared, but then Brian appeared. He clapped his hands, and the birds backed off.

'Big buggers up close, aren't they Dave?' he said.

He had the bag of bread with him. He squatted next to me and we hurled doughy pellets into the water, laughing at the birds fighting for them, quacking and splashing.

Brian shook the last crumbs out of the bag when something – some noise? Or was it a sudden silence? – made me turn and look back to the playground. What I saw was an image that froze into the vision of icy clarity that would lodge in the recess of my deep consciousness forever.

Dad was crouched on the ground, huddled over something. He was motionless but I could sense pent-up energy. A trembling, an urgency. Brian too had turned to look up the hill. The empty plastic bread bag hung limply from his fingers then fluttered to the ground. Next thing he was running. I tottered after him, knowing even then that this was no longer a normal trip to the park, and that the day had abruptly and massively changed. I ran with tears welling up, my mittens still swinging and breadcrumbs sticking to my fingers. Brian was way ahead of me now, yelling.

'Janice! Janice! Janice!'

Brian and Dad knelt over her. She lay on the concrete next to the slide, crumpled on her side, her left arm twisted grotesquely beneath her. She wasn't moving. Straightaway I looked up at Tony. He was standing on the little platform on top of the slide. His face was white. His arms were rigid, gripping the bars. Our eyes met. He looked away. While Brian was patting Janice's cheek, repeating her name, Dad's head jerked up and he hissed something at Tony and waved at him to come down. Tony backed down the ladder, slowly, one rung at a time. He stood with his hands in his pockets. Later I wondered why he didn't slide down the slide. Why come down the ladder? Perhaps he already sensed the enormity of what he had done, and that to have slid down would have been an act of unspeakable frivolity.

Dad and Brian talked, hushed and desperate, looking round wildly. Brian pushed Janice's eyelid back with his thumb, revealing only a shiny white orb, like a hard-boiled egg. I wish to this day I had looked away first.

'I'll find a phone,' Dad said. 'Stay here!' he barked at me and Tony.

He sprinted towards the park entrance and the street. I'd never known my dad could run so fast.

Brian scooped Janice up and followed Dad. I didn't want to disobey Dad, but didn't want to stay at the playground. I looked at Tony for a lead. He waited a few moments before trailing after Brian. Janice's head bounced horribly as Brian half walked, half ran. When we reached the road, Brian was pacing the pavement and Dad was running towards us, out of breath and red faced.

'Ambulance on the way,' he panted. 'Has she moved?'

Brian shook his head. 'Jesus,' he said. 'Hurry *up!*'

I was crying properly now, the tears running hot on my icy cheeks, snot bubbling in my nose. My ears and fingers ached with cold. Tony stood apart, his face pale, his mouth open, and his eyes on the ground.

I can't remember much of the rest of that day, except that it was bad. Mum saying she should go to the hospital and trying to ring Mrs Dawson and generally being hysterical. Tony and I slept in bunk beds, me on the top. After we'd climbed into bed that night we lay quiet for a long time. But he was still awake. He was snuffling and lying too still to be asleep. I leaned over the edge of my bunk.

'Tony?' I asked into the darkness below.

He stopped sniffing, but didn't reply. I didn't know what I was going to say to him anyway. Perhaps I just wanted to hear his voice. I rolled onto my side, facing the wall. Tony's mattress creaked and the bed frame shook as he hauled himself up and stood on the edge of his bunk. I inched nearer to the wall. Tony curved his arm up and across and punched me hard in the middle of my back. Despite the pain and shock I didn't say anything. He quietly got back into bed. Soon he was asleep. I cried for a long time, but silently.

Mum fluttered into our bedroom early the following morning. Her face was puffy and red, but she brought good news.

'Janice has woken up! She's got a broken arm. But the doctor says it'll heal quickly. And she's got to stay in hospital for a while.'

I started quivering and crying. Mostly shock and relief I suppose, but also the sheer strangeness of it all. For the first time, I'd seen adults in a crisis. My little world had been tilted briefly off its axis. I was barely four years old, after all. But now everything was going to be alright. Mum leaned over and gave me a cuddle. As she was doing so, Tony slid from his bunk and tugged her leg.

'Mum, can I have eggy bread for breakfast?'

'Of course you can, love. Since this is a special day.'

She knelt and gave Tony a hug. The roots of her blond hair were dark brown, almost black. I'd never noticed this before.

'Your dad's told me what happened, love,' she murmured to Tony. 'How you were helping Janice on the slide. And then she accidentally slipped.'

She tilted Tony's chin up so she could look him in the face.

'Probably she was just trying to follow you, eh, and went too fast.'

Tony nodded, and wriggled free from her grasp.

'Can we have eggy bread now, Mum?'

'Yes. Off you go and wash your face first.'

His footsteps clattered down the stairs.

****

For many years, I was uncertain about what I actually remembered of what followed that awful day and what was just me applying logic to piece together what must have happened, supported by a few snatched images. The sequence of events, the order of cause and effect. But now the fog is lifting. A few details still elude me, but what was previously no more than a jumble of images and emotions is now mostly clear.

Brian came to our house a few times in the days after Janice's accident. He was as kind to me as always. I don't remember Tony being around. Probably he stayed out of the way. I like to think that Brian and Dad restored their friendship. Janice's arm would soon heal. Perhaps Brian pretended that it had been an accident. Perhaps he even convinced himself that it had been. But then the terrible truth about Janice's brain injuries emerged, and Brian never visited our house again. I pestered my parents about this, demanding to know why Uncle Brian didn't come round anymore and show us his tricks. They said he was too busy because of Janice. Tony was quiet during this period. One day he was sent home from school for being in a fight. I remember dark blotches of blood down the front of his grey jumper.

My parents argued a lot. Night after night Tony and I heard shouting downstairs – 'why, Eric, for god's sake, just tell me why' – and doors slamming. Mum at breakfast with red eyes and a too-bright smile. Evidence of her distracted state was plain. She didn't get cross when I poured myself too many Golden Nuggets at breakfast and couldn't eat them all. So I was spared her usual lecture about wasting good food when there were starving children in Africa.

'It doesn't matter love,' she'd murmur. 'Just leave them if you don't want them.'

Housekeeping standards declined. Our bedroom became a glorious junkyard of toys. Tony's Action Men slumped over cupboards or lay as battle casualties on the floor, limbs missing. My dog-eared books were scattered across the floor instead of stacked in the bookcase. Playdoh was ground into the carpet in lurid blotches.

The full impact of the news about Janice emerged over a period of weeks, if not months. I recall Mum saying 'brain damage' in a hushed voice to Auntie Sandra amid lots of weeping. We began to hear the words 'oil rig' and 'Scotland' around the house. Dad spent a lot of time on the phone or filling in forms at the kitchen table. I overheard him telling Mum that his 'medical' had gone well. She didn't seem happy about it.

I had no idea what an oil rig was – probably not even what oil was. This was 1971, four years before North Sea oil started flowing ashore and before it became a newsworthy commodity when the OPEC crisis led to power cuts and three-day weeks and mile-long queues for petrol. I asked Auntie Sandra about oil rigs and she was surprised I was asking such a thing. So I told her about Mum and Dad. When I asked her where Scotland was she shuddered and made it sound like the North Pole, a faraway land that was even colder than where we lived and people talked in a strange way.

The door slamming worsened. Tony and I spent lots of time at Auntie Sandra and Uncle Ron's, often on the basis that we might like to play with our cousins Sally and Tina. But they were older and occupied a different world. They were only interested in boys and the Bay City Rollers. Tina told me the Bay City Rollers were from Scotland but all she knew about the place was that they wore a funny pattern called tartan. We also spent long periods with Nana Truman, Dad's widowed mother. She lived high in a block of flats from where you could see across the houses to the reservoir. The bad part was the lifts, which didn't smell good.

Several times Nana pestered me about what had happened that day at the park. I always told her the truth.

'I don't know, Nana,' I would whisper. 'I can't remember.'

Once when she asked me I started crying. After a while she stopped asking.

One wintry afternoon at her flat I watched cartoons while Nana had a long talk in the kitchen with Tony. Next time on the way to Nana's Tony lay screaming in the snow and wouldn't get up. Mum took us to Sandra's instead, flustered and teary.

'Why don't you want to go to Nana's anymore?' she kept asking Tony.

But he wouldn't say.

My father must have confided in his mother about what he thought had happened in the park that day. I can see, now, that he would have been desperate to talk to someone about it. To explain, to speculate. Perhaps even to excuse, to justify. Maybe he hoped for reassurance that his suspicions were groundless. I don't think he received it. Nana never thereafter referred to Tony by his name unless actually addressing him. She referred to him as 'your brother' to me, or 'the boy' or sometimes 'buggerlugs' to Mum and Dad.

How must my mother have felt as my father planned his escape? Did she believe the story he must have told — that it was about money? For the good of the family. Probably he told of feeling trapped working at British Leyland. Sick of dishing up watery mashed potato in a factory canteen. Wanting to create a better future for us from the huge wages to be earned out on the North Sea oil platforms.

I doubt he told her how dangerous it was. Perhaps he didn't know himself, in those very early days of North Sea oil exploration. But she probably knew enough. Dad told me something about it not long before he died. Hundred-foot waves crashing right over the rigs. How the wind came screaming out of the night and scoured your eyeballs like grit and you felt like your face was being flayed. How the whole massive platform swayed and groaned like some sea monster. It was only after Dad was gone that I properly learnt about those early cowboy days of North Sea oil. The horrendous conditions. The accidents. The divers who went hundreds of feet down into the black water and never came up. Only forty years ago, but the risks they took were unbelievable by today's standards. All for the oil that was going to bankroll Britain for decades and save us from being held to ransom by the mad sheiks in Saudi Arabia.

Dad would have told Mum about the shift system and that he'd be back every two weeks. He'd have tried to convince her that Aberdeen wasn't so far away. Perhaps he joked about how she'd so often scolded him for being under her feet, and she should be thankful he'd now be out of the way.

'But what about me and the boys?'

She would have asked this so many times. He might have looked away, and muttered an answer.

'Love, it's because of you and the boys that I'm doing this.'

And only now do I finally see that he wouldn't have been entirely lying.

He was doing it because of one of his boys.

– 21 –

My old bedroom, a long narrow room upstairs at the back of the house, was converted to a bathroom years ago. So for my stay at Mum's I'm in the spare room, originally Tony's bedroom. Sleeping there, with its ghosts of him and girlfriends past, is as close as I'm going to get to seeing him. I'm sure the story he gave Mum about being away on a management course is untrue. He ignores my emails and phone messages. Usually his phone – home number and mobile – just goes straight to voicemail. Probably he recognises mine or Mum's numbers, and just doesn't answer.

But I've come ten thousand miles to talk to my brother, and the days are slipping away. And there's something else now that I need to talk to him about: the guilty secret in his past, the truth that had lurked just beyond my reach for so long. I don't know what I'll say, or how, but I can't just go back to Australia without confronting him. So one evening after dinner I grab the car keys and drive over towards Solihull. I get lost a couple of times. Then I can't find their street which is in a new estate on the city fringe, out towards the M42 motorway. Finally I stop at a petrol station and get directions to Elderberry Crescent.

Tony and Gail's new house is surprisingly big. It's what in the 1980s was called 'Executive Housing': detached, double garage, but overdone with fussy patterns in the brickwork and hints of mock Georgian with a twin-pillar porch over the front door. I cruise past, noting the two Audis in the driveway, and park twenty yards away. I turn the engine off and sit for a moment. I hold both hands up as if playing the piano. There's a slight tremor in my right, but maybe there always is. I crunch up the gravel driveway and press the doorbell.

The *EastEnders* theme music blares out as the front door opens. Gail is wearing a flowery skirt and a singlet. Her bra straps bite deep into her shoulders.

'Dave! My God!'

'Hi Gail.'

'Tony's not here,' she blurts.

Half relief, half frustration washes through me.

'Will he be long?'

'Ages. It's his pub quiz night. Then they go for a curry afterwards.'

'Oh.'

Gail sees something in my face or the slump of my shoulders and springs to life, flapping her hands.

'Look at me, aren't I rude! Come in.'

And so for a while we act as if Sydney never happened. She ushers me inside and we sit in padded lounge chairs out on the patio. Gail launches into a breathless twitter of inane questions.

'How was your flight? Have you still got jetlag? Isn't this drought unbelievable? Tony's cross that he can't wash the cars. He can't believe we can't just get more water from Wales or somewhere.'

She pauses for breath, but I'm not quick enough.

'It's so hot, isn't it?' she prattles on. 'But I bet it's still colder here than it is in Australia, even though it's your winter! Or is it spring now?'

I nod and smile and let it flow around and through me, not saying anything. Starlings preen dusty wings on a rooftop opposite, the sky melting from blue to pink behind them.

'It's such a shame Tony isn't here,' she says. 'He'll be so sorry to have missed you.'

I look at her, aghast, and she goes quiet, staring into her drink. Now she sounds guarded, wary.

'Is it true Dave? What Tony's saying?'

'That depends on exactly what he's saying.'

'That you and your friend set off that firework.' There's disbelief in her voice.

'Well, there was a lot more to it,' I say, 'but basically yes, it's true.'

'Oh, Dave,' she says.

'How is Tony? Apart from still angry with me, obviously.'

'Angry... I've never seen anyone as furious as he was that day. He rushed me out of your house without even letting me pack properly. He wouldn't tell me anything.'

I shiver at what would have happened if I'd been there when Tony found Tracey's hat in my study. Or if they'd still been there when I got home.

'But when we eventually found a hotel – it was one of those lovely ones at Darling Harbour – things got ever so bad,' Gail continues. 'He was rude to everyone and the hotel almost refused to take us. He made me go and get him beer and a bottle of whisky. He drank all evening. It took him a while to fully compute everything. I begged him not to, but he swore he was going to see you next day, to have it out. He said some terrible things.'

Her voice is choked with tears.

'But next morning he had a terrible hangover. He had to stay in bed all day. Luckily that calmed him down, being so sick.'

Luckily for me, she means. The horror still sounds in her voice. Tony's capacity for vengeful anger would have come as a nasty shock.

'I thought he might have gone to the police,' I say. 'When you got back here.'

'And yet you still came back.'

'Yes. I had to.'

'Well, you were lucky. He was going to go to the police. He talked – or ranted, more like – about nothing else on the plane on the way home, even when I was trying to sleep or watch a film.'

I swat away a dancing cloud of midges. I'd forgotten how warm an English evening can be, although there's a hint of chill in the air now, the heat draining from the earth.

'Why didn't he?'

'Well, it goes against his nature, doesn't it? God, he still calls them pigs. No, in the end he said it would be a waste of time, they wouldn't do anything anyway.'

Her voice sharpens. Now Gail is on home ground there's no hint of that gushing eager-to-please innocence of her Sydney visit, and from when she first opened the front door earlier.

'I didn't tell Tony this,' she says, 'but he's wrong about the police not being interested in something from so long ago. My sister-in-law's the admin manager in CID headquarters in Wolverhampton. She said that if the police were given a name about an unsolved case, they'd be obliged to talk to that person. Interview them. They'd have to.'

'I suppose I'm lucky then.'

'Because you'd got his girlfriend's burnt hat, Tony worked out that you must have been at the fireworks that night, and that you stayed until the end. Then he remembered that you lied to him at the time.'

'Yes, I realise that.'

'He put two and two together and guessed you must have had something to do with the accident. He kept saying, "I knew it! I effing knew it all along!"'

She shakes her head and shudders.

'What made him go crazy, back at your house, was finding that note. Inside the hat. Up until then he was just sort of puzzled. He sat in your study for ages, looking at the things he'd found. Then he found the note. He wouldn't let me read it.'

'It was a love letter. From his girlfriend.'

'Oh.'

She looks at me sadly.

'But Dave,' – and now there's a clear warning in her voice, and a trace of fear – 'he mightn't be so angry if he knew it was the other boy's fault, not yours. Tony says this other boy was a tearaway. A troublemaker, from a bad family. He reckons this boy must have been to blame, that you just went along for the ride.' Gail says this in the Australian way, with a rising inflexion so that it sounds like a question.

'Does it matter? It was an accident. But we were both there. It was both our faults.'

'But the only guilty one is the one who actually set the firework off, isn't it? Literally the one who lit the fuse. And that was your friend, wasn't it?'

I shrug, and close my eyes, and Gail isn't there anymore. And neither am I. I'm circling high above a dark hillside, looking down. The cold night air is thick with fog and swirling smoke but for the first time in thirty years I can see clear through it in sharp focus to the frosty grass and the vivid outlines of two figures.

I squatted and looked closely at the rocket. It stood almost three feet tall. I yanked off my glove and ran my finger along its length, from the red plastic cone on its nose, down its fat cylindrical body with its red and yellow oriental dragon design to its rough square-cut wooden tail. It was true, it did have 'Big Boy' written on it in fiery yellow script. I sniffed the powdery residue on my finger, and licked it. A chemical tingle danced on my tongue.

'Come on, Dave,' said Pete, 'get on with it before I change my mind and light it myself.'

'No, go on, you do it Pete.'

'Are you scared?'

'No! It's just… I dunno.'

'Lighting it's the fun bit. You'll see.' He held up the box of Swan Vestas and shook it. 'And watch it,' he said. 'That plastic bottle's wobbly. We really needed a proper glass bottle instead.'

He tossed me the matchbox, which bounced off my palm before my frozen fingers could close round it.

'Quick,' Pete said. 'Pick it up before it gets wet.'

I retrieved the box from the sodden grass. The rocket was pointing up at the night sky, waiting for me. It was such an inert, dull object: just a cardboard tube on a rough wooden stick. Yet it held such promise, such thrill, such beauty. The protruding twist of blue touchpaper looked too short and I thought of Tom and Jerry cartoons with the bombs like bowling balls and the fuse that burns for ages but always explodes in Tom's face, leaving only his singed whiskers and wide white vengeful eyes.

My stuttering fingers pushed the matchbox's sliding tray open. The box was crammed and the two flaps that folded in on its long sides made it difficult to extract a match. Several fell onto the grass before I got one. I crouched next to the firework again. This was it. Music and happy shouting drifted up from the fairground. I looked at Pete.

'Now?' I asked.

'Yes! Get on with it. Bloody hell!'

'It's bloody hard when you can't feel your hands,' I snapped back at him.

The first match broke in two as I struck it. Pete shook his head with theatrical exaggeration.

Something was making my heart pound now. It could have been excitement, it could have been fear, or it could have been the pressure of not failing again in front of Pete.

This time I took a big risk and lit the match the way Grandpa did, snapping it towards me with a twist of the wrist. It sputtered for an instant before flaring to life, casting a sudden pool of light onto the grass, turning it a lurid green. My heart leapt with the flame, and my arms shook as I jabbed it towards the touchpaper, like I was poking a snake with a stick. But I was crouching too far from the firework and had to lean forward. My centre of gravity shifted beyond the point of return and I tipped forwards. I landed on my left hand, my right with the burning match knocking the rocket and bottle over. The match fizzed out on the grass. I hardly dared look up at Pete.

'You clumsy spaz,' he said. 'Give it here, I'll do it.'

'It's your fault,' I shouted, 'making me take my gloves off! I'll be fine this time.'

'I didn't make you. I only said you looked like a girl. Go on, you try again, but if you stuff this one up I'm taking over.'

He looked at the sky above the looming black ranks of the poplar trees, and folded his arms round himself a few times, his palms slapping on the leather of his coat.

'If I'd known it was going to be this bloody cold,' he said, 'I wouldn't have bothered. I only bought us the firework for a laugh. Come on Dave, let's hurry it up.'

It was harder for me this time because my left hand was now wet as well as frozen. I stood the bottle back up and placed the tail of the rocket back into it.

I crouched with my back to Pete, deliberately obscuring his view of the rocket. No more stuff-ups. I'd find it easier without him watching every tiny move I made. My thoughts flitted to home, and the warmth of the lounge room, and Mum, and a cup of cocoa. I blew on my fingers a couple of times, hot breath misting on my raw knuckles. Then the match was in my hand and smoke in my nose and the flame was unwavering, steady, the air so still I didn't even need to cup my hand to protect it. Its warmth was beautiful on my fingers. I held the flame beneath the neat twist of blue touchpaper. Two, three, four seconds… the paper glowed red and began to hiss.

Pete would be so impressed that I had managed to light it so quickly this time, although he wouldn't say so. But as I ran back to join him, he frowned and peered over my shoulder.

'Did you jam the bottle back into the ground properly?' he just had time to say.

Then there was the whoosh of the wind sweeping down from the black trees behind us, and Pete's hands flew to his face in horror at what I had allowed to happen.

A lawnmower drones in the distance. Birds flit and chirrup in the hedges. Gradually I realise Gail is asking me something. Her voice comes from far, far away.

'Did you ever get counselling, or anything?' She asks this like she's saying it just for something to say. 'To help you cope?'

'No. No-one had heard of counselling back then, had they? Nowadays schoolkids are offered counselling when their pet goldfish dies. Anyway, no-one knew we'd done it.'

'But what about later?'

'For ages I went to a neurologist, about my migraines and insomnia. He sent me to a psychologist. It was supposed to just help me with relaxation techniques. But the psychologist did try to ask me about my childhood, probing about why I moved to Australia. "It sounds like you've got a monkey on your back," is how she put it.'

'Did you tell her about this guilt? Did she help you?'

'No. I just stopped going.'

'And what about at the time – straight after it happened? Did you tell anyone?'

'Nope. No-one knew.'

'It can't have been easy, living with something like that.' There's no sympathy in Gail's voice; more a vague curiosity.

'It wasn't. Looking back, I can't believe how we kept going. Maybe it was sort of down to luck.'

'How do you mean?'

'Well, we were still too young, or too stupid, to be able to understand what would happen. We thought it would all just go away.'

'You mean you thought you could get away with it.' There's a tone of triumphant reproof in her voice.

'I suppose.' I shrug. 'Even now I wake at night wondering what I should have done differently to avoid what happened. It's easiest just to say that I should have done everything differently. But then I think, from when exactly? What was the first in the chain of events? Was it when Pete bought the firework? I can still see him now, bounding out of that shop with a stupid grin on his face. "Have I got a surprise for us!" he said.' I laugh grimly. 'But there was nothing surprising about it. It was typical of him and I knew it was. So sometimes I think maybe everything began back when he and I first became friends, when we were five years old.'

'That's just silly,' says Gail. 'It's like saying it wouldn't have happened if you'd never been born.'

'There were times when that's exactly what I wished for.'

Again, there's a long silence.

'Were Tony and this girl, Tracey, close?' Gail asks.

'Very close. But it was a long time ago.'

Neither of us has anything more to say. Most of the garden is in deep shadow now, just the left-hand hedge top and upper limbs of an apple tree lit with a coppery glow. I reach out to gather my car keys and phone off the table when the front door slams. Gail jolts upright as if her chair has been electrified. My heart does the same. I pray it isn't him. This was a really stupid idea.

Gail's hands are at her mouth.

'Gail! Are you outside?' Tony's voice is loud, belligerent and rapidly approaching. 'Can you believe it? We got accused of cheating, just because someone saw Johnno fiddling with his phone. Thrown out of the quiz! *Bastards!*'

My heart hammers and I stand, looking for an escape.

He's in the kitchen now, shouting through the open back door.

There's the chink of bottles. The fridge door slams. Gail shoots me a terrified look and scurries towards the kitchen door. In the last second I see a pathway down the side of the house. I'm off the patio and down this dark passageway like a scared rabbit. It leads to the front driveway where there is a padlocked timber gate, its upper edge at head height with three strands of barbed wire on top. I've got one foot on the door's cross beam and am about to pull myself up. *Shit!* My car keys and phone are on the patio table. Bugger it, I'll get them later somehow. The gate creaks and rattles under my weight.

'Tony!' Gail's voice is a desperate wail.

'You *fucker!*' His skinny frame fills the oblong of space where the passageway emerges back onto the patio. 'Get off there!'

He strides towards me. His movement activates a security light on the wall behind him and he becomes an instantly menacing silhouette inside a halo of white light. From the woolliness of his voice it's clear he had a good few pints before being thrown out of the pub.

'Oi!' he yells.

He hurls his beer bottle like a grenade, his arm straight and swung from behind his back. It arcs through the air, pissing beer in a foaming curve, ricochets off the wall and explodes on the ground in front of the gate. Pieces of jagged glass glint in the dazzling light.

I've got both feet on the cross beam. I can still make it. A good heave and a commando roll across the top and I'll be gone, with only some barbed wire damage to my chest.

But I hop down and face my brother.

His feet crunch on broken glass. Without breaking stride he puts his right hand up, arm rigid, collects me by the throat and slams me back against the gate. His face is mottled, his lip curled. His grip is like a pair of steel pincers.

'Tony! Tony! Get off him!' Gail sobs behind us. He ignores her.

'What the fuck are you doing here?' he screams. 'I don't want to see you ever again. Piss off back to kangaroo land!'

He's hurting my throat badly, crushing my Adam's apple back into my neck. Veins and arteries and tubes are being squeezed, twisted. The blood is bursting in my head, pushing at the back of my popping eyes.

'Tony!' I wheeze. 'I only wanted to talk to you, to explain.' My voice is a strangled squeak.

'What's to explain? I know what you did to my Tracey! You and that cunt Sharpe!'

He shifts his fingers on my neck, relaxing his iron grip for a microsecond. Quick as light I swing my arms up and across and bash his hand away from my throat, nearly breaking my neck in the process. The blow spins him through ninety degrees and I push past and leg it back down the passageway towards the patio, passing Gail in a blur.

'Come back here, you fucker!'

'Tony! Put that down! *Please!*' Gail screams.

Jesus. Is Tony coming after me with a broken beer bottle? I accelerate in an adrenaline burst of fear. The patio and garden are black beyond the stark brightness of the lit passageway. As I reach the patio an explosion of pain hits my right shin and I go sprawling.

It feels like someone has swung a baseball bat against my leg, full force. I haul myself to my knees and as my eyes readjust to the dusk I realise I've tripped over a stupid wheelbarrow handle.

'Tony, nooooo!!' Gail again.

I scuttle away like a panicked crab. Tony grabs the collar of my polo shirt and twists it viciously while using our momentum to jerk my prone body forward. I wriggle furiously but can't stop him heaving me like a roll of carpet onto a low retaining wall set in a bed of white pebbles. It's part of a water feature and series of raised garden beds. I inspected it earlier while Gail was getting us drinks. There's a fountain that dribbles over a dome of imitation granite and a crappy Zen-like pebble arrangement with a few overweight goldfish gulping for air in the pool that rings the dome. The retaining wall's sharp edge digs agonisingly into my sternum but that pain and the agony of my leg is forgotten once Tony starts hitting me.

He keeps one knee in the small of my back, grinding my chest into the wall, and works fast, probably mindful of Gail. I'm mindful of Gail too, praying that she comes to my rescue, and soon. With his left hand, Tony pushes my face into the water. It's not deep, I can breathe — just — but my left cheekbone grinds against the slimy pebbles on the bottom. With his free hand he punches me on the right side of my head and face three or four times. Solid, jarring blows. I haven't been punched properly since schooldays. I've forgotten the hot, numbing, explosive pain of each slamming impact, and the way it spreads like a tingling flush down your neck. I thrash and kick. My arms are pinned uselessly beneath me, and I try to work them into a push-up position, to try to throw him off.

'Fuck off! Get off!' I scream, my voice bubbling from my half-submerged face.

More than the pain I'm horrified at the thought of a goldfish swimming into my mouth. I have a flashback to Tony by the pool at Port Stephens. He has acquired a pot belly but otherwise has the same build he always did. He looks skinny but that's deceptive: more than merely wiry, it is as if his thin limbs are made of steel. Even as a teenager and young man, Tony never had any bulk in his arms and shoulders. But he never needed it.

'Tony, he's your *brother!*'

There is shock and terror in Gail's scream. Then she's crying, gasping sobs somewhere behind us. Sensibly – but unfortunately for me – she's not on Tony's back trying to drag him off.

The punches stop, but the buzzing in my head doesn't. My hearing has gone funny: sound pulses into my damaged ear in painful waves of distorted noise. Tony grabs my hair at the back and yanks my head out of the water. It's only through my left ear that I can hear what he's saying. I can also hear the rasping of his breath and feel its tickly heat on the back of my neck. I shiver.

'Right, Dave. You came to explain. So explain.'

He might have broken my jaw. There is a stabbing pain in the side of my face. My speech is woolly, thick.

'Firstly, Tony, I came to say sorry. I know it's been a long time coming, and it means nothing now, probably, but I'm sorry for what we did. All I can tell you is that it was an accident. A complete accident.'

'Aha. And what, exactly, did you do, Dave?'

'Tony, we were just kids, I can hardly remember...'

'Oh yes you can.'

Water drips from my nose and chin. It tickles.

'Okay. Well, we set off a rocket. It was meant to go up into the sky, like normal. But we could only find a plastic bottle to stand it in. It blew over just as the rocket went off, and flew off sideways. Tone, let go of my head will you.'

'Dave, you're not listening. What, exactly, did *you* do?'

'Dave! Tell him! Go on! Tell him how it was your friend who set off the firework.' Gail has stopped sobbing. Her voice is urgent, encouraging, and desperate.

'Is that right Dave? Was it Sharpe who set the firework off, like I knew all along?'

I say nothing. My neck muscles are screaming. All I can see is the roof of the house opposite and the near-black sky.

Long seconds tick by.

Tony abruptly releases my head. My face slams down into the water. I brace for more punishment. But there's nothing. Several electric spotlights abruptly come on in the water feature, dazzling me, greenish-white. They must be on a timer. Scarlet tendrils of blood stain the water.

'Well, that's it then. At least we know.' Tony's voice is flat.

I raise my head. He sits on the ground with his back against the retaining wall, his legs splayed in front of him. I heave myself up and sit on the wall, out of punching range. I run my hands through my hair and dry my face on my sleeve. I'm shivery from pain and cold and shock.

Gail sits on the wall next to Tony. Initially she looks like she's going to sit between us, but at the last minute she ostentatiously veers off and sits on his other side, away from me. She's still sniffing and gulping. She strokes the back of Tony's neck.

'One last thing, Dave.' Tony's heels crunch deep parallel grooves in the pebbles as he draws his knees to his chest. 'Why didn't you give me Tracey's note? Why did you keep it?'

He mutters these words into his kneecaps, and I'm glad. I'm glad he's not looking me in the eye. What do I say? Because you didn't deserve it, Tony? Because you didn't deserve Tracey?

'I forgot about that note in the chaos after the accident, until I found it again much later in my pocket… and then, I couldn't give you it, could I? It was too late. We'd got so tangled up with the lies we told. I'm sorry.'

Another long silence. I rub my arms and hug them to my chest. My teeth are chattering. This hurts because I think Tony has loosened some of them.

'Anything else you want to tell me Dave?'

'No.'

'Sure?'

I nod.

'In that case I think you'd better go,' says Gail.

Her prim tone, and her display of unity with my brother, this standing by her man, tending the conquering warrior, ignites a spark of irritation in me. They haven't asked if I'm alright. The right side of my face is already swollen and throbbing. I clench my jaw and a hot stab of agony shoots along it. Irritation becomes real anger. I jump to my feet.

'Don't worry, I'm going. But is there anything you want to tell me first, Tony?'

I'm trembling. But I'm not cold anymore.

Tony lifts his head from his knees.

'What are you on about now?'

'At least what I did was an accident!'

I literally can't stand still. I'm tingling all over. I can feel the blood pumping around my head. I grab a handful of pebbles, just to try to control my hands, and toss them one by one into the strip of garden bed bordering the lawn.

'You're making no sense.' But now Tony's voice is wary.

'Tony, what's Dave talking about?' asks Gail. Like I'm not there.

'I don't know love.' Tony gets to his feet. 'Dave, you need to go. Now.' He points to the way out.

Something deeply buried rises in me like a geyser of fury. He sees it in my eyes and drops his hand in alarm but he's still too slow.

I hurl my fistful of pebbles down the dark garden. They clatter against a greenhouse with a noise like a burst of gunfire.

'I KNOW WHAT YOU DID!' I scream.

I shove him in the chest and he falls backwards across the fountain, his eyes wide, arms windmilling. He slides sideways down the dome and sprawls to the ground, his elbow clunking on the edge of the wall.

I stand over him like a gorilla, arms curved at my sides.

'You killed Dad. You killed my dad.'

Tony sprawls on his executive pebble stones, probably with

a broken arm. Suddenly he looks old, pathetic, harmless. Like a toothless Doberman.

Gail is already kneeling next to him, helping him up, looking at me strangely.

'Tony, what...?' He shrugs her off. She falls silent.

'That's not fair, Dave,' he says.

'Why? Are you telling me it was an accident? That Janice fell off on her own? Only don't, because it wasn't, was it?' I suck cold air over my teeth. It hurts like hell. I want it to.

'You know what I mean,' Tony mutters. 'I didn't make Dad go and work on an oil rig. I didn't make him get in that helicopter.' He grimaces and holds his elbow awkwardly.

'Yes you did.'

'Bullshit Dave! He *chose* to leave us.'

'No he didn't. He had no choice. And all because of you.'

'So have you told Mum this? Are you going to?' Tony sounds tired rather than concerned.

'Dunno.' I curse myself that even now, at the very last, Tony has cornered me, trapped me into revealing an indecision. A weakness.

After a long silence I step away and retrieve my phone and keys from the table.

'Once last thing,' I say. 'Why did you and Tracey have a row? What was it about?'

He laughs bitterly.

'*Chariots of Fire.*'

'Huh?'

'The cinema. She wanted to see *Chariots of Fire*. I wanted to see

Raiders of the Lost Ark. That was all it was.'

I want him to look at me, but he won't.

'Just go, Dave,' he mutters.

I nod. 'See you.'

I walk back into the kitchen. As I pass into the hallway there's a shout of defiance from my brother.

'Don't think any of this makes us even, Dave. Because it fucking well doesn't.'

I'm about to close the front door behind me when footsteps approach in the hall.

'My God, Dave,' Gail says, 'you looked angrier than Tony. What was that about?'

She's back by the foot of the stairs. Keeping her distance.

'Tony knows what it was about. He may not realise it, but he knows.'

Gail frowns at this, but says nothing. She joins me at the door.

'Tony looked at your old scrapbook about your father in your study too, when he found those other things. It was open on the floor.'

'I thought he had.'

'He spent ages going through it.'

It's almost dark now. The sky is deep violet, the street lights fuzzy orange. The traffic on the M42 is a persistent low drone.

'It's loud, isn't it?' I say. 'The motorway.'

Gail smiles. She looks old. Her hair is messy and her face distorted with shock and tears.

'Yes. We didn't realise when we bought the house. Tony

complained to the estate agent afterwards and she said we'd soon not notice it. But you do. The motorway's over a mile away, but the noise is always there in the background, night and day. It sort of gets into your head.'

'I know what you mean,' I say.

'Dave, I've got to go. Will you be all right? Do you need a doctor?'

'No, I'll be okay. I hope Tony's arm is all right. Please do me one favour?'

'What?'

'Tell him I meant it when I said I was sorry.'

I sit in the car in the dark street doing deep breathing and trying to calm myself before driving off. A face checks me out from the upstairs window of the house opposite. Time to go.

I'm glad it is quite a long drive home. I open the window and take deep breaths. What are Tony and Gail doing right now? Is she comforting him, tending his arm? Is she leaving him to cool off? Or is she probing him for information, intrigued by my outburst? I hope not, for both their sakes. Already I half regret screaming those words at him.

But there are still other things I could have confessed to Tony. An explanation of long ago deeds that I will never tell anyone. I don't regret not telling him, mainly for reasons of self-preservation – for a few punches to the head would be a gentle warm up compared with Tony's reaction to this revelation.

Even Peter Sharpe, for once, knew nothing of what I'd done. The only witness to my guilt in this regard isn't going to say anything.

And there were no physical mementoes hidden in my study in Sydney to act as slow-burning clues to the other awful thing I did to Tony even while our firework was still lying dormant in its neat cardboard tray in a locked glass drawer in Mr Minwalla's shop.

Tony had even given me an opportunity to confess as he sat slumped against his water feature with his head on his knees.

Anything else you want to tell me, Dave?

No, Tony.

Are you sure?

Yes.

But at this point I might have reminded Tony about a conversation he and I had thirty years ago, in the early evening of the night that changed our lives. And I might then have told him about another conversation, one I'd had earlier that same day.

'Are you going to the fireworks as well, Tony?' asked Mum hopefully.

The television cast a blue glow on her face. The lounge room was hot and smoky.

Tony looked at his watch as if with massive effort, and sighed.

'Dunno, Mum.' He turned to me. 'Have you seen Tracey today at school? Has she said anything about going to the fireworks tonight?'

I thought back to that morning. Tracey and I had stood shivering on the edge of the school playground, dodging the running kids and the flying footballs. She had intercepted me on my way back up from the woods with the smokers and shyly asked if she could talk to me.

'Dave, do you know if Tony's going to the fireworks tonight?'

My first thought was: why don't you ask him? My second was: so they're still not speaking to each other, after three days. Incredible. Maybe their falling out, into which I had stumbled so embarrassingly in our living room, was more than a mere lovers' tiff.

'I don't know. Probably.'

Boys looked at me enviously. Few boys below the sixth form could hope to have a one-on-one conversation with Tracey Downey, the school's undisputed pin-up princess, the catalyst of a thousand dance floor scuffles.

'I hope so, Dave.'

For a terrible second it looked like she might be about to cry. Her face was pale and tight, though it could just have been the cold.

'I'm going to be there,' she said. 'Maybe you can tell him, you know, encourage him to come? I'd be ever so grateful.'

She put her hand on my forearm. I folded my arms tight across my chest, pretending to be colder than I was.

'Sure. I'll try and twist his arm. Leave it with me.' I hoped I sounded competent, bold, decisive. *Leave it with me.*

'Thanks.'

She smiled feebly, and I felt a rush of pity for her, knowing she hated asking this. How could Tony behave like this? What was *wrong* with him? How could anyone be indifferent about having Tracey Downey for a girlfriend?

'Dave? *Dave!* I'm talking to you!' Tony's voice jerked me away from the memory of Tracey's face that morning and back to the lounge room. He rolled his eyes and raised a hand to his forehead, as if in severe pain. Then he spoke infuriatingly slowly, as to a child.

'Have. You. Spoken. To. Tracey. About. Tonight?'

'No, I've not seen her at all, the last couple of days.' I held his eye, praying for him to turn away.

'Tony love, why don't you just phone her?' said Mum. 'Say sorry. Make the first move. You'll be glad you did.'

He shook his head, his eyes not leaving the television. A muscle in his jaw stood out. 'Nah. And I'm not going out tonight.'

Lying to Tony had been easy. As I walked the dark streets to meet Pete on the way to the park I further justified it by reminding myself that Tony wouldn't have gone to the fireworks anyway, however badly Tracey wanted him to. I didn't know the reason back then, but Tony never went anywhere near that park.

I know now of course.

– 22 –

'Your dad used to love it here,' my mother says.

'What, this place?' I reply, indicating the bistro where we're having lunch.

'No, silly, this restaurant wasn't here in those days. I mean Stratford, the town. He brought us here a lot. We'd have picnics on the grass, go on the river. Don't you remember?'

'Sort of,' I say.

I can recall scraps of images. Chasing ducks into the water. Ice cream dripping over my fingers. Mum and Tony and me splashing Dad as he rowed us down towards the weir. Drops of water in his beard catching the sunlight. Do I even remember kicking a football around with him and Uncle Brian?

I wanted to take Mum somewhere she would consider posh so we are having lunch at a riverside bistro. She's been depressed for the last couple of days. This might be due to me leaving tomorrow or because she didn't have the family dinner she had craved. A phone call with Tony the day after my visit to his house made her realise that a family reunion was not going to happen. I don't know what was said. I hope she isn't suspicious about my swollen face, but doubt she believed my excuse about parking the car on a steep slope and the door slamming back onto my head.

We're sitting inside because there is a cool breeze coming off the river and because Mum saw a wasp buzzing around outside. To make this a special occasion I got her a glass of champagne, which she loves but thinks it's something you only drink at weddings. Or unless you're rich, or French. At her first sip she giggled at the sensation of the bubbles going up her nose, the ridges of loose flesh under her arms wobbling. By the time our food arrives – Dover sole for Mum (my suggestion, saying it's Friday so we must have fish, like she used to insist) and seared Atlantic salmon for me – she's well into a second glass. But the giggling has subsided along with the bubbles, and she's getting maudlin and talking about Dad. Better I suppose than asking me about Tony.

'Once your dad started working in Scotland,' she says, 'we stopped doing things like this. Weekend outings.'

'Why? Apart from he wasn't home as much, obviously?'

'Well, even when he came back each fortnight, the changeover day was the Friday, so that first weekend he'd be exhausted. And then he spent a lot of time with you but with Tony… I don't know, he seemed happy to let your brother just do his own thing. Poor Tony didn't complain. So if your dad was doing something with you, I always made sure to be with Tony. When Tony wanted me to, that is. He was older and often just wanted to be out with his mates.

You remember, don't you? Your dad would take you to the football, and I'd take Tony to the shops. Buy him something nice.'

One of the waiters – presumably having seen her dismayed look when a whole fish was put in front of her – saunters over and asks Mum if she would like him to fillet it for her and remove the bones.

'Yes please,' she says. 'I don't know where to start with it.'

I give the waiter a tight smile of thanks and because I'm embarrassed that it's obvious my mother has never had Dover sole before. When he's finished, she pushes some white flesh onto her fork and tries some.

'Nice?' I ask.

She nods and smiles, but looks no happier than the fish. She puts down her knife and fork.

'Why do you think your dad left us, Dave?'

I half-guessed it was coming but her question still hits me hard.

'Mum, I don't know. Honestly. I was five years old. I barely remember it happening. I guess it was for the money, wasn't it? Or boredom, those years working at Longbridge. Maybe it was him falling out with Uncle Brian. Maybe all of the above.'

The waiter glides towards us but I raise a hand and he veers away.

Mum rests her handbag in her lap. I expect her to reach for a tissue, but she doesn't. She just cradles it, as if needing the security of a familiar object.

'It gnaws away at me,' she says. 'Every day. I still wonder even now if he left because of me. Sandra says it was for the money. But it's the way she kept labouring the point that made me suspect something else. Something I did. Or another woman. Something I don't know about.'

We're in territory far beyond any frontier I've previously crossed with my mother. But I can't just change the subject and ask to see the dessert menu.

'Don't be daft. I know Dad wasn't always happy at that time, but he was always happy with you. That much I can remember. Like Sandra says, it was probably about money.'

'Money,' she says sarcastically. 'We didn't need more money. We weren't well off, but we were fine.'

'By the way, did you get compensation for the accident from the oil company?' I've always wondered about this.

'Oh, they threw each bereaved family a few thousand, but it wasn't like today. Class actions, hiring lawyers, getting millions – those things didn't happen back then.'

'That mightn't mean you couldn't sue them now. The oil company still exists, doesn't it? Do you want me to find out? I could ask Jeremy. His law firm's got a London office.'

She smiles and shakes her head. 'No thanks, Dave. What would be the point?'

She gives me a look. One from long ago. One I'd forgotten.

'You are telling the truth, aren't you Dave,' she says, 'when you say you don't know why he left? I could always tell if you weren't telling me the truth, when you were a boy. Tony was different. But you were a hopeless liar. Probably that's why you didn't tell many lies.'

I can't meet her gaze.

'Yes Mum, I'm telling the truth. If I knew, I'd tell you. But would it make a difference, knowing why he left? It was forty years ago.'

'You sound like Tony,' she says, a touch bitterly. 'He's always telling me I shouldn't live in the past. He means I should forget about your dad, like he seems to have done. But I just can't. When the police catch a murderer I can understand why the victims' families are so relieved. Sandra would say it doesn't matter who killed the person, it won't bring them back. But I understand. It's that stupid word, closure. That's how I feel about your dad. If something drove him away to go and work in Scotland, then that's what killed him.'

'Oh, Mum. It definitely wasn't anything to do with you.'

'I know. Deep down I know it wasn't because of me. He used to say I was the love of his life.' She looks me in the eye. 'I'm not embarrassing you, am I Dave?'

I smile and shake my head.

'We were happy,' she continues. 'What hurts is the thought of getting to the end of my life, and still not knowing.'

I'm acutely aware that this is a point at which I might say something reassuring. Meaningful. Memorable.

The moment passes.

She looks down at her plate, at the almost untouched disc of pale fish with its empty eye socket and downturned mouth, the congealed buttery sauce.

'Sorry love, but I'm not hungry anymore,' she says. 'What a waste.'

'It's fine.' I force a smile. 'Let's go and get some sunshine.'

I pay the bill and we stroll across the riverside recreation area opposite the red brick façade of the Shakespeare theatre and its tower like a glass factory chimney. The rec's vast expanse of grass, normally deep green, is as drought-affected as the city's parks and is suffering badly from the thousands of tourist feet and picnicking families. It is a weekday, but still busy. Toddlers weave across the grass, trying to kick footballs. Some veer dangerously close to the river and are headed off by their mothers. Elderly people line the benches and sit in folding chairs on the grass reading newspapers.

We lean on the parapet of the ancient stone footbridge. The river looks treacly and sluggish, like it has given up the effort of flowing. The ducks and swans seem to expend extra effort to swim through it, their necks straining forward, the ripples of their wake lingering for ages.

Mum links her arm through mine, the old-fashioned way.

'I wish you weren't leaving tomorrow, love,' she murmurs.

Whose arm is she really clinging to? Are those words meant for a son or a husband, as the sunlight shoots silver needles across the water, too dazzling for the eye?

'I know. Me too.'

A rowing boat glides out from under the bridge. It's overloaded with one family. The father is rowing. His teeth flash white in his face as he laughs. His two young sons are rocking the boat, slopping water over the sides. Their sari-clad mother shrieks and laughs and begs them to stop. She's like a colourful bird.

'Come on, faster, Dad,' the boys yell, their voices echoing up.

We laugh. The boat emerges from the bridge's dark shadow into the bright dancing light and heads unsteadily downriver.

'Could you really always tell when I wasn't telling the truth, when I was young?'

'Every single time.' She touches my swollen face. 'I still can.'

I jerk my head away.

She grips my arm tighter, pulling me close, and gives it a shake.

'Don't be like me, Dave. Don't spend your whole life worrying about things that happened years ago, and that I'm sure weren't your fault anyway.'

All I can do is nod, and look at the river, and try to keep it all in.

****

We're quiet in the car on the way home. I settle my mother in an armchair with a cup of tea and her feet up and nip to the supermarket to buy a few things to take back to Australia with me. Just a few nostalgic childhood treats. Marmite. Ploughman's Pickle. A Curly Wurly. Silly, since they're heavy to carry and Marmite at least you can get in Sydney, although not easily. But I've travelled light and have plenty of room in my suitcase.

I could have bought what I want at any supermarket, or even just at the corner shop at the end of Mum's street. But there's a reason I've come to this particular store. There's one more thing I want to do before I leave England and the past.

The shop is crowded. Perhaps it is pension day because lots of old people block the aisles, their trolleys empty save a couple of packets of biscuits and some cat food. Finally I'm in the checkout queue, prodding my basket along the floor with my foot. Shoppers bark at their fractious children or flick through the magazines on the racks by the checkouts while they wait. Surprisingly, this supermarket still has staff helping people pack their bags and load their trolleys.

A middle-aged woman packs bags at my checkout. She laboriously licks her forefinger and thumb to separate a new plastic bag from the stack. She's a big woman with raw beefy arms and thick dark brows above wide blue eyes. Her dark but greying hair is curly and completely unstyled above her round pale face, piling up in an untidy frizz. A plastic hairclip shaped like a butterfly swings loosely, serving no useful purpose. She wears the same orange nylon pinafore dress as the rest of the female staff. But she's missed a button so that her dress bulges at her midriff and the hemlines are lopsided. She has the wide smile of someone absorbed in their work. Periodically she raises her arms rigidly and claps them together two or three times, hard, her palms clashing together with a hard bounce between the heels of her hands.

My queue shuffles forwards until I'm next in line at the till. The woman is loading another sliding cascade of groceries into plastic bags and boxes. Another staff member hovers nearby. Abruptly she steps forward and whispers in her ear. The woman unpacks items from one of the bags, where she's put frozen foods in with some toiletries. Her lower lip trembles. The supervisor steps back and nods encouragingly.

'That's better,' she says. 'Remember? The cold things stay together.'

The woman snorts and giggles, her knuckles pressed to her mouth. She lunges at the supervisor, her arms spread, and gives her a bear hug. The supervisor smiles and pats her back, and the woman resumes her work. The supervisor drifts away. But not too far. The girl on the checkout till is a thin-faced teenager with a stud through her nose. She rolls her eyes at the customer she's serving and gets a sympathetic shake of the head in response.

When my turn comes, the woman rapidly shoves my few groceries into a bag.

'Hello Janice,' I say, with a wobbly smile.

But she has lost interest and is already eyeing the laden trolley of the customer behind me.

– 23 –

On my last day in England I pull on my gear and tell Mum I'm going for a run, saying I want some exercise before my evening flight to Sydney. This is a lie because my face still hurts from Tony's beating, and running jars it painfully. I really just want a walk but can't risk my mother saying she'll come too.

It's only fifteen minutes away. I stand on the corner by a tall privet hedge and look along Brindley Close to a house fifty yards up. It's a bright, warm Friday afternoon. Schoolkids wander home, pushing and shoving. *Greensleeves* jangles from an ice cream van in the distance.

The last time I stood on this spot was also on a Friday. A freezing night in December 1987 when the pavement glittered with frost and Tracey Downey clung to my arm after a boozy evening at the Gun Barrels pub.

'Would you like to come in for a coffee?'

I opened my mouth to mutter some excuse.

'*Please*, Dave. I'd love it if you did.'

She was giving me the old smile.

I was drunk. And confused. But I could have said no. I should have said no.

I could only vaguely guess the time. With my student lifestyle I didn't see many early mornings. Tracey was jammed against me in her single bed. My head hurt, badly. My mouth was like sandpaper. Rivulets of condensation ran down the window. Wintry morning sunshine slanted into the room through the gap in the purple curtains in a dense bar of light, casting an orange glow over a huge poster of The Human League. On the shadowed opposite wall hung a poster of Echo & The Bunnymen, dark and sullen.

The room was unbearably stuffy. I felt the radiator by the bed: it was too hot to touch and I jerked my hand away, making Tracey stir. I froze, my hand hovering in midair. She snuffled and opened and closed her mouth with a soft 'clop', then resumed a gentle snoring.

Tracey's bedroom decor was mostly purples and pinks. A row of stuffed toys covered with a skein of cobwebs peered down from the curtain pelmet. A dressing table stood opposite the bed. Above it was an arch-shaped mirror rimmed with stickers and photos and magazine clippings: Simon le Bon, CND, Miss World in swimsuit and sash. Piled on a desktop were school exercise books – I recognised the dark grey – and some text books. A wardrobe door stood ajar, but it was too dark to see inside. But hanging there would be a grey pleated skirt, white blouse, navy and white tie and grey jacket with our school crest on the breast pocket. Waiting for Tracey to put on when she dressed for school on the morning of Friday 6 November 1981, her ears still ringing from an evening of fireworks fun, her lover's tiff with my brother all forgotten.

Tracey flopped onto her back. Her left cheek and eye were three inches from my face. The curtain of hair had moved aside, dragged under the back of her head as she rolled over.

At first I couldn't focus. Then I still couldn't register what I was seeing. It was like one of those puzzles where you stare at a vague pattern until an object emerges. The makeup that had hidden her cheek last night had been smeared off onto the pillow, revealing a shiny, frozen, red and white scarred area centred on her cheekbone, as if her skin had been cut and twisted. Her eyelashes were false and were dislodged, as if about to come away completely. The pencil line of her eyebrow was exactly that, a painted-on strip on the shiny, puffed area above her eye.

Pinpricks of sweat itched on my scalp and chest like crawling insects. My head throbbed as if a chisel was being thrust behind my eye. I had to get a drink of water. I slid my legs sideways and sat up, trying not to disturb Tracey. The movement this entailed and the thought of a chisel behind my eye brought on a wave of giddy nausea. My legs trembled. I tried to breathe slowly, my hands clasped to my clammy forehead. Tracey hadn't woken but had stretched out into the vacated space so that one bare leg, from the upper thigh downwards, now protruded from the duvet.

Dully I registered that her leg was startlingly white, and that she had cellulite. Or were they stretch marks? Tracey shifted back onto her side, and the front of her thigh became visible. A livid, wavering six-inch scar ran down it, the skin puckered along its length. At each end the scar broke into three or four short extensions, like the deltas of little red rivers. Skin from there had ended up on her face. I thought of the famous newspaper photograph of Tracey, the Miss British Leyland beauty queen picture. The perfect creamy smoothness of her thigh, unblemished by even the tiniest mole. The tight fabric of her swimsuit. The angle of her raised leg as she reclined on the car bonnet.

Clamminess broke out all over my body. My stomach heaved. I needed water.

In Mr and Mrs Downey's bathroom, hunched over their toilet, wiping drool off my face on their towel, using their soap to wash my night with their daughter off my hands, I felt more intrusive than any burglar.

A picture on the landing wall caught my eye as I scurried back to the bedroom. It was a framed colour photograph of a group of soldiers in camouflage trousers and olive green t-shirts, posing in two rows like a sporting team. The men in front sat with arms rigid and hands clasped on knees and those standing behind had their arms sternly folded, pushing out their biceps. A couple of faces were smiling but most were grim and hard. Nearly all had crew cuts and moustaches. One man at the front was grinning as he held a pistol to the head of a small green doll, which it was just possible to make out as a leprechaun.

The photo's caption read: *D Company. Crossmaglen, March 1974.* Beneath ran a list of the soldiers' names. In the front row, next to the pistol-bearer, was Sgt. J R Downey. Tracey's father looked like the others: squat and unsmiling, his cropped hair and moustache very dark and his eyes crinkled into slits.

Tracey's parents were away for the weekend. But how far had they gone? What if their plans changed? Quickly and quietly I returned to the bedroom and began to dress, retrieving my clothes from their scattered positions around the room. One of my socks was draped on the chair next to the desk. I picked up a couple of the textbooks. *Twelfth Night, Or What You Will*. *The Ice Age in Britain*. Subjects we had been studying in the autumn term of our school fourth year. Six years ago.

'Hey Dave.'

I jumped, dropping the book.

She had rolled over and snuggled up, the duvet clutched to her chin.

'Sorry about this,' she waved her hand at the room. 'Mum always keeps it just as it was. I know. Weird.' She giggled. 'God, I've got a headache.'

'Me too. Sorry about this, but I've got to go.' I hopped around, pulling on my sock.

'What, right now? It's so early.'

I nodded. My head screamed. I couldn't think of any plausible excuse. It was the university holiday. I had no job to go to.

'Yeah, I'd better make a move.' I said this to the floor.

'Okay.' Tracey rolled onto her back. 'Probably see you again soon.'

I felt too ill and too confused to tell at the time, but afterwards agonised over whether this was a question or a statement. Not that knowing would have helped any of us.

'Sure.'

I hovered at the door.

'See you then,' I said.

She poked an arm from the duvet and waved. As she did so a tiny triangle of golden sunlight reached the corner of her pillow.

****

13 July 1988

Dear Dave,

I don't know why you won't reply to my letters, and I stopped expecting that you might return my phone calls ages ago. I've decided I'm not going to write any more. You're probably relieved to hear this.

All I ever wanted Dave was to understand. I didn't want nothing more from you. I knew you probably had a nice girlfriend back at university. Maybe that's why you felt guilty. Maybe you still do.

Doreen says I have to move on, look to my future. But the trouble is I can't. Not unless I never look in a mirror again. It's like my past is wrapped around my future, always in the way.

But I hope you have a happy future Dave. London must be a pretty exciting place to be, I should think. I've only been there once, on that school trip in the third year. Do you remember? Peter Sharpe got in trouble in Madame Tussauds for lifting Raquel Welsh's skirt.

Like I said, this is the very last letter I'm ever going to write.

Tracey

– 24 –

The taxi pulls away from the kerb, scattering a gang of pigeons. At the end of the street I look back. My mother stands outside the house. Her hand is still at her face, clutching the shredded remnants of a pink tissue. Our goodbyes were brief and tearful. I haven't told her that I don't plan to come back again for a long time, but she knows this anyway. She gives me a quick wave. The taxi noses out onto the main road then turns and gathers speed.

About a mile from the house we drive down a long straight road. It's bordered on our left by a high yew hedge so dense and perfectly trimmed it looks like a concrete wall painted dark green. Ahead of us is a pair of iron gates, standing open. They've worn deep curved grooves into the bitumen. I ask the driver to stop. From this main entrance, a long straight grey driveway extends into the heart of the cemetery. It ends at the chapel and crematorium. The neat rows of graves branch off at right angles and extend down the curve of the slope on each side like a giant ribcage.

I know roughly where she is, even though none of us went to the funeral. Her parents had insisted it was to be immediate family only.

Probably they wanted no-one there — especially old school friends — who might remind them of how things had once been, before. Or perhaps it was their shame. Catholics. The manner of her passing, as they say. Doreen and a few others made their feelings known. Complained about not being able to pay their respects. Say goodbye to Tracey. But Tony and I, for different reasons, were so desperately relieved not to have to go.

The driver twists in his seat. He's a young black guy with a scarred face. He asks where I'm flying today.

'Sydney.'

'Australia!' he says. 'It's all just desert, isn't it, and dangerous animals an' stuff?'

'Pretty much,' I say, just for the hell of it.

'What made you want to go and live down there?'

'I don't know. Maybe I thought that if I went away, all my problems would too.'

There's a long, long silence.

'So what's happening, boss?' he eventually asks. 'You going in there, or not?' He indicates the cemetery gates. 'Makes no odds to me, meter's running.'

Something — a twig or pine cone — drops from an overhanging tree and pings on the roof.

'Shit, what was that?' says the driver. He peers up through the windscreen. 'Hey, you know what man?' He turns to me, beaming. 'Think it might be going to rain.'

****

Three hours later the plane bumps off the tarmac and climbs into the summer twilight. I peer down with my cheek pressed to the window as the plane banks steeply over the city, setting course for the south-east and half a world away. The suburbs are spread below me: the commuter roads and the roundabouts, the crescents and the cul-de-sacs. There's a flat silvery gleam far off to the west which could be the reservoir, but I can't be sure. Tower blocks send long parallel shadows creeping over yellow grass and grey concrete.

The plane banks again and the city falls away to be replaced by a cloudless indigo sky. I lean back and close my eyes. The words of Tracey's final letter spool past my eyes like tickertape. I burnt the letters she sent me, unlike the other mementoes in the box that Tony found in my burgled study in Sydney. But I can exactly recall the words of that final letter, despite trying so very hard to forget them. The act of setting fire to the paper on which they were written served only to burn the words themselves into my memory forever. Soon a familiar image swims into focus in place of the words. I don't try to fight it away: there's no point. I learnt that years ago. It's an image that has visited me all too frequently since that last time I ever saw Tracey Downey, waving sadly from her time-warp teenage bed that December morning as I hovered in the doorway.

I see her continuing to wave after I turn my back and leave her alone in bed, and as I run down the stairs two at a time. She keeps waving even as the front door crashes shut behind me, and as my footsteps die away down the frosty garden path to the street, and as her whole bed becomes bathed in golden winter sunshine.

Acknowledgements

Thank you for reading *Where There Is Darkness*.

There are many people to whom I'm grateful for their contributions in helping my story become a finished product. In particular I thank the core members of my decade-old writers' group, *The Beak*: Jon Steiner, Lynne Blundell and Zoe Sadokierski; fellow UTS alumni Mark Rossiter and Nigel Bartlett; and Mandy Newman and Kerry Littrich, who were there when it all began. Jon and Mark I thank particularly for giving such comprehensive feedback on early drafts of the story and Zoe for her expert advice on book design and printing.

I owe a huge debt to Associate Professor Debra Adelaide of the MA Creative Writing program at the University of Technology Sydney for helping me turn my half-baked idea for *Where There Is Darkness* into something fit for human consumption, and for so tactfully highlighting the many deficiencies in the early drafts.

I thank my sister Alison Waters for proof-reading the manuscript.

Finally, and above all, I thank my wife Vanessa and my daughters Sophie and Anna – the latter two for staying out of the way so I could finish the novel and the former for making sure they did so; and for so much else besides.

17432770R00177

Printed in Great Britain
by Amazon